ALLOUET

Allouette's gaze shot up to ... ...st-ing her features. Then she recognized Gregory and the sight of his face waked her from the trance. She leaned against him but was still stiff as timber.

"Poor love, you must have seen horrors indeed! Was it a glimpse of genes gone awry, twisted into an angry knot? Or of a tumorous brain yielding distorted . . ."

"It was an invasion!" Her fingers bit into his arm. "Tribes of monsters, horrid and scaly, revolting and tentacled, brandishing weapons of strange design but sharp enough to hew our people in half! Behind them rode armies of humans on mounts obscene and savage, warriors driving the monsters onward to conquer our land! Nay, not simply to conquer, or even to rape and loot and pillage, but to slay and slaughter each and every one of our people!" She broke into sobs again . . .

Ace Books by Christopher Stasheff

The Warlock Series

ESCAPE VELOCITY
THE WARLOCK IN SPITE OF HIMSELF
KING KOBOLD REVIVED
THE WARLOCK UNLOCKED
THE WARLOCK ENRAGED
THE WARLOCK WANDERING
THE WARLOCK IS MISSING
THE WARLOCK HERETICAL
THE WARLOCK'S COMPANION
THE WARLOCK INSANE
THE WARLOCK ROCK
WARLOCK AND SON

Heirs to the Warlock Series

A WIZARD IN ABSENTIA
M'LADY WITCH
QUICKSILVER'S KNIGHT
THE SPELL-BOUND SCHOLAR
HERE BE MONSTERS

HERE BE MONSTERS

CHRISTOPHER STASHEFF

ACE BOOKS, NEW YORK

This is a work of fiction. Names, characters, places, and incidents either are the product of the author's imagination or are used fictitiously, and any resemblance to actual persons, living or dead, business establishments, events, or locales is entirely coincidental.

HERE BE MONSTERS

An Ace Book / published by arrangement with the author

PRINTING HISTORY
Ace mass-market edition / September 2001

All rights reserved.
Copyright © 2001 by Christopher Stasheff.
Cover art by Eric J. W. Lee.

This book, or parts thereof, may not be reproduced in any form without permission.
For information address: The Berkley Publishing Group, a division of Penguin Putnam Inc.,
375 Hudson Street, New York, New York 10014.

Visit our website at
www.penguinputnam.com

Check out the ACE Science Fiction & Fantasy newsletter and much more on the Internet at Club PPI!

ISBN: 0-441-00851-8

ACE®
Ace Books are published by The Berkley Publishing Group, a division of Penguin Putnam Inc.,
375 Hudson Street, New York, New York 10014.
ACE and the "A" design
are trademarks belonging to Penguin Putnam Inc.

PRINTED IN THE UNITED STATES OF AMERICA

10 9 8 7 6 5 4 3 2 1

PROLOGUE

Allouette gazed out the window as Gregory lit the incense in their meditation room. "How curious!" she murmured.

"What is curious, my love?" Gregory came up behind her to follow her gaze. His hand seemed to rise of its own accord toward the satin-draped curve of her hip, but he forced it back by sheer willpower; his fiancée did not need any distractions if she intended to meditate.

He exerted more willpower to turn his gaze to the meadow below their tower, rather than toward the beauty of her profile, the more beautiful because it was radiant with happiness—at last, after a decade of exploitation.

"That is the fifth couple come to build in our meadow." Allouette pointed to the ground around their ivory tower that had so recently sprouted four sturdy thatched cottages. The young folk who lived in them were helping the new arrivals build a cottage of their own. They had already set up the posts and were weaving the wattle branches among them.

"I had cherished our solitude," Allouette told Gregory. "Why must they come here? Can they not study as well in their own villages?"

"They cannot," Gregory said regretfully, "for few peasants understand their hunger for learning, and their lords are quite impatient with their ways of passing the winter days."

"I must strive to understand that," Allouette said thoughtfully. "I was fortunate in that, at least—that my foster parents did provide me a school, and encourage my desire to learn—nay, nearly force me to it." Her mood darkened at the memory of a happy childhood turned harsh in her teens. She shrugged it off with an effort and made a face (Gregory thought it was charming). "I may view them with sympathy, but I have no wish to be lady of the manor. I have had my fill of ruling others."

She had indeed, young though she was. She had been trained to be a secret agent for an interstellar organization of anarchists—trained also to be an assassin and to do whatever was necessary to gain access to her assigned targets, including seduction. When she had realized she was being used—not only as a tool, but also as a toy for her superiors—she determined to become the one who did the using instead, and seduced and murdered her way into becoming the chief of her spy ring.

Her assigned targets had been the Gallowglass heirs—Gregory, his older brothers, and his sister. If she couldn't kill them—for, powerful though she may have been as a projective telepath, she found that the Gallowglasses were stronger—she was to keep them from reproducing.

She had accomplished this most effectively with the eldest, Magnus, maiming him emotionally and imprinting him with a horror of intimacy. She had tried to steal Cordelia's beau, Prince Alain, which would have had the advantage of bringing her to the throne, an excellent position from which to sabotage the government—but Cordelia proved too strong for her, as did Alain's love. She might have managed to ensnare the middle son, Geoffrey, but he had captured a fiery young female bandit, Quicksilver, who had captured his heart in return.

Still, one out of three wasn't bad—but she had tried to make it two out of four, doing her best to seduce Gregory away from his beloved books and enslave him with chains of love. In this she had succeeded—all too well, for his probing intellect had seen through her disguises to the woman underneath, knowing her for what she was but loving her anyway. Logic dictated that he execute her, in love with her or not, but his sister Cordelia had pled the cause of mercy and reformed her with the aid of their mother. Gwendylon had used telepathy to probe deep into the woman's mind and found that the causes of her homicidal tendencies had been carefully ingrained by the anarchist agents who had reared her. Gwendylon enabled her to confront her fears and convictions of worthlessness, and helped her cure herself. In the process, she had discovered how completely the anarchists had victimized her, realized how thoroughly the political convictions with which they had reared her had been based on lies, and had rejected their philosophy in disgust.

Remorseful and lost, she had turned to the man who loved her, had traveled with him and fallen in love with him, and helped him build the ivory tower where the two of them studied the operation of the extrasensory powers that made up the "magic" of Gramarye's "witches." They threw themselves headlong into research—and one another. She was not quite willing to marry but was even less willing to leave the ivory tower and her scholarly swain, for she had to admit to herself that she was already addicted to Gregory.

Now, though, it was time for study, not lovemaking. She turned away from the window and went with Gregory back to the center of the room, mind already turning to the cluster of neurons she had identified as a possible source of telekinesis, the power to move inanimate objects by thought.

Gregory, not yet so pragmatic, was still enmeshed in trying to discover whether ESP was actually a characteristic of the brain or was simply a mode of thought. In their discussions, he had already conceded that if it could be inherited, that mode of thought certainly had its source in the brain itself—but he was content to leave neurons and synapses to Allouette while he tried to trace the convolutions of thought, the brainwave forms, that actually made the witches and warlocks of Gramarye able to fly (by telekinesis), to disappear in one place and reappear in another (by teleportation), to read one another's minds and project thoughts and images into others' minds, and to sculpt and animate the strange Gramarye fungus called "witch-moss." Each had already read every book written on the subject, which were few, and had interviewed the few people who knew anything. That, however, gave them plenty of information to organize and analyze—food for many hours of thought.

So they settled down, sitting cross-legged at right angles to one another—Gregory had found that, if Allouette were in his line of sight, he could concentrate on nothing else. On the other hand, if she weren't with him, he couldn't concentrate for worrying about her welfare—so they meditated together, backs straight and hands on their knees, closing their eyes, envisioning the images that represented the problems they were studying. Their minds drifted into the rapturous haze of association and correlation, searching for patterns and testing them for soundness, sorting and rejecting, hoping for the inspiration that would make sudden simple sense of a complex knot of facts.

Then Allouette drew a long, shuddering gasp, her eyes opening, seeing not the room around her but the horrors that had invaded her mind.

CHAPTER
-1-

Allouette's groan penetrated Gregory's trance in an instant, and the images of his mental constructs fell to shards. He didn't even give them a thought—he was already at her side, chafing her hands to restore contact with the real world, speaking in a low but intense voice. "My love! My love, come back! From wherever you roam, return to safety!"

Allouette's gaze shot up to his face, terror twisting her features. Then she recognized her fiancé and the sight of his face waked her from the trance. She leaned against him but was still stiff as timber.

"There now, it was all a dream, only your own imaginings, only nightmares of the past twisted into new and horrible forms," he soothed. "No matter how horrible, it is not real."

She stayed stiff a moment longer, then went limp, collapsing into his arms and sobbing bitterly. Gregory held her and stroked her back and shoulders, marveling at his impossibly good fortune in having so wonderful a creature in his arms. He glowed with a feeling of power and purpose because he was able to comfort her.

At last the sobbing slackened and he tilted her chin up enough so that he could wipe at her tears with the hem of his sleeve. "Poor love, you must have seen horrors indeed! Was it a glimpse of genes gone awry, twisted into an angry knot? Or of a tumorous brain yielding distorted—"

"It was an invasion!" Her fingers bit into his arm. "Tribes of monsters, horrid and scaly, revolting and tentacled, brandishing weapons of strange design but sharp enough to hew our people in half! Behind them rode armies of humans on mounts obscene and savage, warriors driving the monsters onward to conquer our land! Nay, not simply to conquer, or even to rape and loot and pillage, but to slay and slaughter each and every one of our people!" She broke into sobs again.

Even as she spoke it, her mind leaked fragments of the nightmare—giant slug-like creatures with vaguely human faces twisted with obscene glee as they slashed with swords held in four arms, creatures that looked like bears become human riding on great horned lizards and slashing about them with battle axes, giant insects with human faces and razor-edged wings . . . Gregory knelt, frozen in shock, his hand stroking her back automatically as his brain reeled with the vision. At last he said gently, "It was a nightmare, nothing more, some deeply buried—"

"It was not! It was a sending!" Allouette glared up at him. "Ask me not how I know, but I do! They have blazoned this vision before them to weaken us with horror, to render us unable to resist them!"

Gregory knelt frozen a moment longer, then spoke with iron resolve. "If it is indeed a sending, then I too must perceive it."

"No!" Allouette stiffened in panic, then clasped his face between her hands. "Not you, my good and gentle love! 'Tis bad enough that I have had to see this nightmare—I, who have been accustomed to bloodshed from childhood and to murder since I was grown! If it has wracked me so, what will it do to *you*?"

"I am somewhat more durable than I seem," Gregory assured her, "but if there is truly a threat to the land, one sentry alone will not suffice to raise the alarm. I shall have to see what you have seen. Accompany me if you will, ward me and strengthen me, but I must witness it." With no further ado, he gazed off into space, eyes losing focus as he concentrated on the terrible vision he had glimpsed, followed it back into her mind, and opened himself to it, hearing her voice from a distance crying, "Gregory, no!" but following the thought back along a line that reached from her to . . .

To a foggy landscape, a blasted heath with skeletons of trees barely seen through the mist, which gathered into a gray whorl that churned and roiled and opened like a whirlpool, a funnel that spewed distorted nightmare forms hooting and howling with glee as they charged out, waving blades of unearthly design, bloodthirsty and ravenous, seeking human prey.

The vision rippled, and Gregory saw the monsters charging down upon a human village too quickly for anyone to lift even a scythe in defense, saw what those whirling unearthly blades did to the peasants, saw what the warriors who followed the monsters did to the few villagers who remained alive, hooting and calling in mocking tones, "Gregory! Come and join! Come back for slaughter! Come back . . . come back . . ."

Then the vision thinned, separating from his mind, becoming only an obscene picture of turmoil and bloodshed apart from him, away from him as though in a frame, and it was Allouette's voice that called, "Gregory, come back!"

He followed her voice, followed the pattern of her thoughts, feeling as though he were swimming up through dank and fetid water, away from skeleton-haunted wrecks of ships wrapped in dying weeds, toward light and air and freedom. Then he was clear, back in their sun-filled meditation room, and drew a long shivering gasp, clutching something, anything, so long as it was real and part of the living world.

Looking down, he saw it was Allouette's hand.

"Speak, love," she said, her words caressing, soothing. "Was it so bad as to shake even a wizard of your renown?"

Gregory nodded, took another gulp of air, and said, "Worse than anything I've ever seen—and I have witnessed some horrors, when my family and I have needed to save the common folk from oppressors."

"Worse even than you saw in my mind," she whispered.

Again, he nodded. "Tribes of monsters and armies of ruthless humans advancing not only to conquer Gramarye, but also to slay all who live here. They came spewing out of . . . of a sort of whirlpool, only it whirled in fog, not in water— and what they did to the villagers they found . . ." He shuddered. "Pray Heaven no such thing ever really comes upon us!"

"But it is real, and you and I both know it."

Startled, Gregory turned to meet Allouette's eyes and found them sympathetic, but also grave—and very determined. "We must hunt them down, Gregory," she said softly. "We must track them and send every single one back into their whirlpool, or forever despise ourselves for not saving people whom we could have spared this agony."

Gregory sat still for a moment, bowing his head and letting her words sink in. At last he gave a single nod and said, "You have it—we must. But let us rest a day first, to rid ourselves of this frightful vision and fortify our souls against worse to come."

"It shall not take us so harshly again." Still holding his hand, Allouette pressed it more firmly. "It was the surprise as much as the brutality that shocked us."

"We shall be inured," Gregory agreed. "Come, now—let us consider what sorts of phenomena we are likely to meet, and how to encounter them."

They spent the rest of the day in research and planning, and the night in lovemaking, as much for reassurance as for pleasure. Gregory had promised Allouette that they would have a grand wedding when they both felt ready. She had retorted that he was promising it to himself, for she had no need of it—but secretly in her heart, she didn't really consider herself good enough to become his wife. It never occurred to her that Gregory was certain he wasn't good enough for her, and was planning their wedding for the future—at a time when, in his own mind, he had proved himself worthy of her love.

Nonetheless, neither had any doubt about their commitment to the other.

Waking the next morning, Gregory looked up over a steaming cup of tea and said, "Yesterday we held a council of war, did we not?"

"If two people can be said to be an army," said the former Chief Agent of Gramarye's anarchists, "we did, yes."

"I had thought as much," Gregory said with a grim nod. "Ere we leave, then, I shall tell a warrior where we go, and why."

Allouette stiffened, for the warrior in question could only be Gregory's older brother Geoffrey, whom she had tried to seduce away from his fiancée Quicksilver—and the fact that they had not yet been engaged, or that Allouette had failed, did not lessen her feelings of remorse one jot.

Gregory's gaze had lost focus, and though he sent his thoughts to his brother in the family encryption mode, Allouette had long ago learned to decipher it and heard them as easily as though he spoke directly to her.

Gregory, old son! Geoffrey cried with delight. *What moves?*

Monsters, brother, Gregory returned. *We go to hunt them.*

Monsters? Again? Geoffrey said with overtones of boredom. *What manner, and where are they?*

Not in this world, Gregory answered, *and as to the manner, look and see—but brace yourself to hold down your gorge.*

So bad as that? Geoffrey's tone was much more interested. *Well, show me, then.*

Gregory did.

Exasperated, Geoffrey Gallowglass strode down the hall of the royal castle. The guards at the door of the heir's suite eyed him askance and didn't bother challenging him—one simply said, "If you will wait a moment, my lord, we will announce you," even as the other was knocking, waiting for the response, then entering to announce, "Lord Geoffrey to see Your Highness."

Prince Alain looked up with a smile, laying down his quill. "Well, bid him enter, of course!" As Geoffrey came in, Alain rose from his desk, saying, "What moves today, my friend? A wolfhunt, or . . ." Then Geoffrey's expression registered and he said, "What moves indeed!"

"My addlepated little brother," Geoffrey answered, "and his devious betrothed . . . well, all right, wife. They have seen nightmares in their trances and are off to scour the land to make certain their dreams will not come true."

Alain tensed; anything affecting the welfare of the land and the people affected him. "What manner of nightmare was this?"

"A cascade of monsters pouring from a whirlpool of fog," Geoffrey answered, "and a bloodthirsty horde of people riding distorted mounts behind them, hell-bent to ravish and slay all the folk of Gramarye."

Alain paled. "Could there be any truth in so horrible a vision?"

"I cannot believe that," Geoffrey said, "but I dare not take the chance. If there are monsters loose, I shall not let my little brother face them alone—nay, nor even with his bride beside him."

Neither of them had to say that they did not yet entirely trust Allouette.

"If you ride, I ride," Alain said with determination, "you to ward your brother, I to ward my people."

Geoffrey scowled. "We dare not risk the heir to the throne."

"That old song again?" Alain sighed. "It was worn thin when first my mother began to sing it—and now you? Have you sewn patches on it?"

"Still, as your vassal, I must protect you," Geoffrey said stubbornly, "not lead you into danger."

"And as your suzerain, it is my duty to protect *you,*" Alain retorted, "you, and all my people."

"But what if . . ." Geoffrey bit off the question before it was too late.

Too late it was; Alain grinned in answer. "If I were slain? Who would rule? Come, you know the answer! There is an heir and a spare." He frowned. "Come to think of it, the spare should know where I go and the reason for it. Do you bide here while I speak to him."

Neither even mentioned the king and queen, who would have forbidden the foray on the spot—but Geoffrey reminded Alain, "There is someone else to whom you should speak of this."

"I shall tell her indeed." Alain braced himself visibly. "Somehow I think there may be more danger in your sister than in your brother's monsters. Wish me well, comrade."

Diarmid was a slender young man some four years younger than his brother, almost as tall, almost as blond, even more serious—but there the resemblance ended. Diarmid was lean where Alain was stocky, wiry where Alain was muscular, quiet and reserved where Alain was open and direct.

"Ever the knight-errant, brother?" Diarmid actually smiled. "Well, good hunting to you."

"Thank you for kind wishes." Alain returned the smile, then turned serious again. "You know, Diarmid, that if I should fail to return, you would be heir apparent."

The younger prince shuddered. "Heaven forbid! That I should have to forgo my books and spend empty hours in entertaining ambassadors and enduring the debating of lawyers! Take good care of yourself, brother, for I long to be back on my estates in Loguire, where folk speak to the point and do not waste my time in bandying words."

"Ever the scholar," Alain said, amused. "We must watch you closely, brother, or you shall be off to build a cottage in the shadow of Gregory's tower and spend your days in study."

Diarmid's face turned gaunt with hunger. "Do not tempt me, brother."

Alain was taken aback by his intensity and resolved never to mention the ivory tower again. He changed the subject. "I cannot understand how you can administer the whole of a dukedom, and administer it well, in only six hours a day!"

Diarmid shrugged. "It is only a matter of delegating authority—and of choosing good people in whom to entrust it."

"You may yet prove more fit to govern than—"

"Do not say it, my liege-to-be," Diarmid interrupted, "for the plain and simple fact of my efficiency in governance is that I do not really care tremendously for the people or the land."

"Diarmid!" Alain cried, shocked.

Diarmid shrugged. "I do what I do out of duty, brother, not fascination. You, on the other hand, care for the common folk so deeply that you will spend hours agonizing over a ten-minute matter to be sure your decision is as right as it can be." He shook his head, smiling with amusement. "I do not truly understand it—and have no doubt that you will be a far better ruler than I."

"I thank you, brother." Alain clapped him on the shoulder. "Soothe our parents for my absence, will you?"

"As well as I can," Diarmid promised. "Give me the note you have writ for them."

Alain handed him the scroll, then left, squaring his shoulders and bracing himself to confront Cordelia.

Diarmid looked after him with a pensive frown. If the horrid visions had been enough to rock Gregory from his studies, they must have been vile indeed—and there was a chance, no matter how slight, that Alain might find himself in greater danger than he knew. Diarmid made up his mind on the instant, for blood is thicker than ink. He would miss his books, but he couldn't take the chance that Alain might be slain. He would follow him in case he needed to be pried loose from trouble. After all, he had only one brother.

Then, too, he really did not want to have to become king.

Prince Diarmid had been easy to tell; he took it in stride, used to his brother's gallivanting in Geoffrey's wake and quietly certain that the issue was more a matter of young men adventuring than of any real danger to the realm. Cordelia was another matter.

"Now? A month before our wedding? Have you a crack in your skull, that your brains could leak out and let you think of such a thing?"

Alain caught his breath at the vivacity of her, the way she seemed to glow with anger, her face only inches from his . . . He forced his mind away from that train of thought and said firmly, "If my people are endangered, I must go."

"Aye, *if*! But what chance is there of that 'if' being true—and how great is the chance of your leaving me standing alone at the altar while you and my scapegrace brother go jaunting about the countryside?"

"I doubt highly that we will be gone more than a week," Alain told her, then remembered what Geoffrey had told him about courtship and let his feelings show. He dropped his voice a few notes. "Besides, I am near to losing my wits with being so close to you, and so close to being your husband, and able to do nothing about it."

Cordelia thawed on the instant. "There are always kisses," she breathed, swaying even closer.

Alain took the hint, and the kiss—it lasted a long time, but as it ended, a groan escaped his lips.

Cordelia was instantly on fire again. "Are my kisses so distasteful as that?"

"No," Alain gasped, "but they ignite a pain within me that shall not be quenched for a month and a day."

"A day?" Cordelia stared at him, almost affronted. "Why the day?"

"Because I suspect you shall be exhausted at the end of your wedding day."

Cordelia's eyes lit with a different sort of fire. She pressed her cheek against his chest with a husky laugh. "Have more confidence in me than that, my love. I have more energy than you think."

Alain's moan was halfway to a mew.

Instantly Cordelia was three feet away from him, eyes downcast, the very picture of the chaste and demure maiden.

"I shall not taunt you, then. Nay, it is wrong of me to tease you." She looked up, meeting his eyes again. "And wrong of me to withhold you from your duties. Go assure yourself that all is well with your people, and that Gregory's . . . betrothed . . . is only beset by megrims."

"Take heart, my love," Alain said softly. "If you do not yet trust Allouette, be sure that I do not either."

"It had crossed my mind that she was enticing you both away at a most inopportune time," Cordelia admitted, "but it is an unworthy suspicion. Go, my love. Chase phantasms for a fortnight—but do not dare be a single day longer, or you shall face a far more terrible monster than ever my brother could dream!"

Quicksilver was practicing jousting, riding at the quintain with a blunted lance. She knocked it spinning, turned her horse to trot back for another pass—and saw her true love riding toward her with bulging saddlebags and simmering anger in his eyes. Her heart dropped and she kicked her horse to a canter, rushing to meet him. "Geoffrey! What troubles you?"

"My idiot brother," he said, fuming. "He and Allouette have endured a waking nightmare, seeing monsters come ravening out of some fantastic whirlpool of fog to despoil all of Gramarye. Now they have ridden to discover its whereabouts and have left me with a warning to be on guard."

"Gone on a quest?" Quicksilver cried. "But it is only a month until Cordelia's wedding!"

"All the more reason, says Gregory, to rid the land of whatever menace seeks to disrupt their nuptials," Geoffrey said grimly.

Quicksilver caught his undertone and frowned. "You suspect something."

Geoffrey went still, then nodded sheepishly. "It is wrong, I know, but it did occur to me that this might be some stratagem of Allouette's to avoid having to face the whole family at the wedding."

Quicksilver frowned, reviewing what she knew of Allouette and assessing it in a flash.

"Surely we shall have riddled out this muddle in a fortnight! And if we fail to, fear not, sweet one." Geoffrey leaned forward and kissed her, then assured her, "I shall haul Alain home in good time for the wedding if I have to knock him senseless to do it—not that he is showing overmuch sense as it is. Farewell!"

With that, he turned and rode through the gatehouse, leaving Quicksilver staring behind him, trying to decide whether to laugh or to shout in anger. She bit her lip in uncertainty, not willing to admit a lingering fear that Geoffrey might have wearied of her. Nonetheless, the feeling nudged at her, and to quell it, she kicked her horse to a canter, pulled him up at the door of the keep, tossed the reins to a groom, and strode up the steps to rally Cordelia.

Rally? She came into Cordelia's room to find her in a sturdy traveling gown, packing her saddlebags. "How now, sister-to-be! What will your prince say if he finds you on his trail?"

"Naught, for I shall make certain he does not find me," Cordelia said, thin-lipped, "until he has need of me."

"Sound enough," said Quicksilver, "but what if he does not?"

Cordelia shrugged. "Then he will be none the worse." She looked up. "This is no surprise to you. Has Geoffrey, then, already bade you *au revoir*?"

"He has," Quicksilver said grimly, "and in so swift a fashion that I could scarcely protest—especially if the common folk are in danger." She was herself the daughter of a squire and had grown up learning to care deeply about the land and the people. The common folk had repaid her by joining her outlaw band when the only choices left her were to go to her lord's bed as she was bidden, or to rebel.

"Well, Alain is certainly not going into danger without me to ward him," Cordelia avowed, "whether he knows it or not."

"Indeed," the reformed outlaw captain agreed. "Why

should we stay at home and wring our hands?" She pursed her lips. "Nonetheless, it might be wiser to let the boys go ahead of us."

"Yes," Cordelia sighed. "They will take it ill if they see us trailing after them."

"They would be affronted to know we doubt their abilities to deal with whatsoever danger they may find," Quicksilver pointed out. "Then, too, if they fall into disaster, they may welcome others who follow to aid them in fighting off the enemy."

"Not if those 'others' are their fiancées, I suppose," Cordelia said sourly. "I will chance that, though, rather than chance their dying."

It never occurred to either of the ladies that they might run into a predicament that the four of them together might not be able to solve.

"But with only a month till your wedding!" Quicksilver protested. "Will not the ceremony fall apart if you do not keep the arrangements in train?"

"It will fall apart even more if my fiancé does not come back," Cordelia said sharply. "If I wish to be sure of a wedding, I must see to it that my groom stays alive!" She leaned closer and confided, "And truthfully, I am nearly driven to distraction by all this fuss about the church and the food and the gown and the guests! My wedding will proceed just as well for a week gone, and I shall be far more likely to emerge sane and cheerful."

"But your lady mother—"

"My mother was once a bride, too, and I have no doubt she will cheer my leaving." Cordelia gazed off into space a moment.

Quicksilver knew she was telepathically discussing the issue with her mother. It still gave her the megrims, to see mind reading used so casually.

Cordelia nodded briskly and finished folding a spare bodice. "She applauds my going and will keep all the preparations in progress while I am gone." She looked up at

Quicksilver, eyebrows raised. "You will accompany me, will you not?"

Quicksilver felt her lips curving into a smile. She chuckled and said, "Of course. What else is a sister-in-law for?"

So the Gallowglass Heirs set off on a quest, Gregory and Allouette forging ahead, blithely unaware that Alain and Geoffrey were half a day behind them, and Cordelia and Quicksilver half a day behind *them*.

None of them could know that Diarmid followed with half a dozen hand-picked men-at-arms, all very loyal to him—so loyal that none of them had breathed a word as to where they were going to anyone except their knight, and had told him only that the Duke of Loguire had summoned them. The knight would therefore not be able to tell the king and queen that both their sons were playing the knight-errant.

Of course, Diarmid was quite sure that they would learn that little detail—when he failed to appear at breakfast the next day, and his valet found Alain's note. In fact, he was counting on their parents' reaction. It gave him a certain sense of security to know that his father would be a day's march behind him with a small army.

CHAPTER
-2-

On the morning of the second day, Allouette and Gregory climbed into some high and rugged hills. The trees grew more and more stunted, the roadside grass shorter and browner, until they were riding through rock and hardened clay bearing only scrub brush and dried grass. By that time, the path had grown so steep that they had to dismount and lead their horses—so as they neared the crest, they were not in the best position to have an ogre step out from a behind a boulder to block their path.

Its bandy legs looked more like the roots of hundred-year-old oaks; its shoulders seemed like kegs set on either side of a neckless head that was all lumps and slashes with a matted thatch of dun-colored hair. Two-inch fangs protruded from the corners of the bottom-most slash—presumably its mouth—and tiny eyes gleamed from two more, higher up. Its log-thick arms were so long that its ham-handed fingers drummed on a knee, and for clothing it wore only a tattered tunic and moth-eaten hose. It roared, swinging high a huge cudgel, and waddled down the slope toward them, pig-eyes ablaze with bloodlust.

Gregory stared. "From what nightmare came *this*?"

"Yours," Allouette snapped. "Step aside! Let the horses deal with it!"

The ogre's rank odor hit the beasts and they reared, screaming, fire in their own eyes, for alien and horrid though the creature might seem, these were well-trained warhorses who knew to strike rather than flee.

The ogre screamed back and swung its club at the striking legs, but one of the horses cracked a hoof against its shoulder and the swing went wide, turning the creature half around—toward Allouette. Its piggy eyes fixed on her and it waddled toward her with menace, club swinging up.

Gregory shouted and leaped into its path. The ogre turned and swung its club at him. Gregory ducked; the club whistled over his head. Then a huge foot caught him in the stomach and lifted him into the air. He landed in a ball and rolled to his feet.

"Caitiff!" Allouette screamed, and snatched a dagger from her belt.

The ogre turned to her with a snarl, swinging its club high again—but her hand swung in a blur and a dagger-hilt seemed to sprout from the ogre's shaggy chest. It looked down in surprise, then wrenched the blade loose, ignoring the gush of blood that followed, and stepped toward her with a howl of rage—but it lurched as it stepped. It looked down with a puzzled frown, as well it might have—for there was a lump of gray goo where its left foot had been, and as it watched, its right foot seemed to melt. It howled in horror as it shrank, its whole form sliding down and flowing in seconds until only a huge gray heap remained.

Allouette drew a sharp breath and said, "Well and quickly thought, my love."

"It threatened you!"

Allouette looked up, surprised; she had never seen Gregory angry before. His eyes blazed, his face had reddened, his whole body was shaking—but she knew the cause and reached up to embrace him. "I was never truly in danger, love," she said softly.

"But that club!" Gregory's voice was muffled by her hair as he pressed his cheek against her head. "It might have hurt you!"

"I was faster than it was, dear—it could never have caught me," she said, her tone soothing. "Still, you thought most amazingly quickly. How could you tell it was made of witch-moss?"

Gregory shrugged. "All monsters are, on this world of Gramarye. Some granny who does not know she is a projective telepath has been telling her grandchildren tales of night-stalkers again, and bits of witch-moss in the forest nearby flowed toward one another until there was enough of them to form the monster of which she spoke."

The substance wasn't properly a moss, it was a fungus, and for some strange reason, natural selection had made it sensitive to telepathic thought. A trained esper could fashion it into anything she wanted, even living forms, since it was already alive.

An untrained one could turn it into anything he could imagine—sometimes with disastrous results.

"It was worth a try," Gregory explained. "If dissociating had failed, I could always have hurled it away with telekinesis."

Allouette thought of the rage she had seen in his eyes and didn't doubt that he could have summoned the emotional power to have lifted the huge mass and thrown it like a twig. The thought was frightening, but reassuring too; she felt a warm glow at the reminder of the intensity of his love for her, the more amazing because she hadn't manipulated him into it.

Not for lack of trying, of course. How could she have known, when he proved immune to all her wiles, that he would have fallen in love with her for herself?

So she stepped away from him with perhaps more gentleness than she might have—just far enough away to lift her lips for a kiss. Gregory was still for a moment, then began to tremble again and his kiss, though feather-light, stunned her with its intensity.

When she caught her breath, she smiled into his eyes, her own glowing, and said, "Come. This creature may have left havoc in its path. We must track where it has been and remedy its devastation."

Gregory looked up in surprise. "Why, even so! How compassionate you are to have thought of it! Come, let us seek!" He turned away, eyes on the ground.

Well, Allouette would have thought of it as caution and self-preservation, but she was quite content to let Gregory think her compassionate—and a trace of the thought lingered, not enough to convince her that he saw truly, but enough which, added to other such remarks he had made, would someday make her begin to wonder. For now, though, she paced the trail beside him, looking for the prints the ogre's huge feet had made, pressed down into the hardened dirt by its massive weight; for rocks showing the darkness of moisture where those feet had overturned them; and a dozen other such signs.

Then she heard a brushing noise in front of her and looked up to see an even uglier face glaring down at her.

Her fingers bit into Gregory's arm. "Do not move, dear, but look up!"

Gregory looked and froze.

She was a parody of the female form, a burlesque, a grotesque. Where the male's hair had been a thatch, hers was a bramble bush, grayed with age, and her face had so many wrinkles it was hard to pick out which ones held eyes and mouth. She wore a giant sack for a dress with neckhole and armholes raggedly scooped out. She was bow-legged and massive of limb and paw, and her mouth opened to reveal the yellowed stumps of snaggled teeth as she let out a roar, lifting a huge club two-handed above her head. Her eyes burned with fury as she swung it down.

They sprang to either side and the vast cudgel slammed into the earth where they had been. "My turn!" Allouette shouted, and glared at the ogre-hag, thinking with all her might of plant cells dissolving their bonds, of molecules breaking away from one another, of candles melting into puddles of wax.

But the huge club was rising again, and Gregory called, "Quickly, my heart!" as he drew his sword and leaped in.

The hag howled and pivoted, club swinging down.

"Gregory!" Allouette screamed, completely losing her concentration—but her lover leaped back, and the weapon hissed where he had been while, behind him, the horses echoed the ogre's shriek.

Allouette almost went limp with relief, then pulled herself together and focused madly on the thought of a snowman melting in the sun.

The horses pounded in side by side, necks stretching and teeth reaching for the ogre. She howled in rage, whirling her club in a roundhouse swing, but the horses reared and the club swished under their feet. Then those iron-shod hooves struck.

The ogre fell back with shouts of pain and bellows of rage. She began to swing her club in a circle overhead, wading back toward the warhorses, not realizing that she was sinking lower and lower with each step until she could no longer move. Only then did she look down, but before the horror of her dissolution could really break upon her, Allouette poured all her emotional energy into a vision of the snowman collapsing into slush, and the ogre disintegrated into a gelatinous mound.

"Well done!" Gregory embraced her, crowing with pride— so that she need sacrifice none of her own if she clung to him in dizziness or distress. "Oh, well and bravely done, my heart! Subtly and quickly, and the *coup de grace* delivered like a thunderclap!"

"But . . . but she was alive!" Allouette gasped. "And not slain, only . . . dissolved!"

"But so suddenly that she never knew," Gregory pointed out. "Besides, my love, what was the creature a week ago? Only this same mound of fungus, nothing more."

Allouette's trembling lessened.

"Besides, we could not leave it loose to gobble cattle and

smash the peasant folk," Gregory said with practicality, "and this was more merciful than slaying her with swords or horses' hooves."

"That is so." Allouette smiled up at him, tears drying on her cheeks. "Praise Heaven I have you to console me!"

He beamed and lowered his head a little more, to kiss her.

They went on their way, their horses side by side so that they could ride hand in hand. Inwardly, Gregory exulted that Allouette's heart had softened so much that she could weep for an enemy she had vanquished, even one so hideous and bloodthirsty as an ogre.

Scarcely an hour later, though, they encountered a peasant family, pacing beside an oxcart loaded with their household goods, their faces grim and grief-stricken.

Allouette reined in. "Hold, good people! Wherefore do you flee your home?"

"Why, because three ogres have come upon us, lady," the woman said, and dabbed at reddened eyes with her sleeve. "They have feasted on our cow, and we have no wish to follow her down their gullets."

"Heaven forbid," Gregory said.

"Heaven grant they have not gone ahead of us!" the husband returned.

"Be easy in that," Allouette told him. "Two of them have indeed gone before you, but they are slain."

"Slain!" Husband and wife exchanged a glance, and the children stared wide-eyed at the fine lady. Then the wife turned back to Allouette and stammered, "But how? Such great grisly things as those—who could dispatch them?"

"Is there some knight-errant who has come to slay them?" the husband asked. "But what weapon could dispatch such monsters?"

"Magic," Gregory answered, "and its wielder was no knight, but a witch."

"A witch!" The family shrank together, the mother's arms going instinctively around her children.

"Peace, peace," Allouette said, smiling. "She is a good witch, not an evil one, as you may see by her dispatching such villainous creatures as these. Moreover, she goes her way; you will certainly not encounter her ahead on the trail."

"If . . . if you say so, lady." The husband moved a little away from his family. "You have seen her, then?"

"She has come within my glance," Allouette admitted.

"Well, if you should see her again, give her our thanks," said the husband.

"Aye!" said the wife. "She may have slain them, but she has most likely saved our lives!"

Allouette stared at her, then looked up to find Gregory's gaze on her, glowing. She blushed and looked down again. "I rejoice to hear it. Go your ways, now, with no fear of either ogre or witch."

"But what of the third monster?" the wife asked. "We dare not go back to our cottage!"

"Where is this third one now?" Gregory asked.

"We only know that we saw it near our cottage," the father said.

"That is some help, at least," Allouette said. "Where did they come from?"

The parents spread their hands and shook their heads, at a loss, but one of the little girls piped up, "I saw them!"

"Hush, Essie!" the biggest boy hissed.

Essie rounded on him. "If Mama and Papa told us never to go there, Chogie, it was surely not because they feared ogres!"

"How is this?" the mother asked, frowning.

Essie looked up in alarm, then tucked her chin in truculently, hands locked behind her back. "We only went because the gooseberries are so much bigger and more juicy there."

"As well they might be, where the river overflows in nearly every rainstorm! I will not have you tracking mud all over the cottage!"

"We cleaned the mud off before we came home," Chogie muttered.

"Even so—" Mama began, but Allouette interrupted her.

"By your leave, good woman," she said, holding up a hand, "may we hear their tale? If there is a third ogre near, we must know whence it came, or we may find ourselves beset by more of the creatures."

The whole family looked up, wide-eyed and shocked at the thought.

"Perhaps you would indeed do well to repair to your lord's castle," Gregory said, "as you no doubt meant to. There will be time to come home when he tells you that the ogres have gone."

"If they leave our cottage standing," the wife said, tears in her eyes.

The husband put his arm around her. "There, now, even if they do not, three friends and I can build it anew in a fortnight—but what reason could ogres have to smash a cottage?"

"What reason have they for anything they do?" the wife moaned.

"Hunger," Allouette said. "I do not doubt they were simply hunting and foraging." She turned to the children. "So you went down by the river for gooseberries. What did you see?"

"Mist," Chogie said. "There is always some mist over the river in the morning, but this was much more thick and dense."

"And high," Essie added. "It was not plumes lifting, but a cliff of fog rising up to mask the sun."

"When all else was bright with sunlight?" Gregory asked.

The girl nodded. "A wall of mist, it was! And the ogres came out of it, all three."

"The gooseberry bush was between us and them," Chogie explained. "We crouched down and held our breaths."

"We were too frightened to breathe," Essie added.

"I was not frightened," Chogie said quickly.

"Oh, really!" Essie turned on him again. "Why then were you shaking in every limb?"

Chogie reddened and opened his mouth for a blistering retort, but Allouette quickly said, "Did you stay still till they had gone out of sight?"

"Yes, lady." Chogie turned back to her.

"And saw only three ogres come?"

Chogie nodded.

"Then we ran home and told Mama and Papa," Essie explained.

"Was the fog still there when you left?" Gregory asked.

"No." Chogie frowned, puzzled. "We looked back from the top of the slope, and the mist had thinned and lifted."

"Mist always burns off in the morning," Essie said condescendingly.

Chogie reddened. "Not so quickly! Not when it was so thick!"

"Yes, that is odd," Allouette said, frowning. "Was that only this morning?"

The children nodded. "Then Papa came home to tell us he had seen an ogre shambling across the field," Essie said, "so we took what we most needed to the cart."

"Wisely done," Gregory said.

Allouette turned to him. "Like enough, then, there is only the one left."

"It would seem so," Gregory said. "Still, let us be watchful."

Allouette nodded, then turned back to the family. "Thanks for this news, goodfolk. Go to your lord's castle, then. But be watchful—the third ogre might still be on the road."

"No, lady," the wife said. "We looked back at the turn and saw it breaking a tree."

Gregory and Allouette exchanged glances; Gregory nodded. "After it, then." He touched his heels to his horse's flanks.

"Beware!" the wife cried. "You are riding straight toward the monster!"

"We are indeed," Allouette assured her.

"Had you some thought of going onward?" the husband asked in alarm. "Oh, if you do, gentleman and damsel, do not, I pray you!"

"Have no fear for us," Allouette said, touched. "The witch who dispatched the first two shall surely be equal to the third."

"Has she ridden past us, then?" the wife asked, horrified,

and Essie and Chogie looked over their shoulders in fright.

"Do not fear," Allouette told them. "She rides past you even now."

"Where?" The husband and the wife looked about them frantically.

But Essie and Chogie stared up at Allouette, eyes round as saucers, and Essie raised a trembling finger to point at her. "There!"

"Even so." Gregory reached out and caught Allouette's hand. "The witch rides with me—so fear not, good people. I shall be quite safe from the ogre, and so shall you." With that, he clucked to his horse and rode on, Allouette's hand firmly clasped in his own. She gave one dazzling smile to the peasant family, then turned her eyes and her mind to the task ahead.

They didn't find the third ogre until the slapping of huge feet running up behind him made Gregory shout, "Beware!" as he pushed Allouette's horse away, sawing back on his own reins, pulling hard to the right. His horse reared, screaming in rage as the monster's acrid scent struck its nostrils. The huge club hurtled past it but grazed Gregory's leg—a graze from a club as thick as a ham. It cracked on bone and shot agony through his thigh and knee. He set his jaw against pain and set his mind to thinking of melting, but the pain seemed to send a red haze over everything he envisioned. Somehow, though, the ogre tripped and fell, its whole form shimmering and slumping into a shapeless mass as Allouette screamed, "Caitiff! Cat's meat!" She raged on in the same vein for several minutes, glaring at the flaccid heap. It seemed to wince with her every word. "Swine! Snake! Unnatural son of a lizard and a cow! Strike at my love, would you? Forever be fungoid, then! Worse—be no more than slime!"

The heap flowed outward, turning into a puddle that spread across the road. The horses retreated, nostrils flaring, picking their hooves fastidiously away from the moisture that was already evaporating to leave only a thin greenish coating over the hard-packed dirt.

"Peace, peace, sweet one!" Gregory gasped. "I am not so badly hurt as that!"

"Hurt? You are wounded!" Allouette turned from attacker to victim and touched his knee. "How bad is the pain? Nay, do not seek to be brave—I must know truly or I can do naught to heal!"

"The knee itself is fine," Gregory told her.

Skeptical, Allouette tapped his knee a bit harder.

Gregory shook his head. "No pain there at all. The thigh aches abominably and will no doubt bear a horrible bruise, but I doubt there is any real damage."

"Let me see." Allouette probed the outside of his thigh. Gregory stifled a groan between clenched teeth. She gave his face a sharp glance—then, frowning, set one hand on each side of his thigh as she pressed outward in a spiral. "How far does the pain go?"

Gregory caught his breath, eyes losing focus.

Allouette gave him a shrewd look, then a smile as she took her hands away. "Nay, if you can feel pleasure as well as pain, there is no lasting harm. But I'll not have you confusing the two, so put any thoughts of dalliance out of your mind!"

"I shall not even think of it," Gregory said with exaggerated innocence, "not when we still ride into danger."

"Yes, we do, do we not?" Allouette frowned at the road ahead. "There is the matter of this mist from which the ogres came."

Gregory nodded. "It sounds indeed like something wrought by an esper."

"How would an esper make mist?" Allouette asked, frowning, then instantly answered her own question. "Of course, by making water molecules cling to dust motes!"

"You knew the answer already." Gregory's eyes glowed.

"Oh, be done with your admiration!" Allouette scolded. "Anyone who knew a bit of physics could have worked it out! After all, mist forms when moist air cools and the molecules cling together—so when it is too warm for that, simply have them cling to something else!"

"And your telekinesis is equal to the task."

"Be done with your gloating, I said! I am no special woman to be able to use common sense."

"If you say so, love." Gregory turned back to the road with a covert smile.

Behind his back, Allouette allowed herself a small smile too, one of satisfaction. Gregory was so thoroughly besotted with her, mind, spirit, and body, that it might someday become irritating.

But not yet. Allouette gave a brief and unsparing look within her own heart and knew that her self-esteem was still so low that she could absorb a great deal of admiration before she tired of it.

A mile farther on, they met several families traveling together, looking nervously over their shoulders. When they saw the man and woman riding toward them, they did their best to wave them away with cries of "Forfend!" "Beware!" "Ride swiftly away, gentle folk!"

"Wherefore?" Gregory asked, drawing rein. "What lies ahead that is so terrible?"

"A wall of fog with huge hulking shadows that move within it!" one woman said.

"We doubt not that they wait only for nightfall to come out and fall upon us," a man added.

Allouette looked puzzled. "I thought the ogres came forth in the early morning."

"Ogres?" The peasants stared. "Have they come out, then?"

"Aye, some hours ago," Gregory said, "but banish your fears, for they have been vanquished utterly, and have left only slime behind."

That scared the people even more; they huddled together. "What monster could have vanquished ogres?" one quavered.

"A witch," said Gregory, "who sought to protect the common folk, like yourselves."

Allouette blushed but didn't deny it.

"Will . . . will she come this way?" a woman asked, eyes wide with fright.

"Is she needed?" Allouette asked sharply. "If so, tell me what dangers she must face!"

"Only what we have said," a man told her, "though we did find several sheep torn and half-eaten this morning, by the riverbank."

"The riverbank?" Allouette turned to Gregory. "A water spirit, do you think?"

"Say rather a monster," he answered, "though perhaps no more than a crocodile."

"A crocodile in an old wives' tale would be a dragon," Allouette pointed out.

"A dragon!" the people cried, and tightened their huddle.

"Peace, peace, good people!" Allouette said in a soothing tone. "We do not say that there is a dragon—only that there might be."

" 'Might be' is bad enough," a woman choked out.

"Well, we shall go and see." Gregory picked up his reins. "When you stop for the night, friends, camp on high ground and set sentries to watch all about."

"As you say, sir," said a man with military bearing—a retired trooper, Allouette thought. "But how shall you fare against such horrors?"

"I shall call upon the witch who defeated the ogres," Gregory answered, "and perhaps a wizard, too."

The people looked about them frantically again. "Are they here?" "Where?"

"Hard by you." Allouette reached out and caught Gregory's hand. "Come, wizard. Let us ride to this riverbank."

"Even so, witch," Gregory rejoined, and the two rode away, leaving the peasants staring after them.

The lowering sun gilded all the world as they neared the river—and saw before them the towering wall of fog, glowing like red gold in the sun's rays.

"How lovely." Allouette shivered. "But how menacing, when such beauty may hide horrors!"

Gregory's eyes glazed as he probed the mist with telepathy. Then he shuddered, coming back to the here and now. "There are bloodthirsty creatures within, with mind-sets such as I have never known—but they are few. We shall fare well enough against them."

"Perhaps we ought to call up allies." As Chief Agent, Allouette had been able to call on scores of men and women to aid her in her battles.

"We shall call if we have need," Gregory said thoughtfully, "but I think that you and I together are sufficient for anything that we might meet. Shall we ride?"

"Oh, very well!" Allouette kicked her heels against her horse's sides and rode forward.

The golden mist closed about them and the horses began to become nervous.

"They smell monsters," Allouette said.

"Something foul, at any rate." Gregory wrinkled his nose. "But it has more the smell of decaying plants than of supernatural villainy."

Then the horses stopped.

"Gee-up." Gregory kicked his horse, but it only dug in its hooves and put down its head.

"They are wiser than we," Allouette said, "and refuse to go on—but I confess that curiosity has gripped me now, dear heart."

"Let us see if we can lead them." Gregory dismounted and went ahead of his horse, tugging gently on the reins. The animal resisted for a minute, then grudgingly began to follow—but slowly.

"The ground squelches underfoot!" Allouette said, disgusted. "We must be nearing the river."

"Nearing?" Gregory stopped for a moment in surprise. "We have ridden far enough that we should have crossed it!"

"How then?" Allouette stared at him, but saw only his silhouette in the mist. Instinctively, she reached out to grasp his hand. "Has the river run away?"

"Rivers always run," Gregory said practically. "Walk warily, love. We may find our steps wetter than we wish ere long."

They started ahead—but Allouette's right boot wouldn't come free. "Gregory! I am stuck!"

"Here, I shall pull you free." Gregory turned back—and nearly fell on his face. "Mine, too! I cannot lift my foot!"

"Foot?" Allouette plucked up her skirts, looking down, and saw with horror that the mud had risen about her ankles. "I cannot see my feet! I am sinking!"

"We have blundered into a bog in the fog," Gregory groaned. "Hold tightly, and I shall try to rise above it!"

He exerted all the strength of his mind in levitation, but his feet scarcely budged.

"There is more than mud holding us down," Allouette cried with the thin edge of panic in her voice. "There is magic in this!"

CHAPTER
-3-

"Now I *shall* call for help," Gregory said, relenting, and set his mind to searching for his brother and sister.

Allouette joined him with all the fervor of the desperate. Just to play safe, she called out, "Help! Any who hear us, come aid!"

"A rescue, a rescue!" Gregory cried.

"Wherefore, brother?" called a voice from the fog. "What could have overcome you?"

Gregory stared. "Geoffrey? How came you here?"

"Why, you called, did you not? Call again, brother, and keep calling, or we shall not be able to find you!"

"We?" Allouette asked with dread.

"Your prince and liege," Alain's voice called. "Sing high, damsel, or we shall blunder right past you!"

Allouette groaned instead.

Geoffrey shouldered out of the fog. His mouth twitched at the sight of them, but he had the grace not to laugh. "Alain, find a long limb of a tree! Our friends are bogged down."

"As you say." The prince materialized out of the mist, saw

them, stared, then gave himself a shake, knowing it was impolite. He extended a fallen branch. "Will this reach?"

"Yes, thank Heaven!" Gregory shoved the stick over toward Allouette.

"Aid me, Geoffrey," Alain said. "Leverage is against me."

"It rarely works *for* me." Geoffrey bent down to take hold of the wood.

"Hold fast, dear," Gregory urged Allouette while his eyes commiserated—it had to be very unpleasant, being rescued by your former intended victim. He wondered if it would be worse if she had been rescued by Cordelia and Quicksilver, her former rivals. With a look that said she did it only to please him, Allouette shivered and took a tighter hold on the branch.

Geoffrey and Alain began to pull. For a moment, there was no sign of progress; then, very slowly, Allouette began to move.

"Heave!" Geoffrey cried. As Allouette began to move more easily, he called out, "Good fortune that you did not go very far into the mud!"

"No fortune at all," Gregory called back. "*You* try taking more than two steps in this glue! On second thought, do not!"

"If you say so," Geoffrey said equably, and started his next pull as Alain ended his. Inch by inch, the two of them hauled Allouette to safe ground. She came up the last yard on her knees, eyes downcast. "I—I thank you, sirs."

"My pleasure," Alain said gravely. "I am glad to be of some use."

"Rare talk, for a crown prince!" Geoffrey slapped him on the shoulder. "Haul in our other fish."

Alain pushed the branch out over the mud again. Gregory caught it, then held on grimly while the two young men pulled. The mud did not give him up easily; he felt as though it were pulling on him just as strongly as his brother and friend. Then a mighty sucking sound announced his liberation and he began to move slowly toward the shore.

"Up with you, now!" Geoffrey yanked him by the collar and lifted, and Gregory came to his knees with solid ground under him. "I was never so glad for honest sod!" he said fervently.

"Nonetheless, I find myself unsure." Geoffrey surveyed his brother critically. "How say you, Alain? Is he too small to keep? Should we throw him back?"

But Alain's gaze was on the woman who sat gazing down at her muddy skirt and boots, clearly fighting back tears. "Aye, a shame it is to see so pretty a traveling cloak and such handsome boots so besmeared with foulness. Yet take heart, damsel—they can surely be cleaned. The skirt is of stout linen, is it not?"

"It is, Your Highness," Allouette said, her voice low.

"I appreciate the courtesy," Alain said gently, "but if we are to be kin, you should call me by name."

"I cannot!" Allouette cried, and the tears flowed. "I deserve whipping at your hands, not kindness!"

Gregory was beside her in two steps, enfolding her in his arms. "Yes, darling, I know—kindness and courtesy can cut worse than hatred. Still, the prince means you well."

"I do indeed," Alain said gravely, "and would rejoice if all citizens of this land could so good-hearted toward one another as you have proved toward Gregory."

Allouette burst into sobs, completely undone not just by the words of praise alone, but by the plain sincerity of their speaker.

Geoffrey for once took his cue from Alain. "I have broken lances with many a foe who afterwards became a friend, and I hope you shall prove such a one."

"I shall, I shall!" Allouette choked.

"Come then, sweet chuck," Gregory said. "You will not break a lance on my brother, I trust!"

The tension of the moment stretched out thin as a thread of silk; then Allouette gave a strange sort of strangled laugh.

Geoffrey grinned, relaxing a little. "Come, shall I call you sister? For you, most certainly, shall call me rogue!"

"I shall call you a brave and courteous knight." Allouette finally managed to look up at him, then turned to her fiancé. "How shall I bear to live among so kindly a family?"

"By being kindly to them," Gregory replied, "and you have made a brave beginning." He looked up at his brother and his friend. "Shall we wend our way onward, then?"

"Why not?" Geoffrey said. "Where had you in mind?"

Gregory shrugged. "I know not, brother, save that peasant folk directed us to this mist. It was from here, they said, that the ogres came."

"Ogres?" Alain tensed, glancing to left and to right.

"We saw no ogres," Geoffrey said, frowning. Then his brow cleared. "But we did find three huge piles of witch-moss! Well done, indeed! I trust they did not injure you before you disintegrated them."

"It was Allouette did that," Gregory said, "and she suffered not at all."

"But he did!" Allouette said. "The last great hulking brute struck him with its club! I wish I could have torn it to bits!"

"I think you did better than that." But Alain's voice was oddly cool.

Allouette glanced up anxiously. Which had put him on his guard again—her skill with telekinesis or her anger?

Geoffrey frowned with concern. "Are you hurt then, brother?"

"It is only a bruise," Gregory said, "though I suspect it may penetrate to the bone."

"Not so far as that." Allouette laid her hand on his arm, quick to reassure. "I probed with thought. It is only in the muscle, and it will heal."

Geoffrey gave her a quizzical glance, as though trying to classify her—friend or foe? "Still, you should ride," he said to Gregory. "We go farther into this mist, then?"

"Aye, but warily," Gregory told him, then turned to Allouette. "Will you lead my horse, so that I can bind my attention to thoughts all around us?"

Now, the last thing Allouette wanted was to be left effectively alone with her two former targets. "Do you lead me, dea . . . sir wizard, and I shall scan."

"Gregory is best of us all at that," Geoffrey objected. "Even his name means 'watcher.' "

"And I have been too much a watcher of life and not enough of a doer, until my love came along." Gregory squeezed her hand. "Nay, brother, my Allouette is quite equal to the task."

Alain eyed her thoughtfully, and Allouette had to resist a very strong impulse to read his thoughts. No need, though, really—she knew he would be thinking, *She kept watch on us well enough, after all.* Still, when he spoke, his voice was kind, though reserved: "I had not known you were as skilled as Gregory, lady."

"In some things, Your Highness." She tried to meet his eyes but failed.

"Come, I am Alain to you now, even as I said." His tone warmed. "Mount and be sentry for us, then, while Gregory leads us through this cloud come to earth."

Geoffrey brought her horse up to her, telling it, "There now, none blame you for not pulling your mistress out of the mire, and certainly not for staying out of it yourself. Do you bear her proudly, then."

Allouette mounted, wishing that she would be able to believe him as easily as the horse did, if he told her she was not to blame. That, though, would never happen—she had done what she had done, and though those actions had been founded on misconceptions, biases she had been taught, and a world made far worse than it needed to be, she was nonetheless responsible for her own actions. Admittedly, once she had confronted those festering memories and discredited them, she seemed to be a different person entirely—she looked back on her days as Agent Finister, at the things she had done and that had been done to her, and the Chief Agent seemed to be a different person entirely.

Still, she could not rebuild her life as though she had never been stolen from her mother and reared with lies, half-truths, and manipulation as ever-present as the air she had breathed. She could, however, accept the responsibility for what she had done as Agent Finister, make what amends she could, and live the future so that it would make up for the deeds of her past.

And, of course, cherish this strange, powerful, but tender man who, against all logic and common sense, loved her so deeply. She wondered if being loyal to love could redeem her.

As they rode, Geoffrey and Alain conferred in low tones. Allouette scarcely noticed, because Gregory had posed her a difficult question.

"There is an old saying, love, that once may be chance, twice may be coincidence—"

"But the third time is enemy action?" Allouette turned to him, puzzled. "But three ogres is surely one mischance, not three!"

"A point well taken," Gregory said, musing. "But the mist persists. What if more monsters come from it?"

"Why, we shall dissolve them again." Allouette shrugged. "You cannot mean to let them wander about the land, can you?"

"No—but I was wondering at the source of a mist that produces monsters."

"But that is no riddle! We have already dealt with it—it is but a matter of gathering moisture into droplets!"

"Indeed it is," said Gregory, "but who gathered them?"

Allouette started to answer, then stopped, brow knit. "You mean that someone may be making mist and monsters both."

"I had thought that," Gregory said. "That would be two incidents, would it not?"

"It could still be coincidence," Allouette said, but her expression belied it. "The mist could be natural, the ogres could have been abroad early, and the children could have put the two together in their minds and thought the mist had borne the creatures when it had really been only happenstance."

"Children would be likely to see such where it is not," Gregory agreed.

"But we must consider the possibility that they did not." Allouette scowled. "Who, then, crafted both?"

"Surely we shall know if we meet a fourth monster," Gregory said, "though since we go seeking them, perhaps we are making the very pattern that we look for."

"Perhaps," Allouette said absently.

Gregory looked at her, realized she was already deep in thought, and said, "I shall bear these tidings to my brother."

"Aye, do," Allouette said.

Gregory turned back to Geoffrey. As he did, Alain pushed his horse forward. In a minute he was riding beside Allouette, who was still deeply concentrating on the problem. Alain knew the signs and rode in silence.

All at once Allouette looked up, eyes widening in alarm. "Your Highness! I had not meant—"

"Nor did you," Alain interrupted. "You were puzzling out our common enemy, for which I am grateful. Have you worked out who or what it might be?"

"There is still too little information to risk an answer," Allouette said with chagrin.

"But enough to raise a question?"

Allouette stared at him. "How did you know that, Highness? You do not read minds!"

"No, but I have spent much time with the Gallowglass family, and I know the signs."

Allouette turned back toward the front, watching him out of the corners of her eyes. "Does the lady Cordelia do such guesswork, then?"

"Constantly," Alain said, "and I have grown to trust her intuition enormously—though she tells me the cost of her intuition is high. However, the education is certainly worth it."

Allouette frowned at him, not understanding, then saw his lips curve upward a little. "It is a jest!" she accused.

"I had to have it explained to me, too," Alain confessed. "I asked her if she would prefer that I spoke of her having a hunch, but she answered that Notre Dame was not her church."

Allouette stared, then gave a peal of laughter, though she tried to muffle it with her hand.

"Ah, I see you know the tale of the bell-ringer," Alain

said, smiling. "I did not, when she first told it me, so she gave me the book and told me to read it."

"Surely that is quite impertinent conduct, from a subject to her prince!"

"But quite appropriate between fiancés," Alain rejoined. "Besides, it was an enjoyable tale."

"And the ringing of church bells will never seem the same to you?" Allouette couldn't help a smile.

"It does have a peal," Alain acknowledged, and grinned as she tried to throttle her merriment. "Pray do not deprive us of the musical sound of so merry a laugh, lady!"

"That must have been your reply to Cordelia," Allouette accused.

"You mean that, like the bell, I might have tolled her so?"

Allouette stared again, then broke into a full and open laugh. "Prince, I had not known you knew how to jest so!"

"Just so?" Alain asked. "Nay, surely, lady—I must have learned something of wit, for I was surely not born with it. I can appreciate its quality, but when it comes to good jesting, I can only sit and applaud, and thereby be—"

"A clapper?" Allouette asked with a covert smile. "Fie, Prince Alain! Must you wring every last drop of laughter from these bells of yours?"

"A touch!" Alain cried with delight. "A distinct touch! I had known you could not be so serious as you feigned!"

"Ah! Fane would I be witty!" Allouette sighed.

So the two former adversaries rode, trading jests and witticisms, and if some of them were far older than either of the two and nowhere nearly worth the amount of laughter they brought, that was all to the better for healing of wounds. But Alain was the sly one in that exchange, for while he distracted the lady with humor, her fiancé was reassuring his brother about her.

"Did she truly dissolve all three ogres by herself?" Geoffrey asked.

"I turned the first one to mush," Gregory admitted, "but she did indeed disassemble the other two, and the third, due to the force of her anger, in a matter of seconds."

"What angered her so?" Geoffrey demanded, then answered his own question. "Of course, the blow that struck your thigh. Is she your fiancée, brother, or a mother bear?"

"She will be a most formidable mother," Gregory said proudly, "if we should be blessed with offspring."

"If you are, bid farewell to concentration and scholarship for some years," Geoffrey warned. "This is not a lady to take all of such a burden on herself."

"Nor would I wish her to," Gregory said placidly. "Still, I know, from the tales Magnus told of my infancy, that a mother who is also an esper has certain advantages in caring for babes."

"Yes, such as crafting toys upon the instant." Geoffrey shook his head. "Her power over witch-moss is most disconcerting, brother. I had known she was a powerful projective telepath, but I had not known she also excelled in telekinesis!"

"She does not," Gregory answered, "but so powerful a projective with even mild competence at molding matter with her mind can be devastating when she wishes."

"I see the sense in that," Geoffrey said slowly, "and can only acclaim such strength—when it is wielded in my defense."

"Or your brother's?" Gregory asked with a smile. "I suspect that she will guard any who are dear to me with almost as much ferocity as my own person."

"I begin to think that she *is* your own person, brother," Geoffrey said with a touch of sarcasm, and when Gregory's only reply was a smug smile went on to ask, "Can she follow the spoor of this ominous mist that we seek?"

"Why should she?" Gregory pointed to a range of hills ahead, their tops sending streamers of mist into the lowering clouds above. "Yonder lies our fog, does it not?"

Geoffrey stared a moment, then nodded slowly. "I think you have the right of it, brother. Let us climb upward and seek."

●　●　●

The roads slanting upward across the slope had been worn hard and smooth, so the companions had no difficulty riding a series of switchbacks into the foggy realm at the peak. They were almost to the summit when a ululating howl sounded ahead, echoed a second later on each side and behind. Alain and Geoffrey barely had time to draw their swords before the ambush closed upon them.

There were no monsters this time, only men and women, though their eyes glared white in faces painted ochre and scarlet. They wore crudely tanned leather kilts and swathes of dun-colored homespun and screamed like berserkers, brandishing flint axes and wooden bucklers.

Alain and Geoffrey met their onslaught with shield and sword, bellowing in answer to the howls and shearing through the handles of the flint axes by the handful—but as the heads fell off, they flew spinning at the ambushers behind, swooping and diving like hawks.

Allouette's face was taut with the strain of guiding so many weapons. Gregory's was, too, as a series of warriors tripped over their own feet and went sprawling. Those behind stumbled over them and somersaulted to the ground.

None of them stopped howling for a second.

"Beware, my love!" Gregory shouted. "There are simply too many of them . . . Allouette? Allouette!"

His answer was a scream. He whirled to see half a dozen mountaineers carrying off his true love, thrashing and kicking and biting. Axeheads flew at them, knocking one after another away, but for every one who fell, another leaped in to take her place.

"Avaunt!" Gregory shouted, and earth and rock exploded before them. They hesitated but kept on going.

"A rescue, a rescue!" Alain shouted.

Gregory whirled, seeing four mountaineers descending on the prince. For a moment he wavered, then realized that he couldn't go after Allouette alone. He shouted. "To blazes with you!"

Gouts of fire shot from the earth, ringing the prince. The

mountaineers' howls slid into shrieks of fear as they fell back.

Gregory spun, glaring at the kidnappers again. Three of them stumbled and fell, but three more leaped in to wrap arms around the struggling woman. One shrieked and fell, clutching at his leg, but a woman hurdled his body to seize Allouette's waist in his stead. Then one of the mountaineers lost patience and swung a club at her head. Allouette went limp.

Gregory went berserk. He screamed like a banshee, and dozens of mountaineers clapped their hands to their heads, stumbling and falling or weaving about, aware of nothing but the fire in their brains. Allouette's bearers stumbled, too, four of them losing hold of her—but the remaining two blundered doggedly ahead. Fire erupted in their path; still they plowed onward. Boulders vibrated, rocked, then rolled down upon them; they dodged and kept going.

Then, suddenly, all the mountaineers were running after them, pounding uphill after the hostage and her bearers.

"They flee!" Alain leaned on his sword, gasping for breath.

"Wherefore?" Geoffrey cried, then saw the bearers with their precious load disappear into a rocky maze. "Out upon them! Gregory, leap and seek!"

With a double explosion, both young men disappeared. They reappeared a split second later, standing upon a boulder high on the hill, looking down into the maze—but wind-twisted evergreens overhung the rocky channels, hiding the mountaineers from sight, and a host of triumphant thoughts shielded those of the bearers from discovery.

Gregory fell to his knees with a scream of anguish and loss.

CHAPTER
-4-

With a bang, Geoffrey was beside him, hand on his shoulder. "Courage, brother! We shall find her, we shall hunt throughout these hills until we have her safe again!"

"I shall tear this mountain apart if I have to!" Gregory's face was twisted with anger and pain. "I shall rend each of them limb from limb if they seek to keep me from her! And if they dare to hurt her, each one shall die a slow and agonizing death!"

Geoffrey blinked, staring in surprise. Never had his gentle little brother been so caught up in rage; never had the abstracted scholar been so wracked with emotion—and it wasn't until that moment that he realized just how passionately Gregory loved. In fact, it wasn't until that moment that he had known his brother was capable of passion.

First Allouette became aware of a crushing headache. She tried to go back to sleep to escape it, but the pain was too severe and wouldn't let her go. In desperation, she reached into her own brain and boosted her endorphin production.

The pain didn't go away, but it became oddly removed, as though on the far side of an invisible barrier; she knew it was there but no longer cared.

That freed her mind to concentrate on causes. Moving through the endorphin-induced haze, she took inventory of her head and found the lump on her crown. No wonder she was in pain! She moved busily but deliberately, mending damaged capillaries, draining the blood that had pooled, and generally restoring the site to its normal condition.

As the pain eased, she was freed to wonder what had caused the bruise—and memory came flooding back: a horde of painted, kilted, unkempt savages. But where were they? Come to that, where was she?

Finally she turned her attention to the outside world—and recognized laughing, boastful conversation, and a general party atmosphere. The accent was thick but she knew she could puzzle it out. Even if she couldn't, she could read their minds—when her headache was completely gone.

But if she found herself in the camp of her enemies, how free could she be? She pushed with her arms and, sure enough, felt restraints. Another push with her feet told her that her ankles were lashed together—and, now that she thought of it, there was pressure on her mouth, considerable pressure, and a knot pressing the base of her skull—a gag, then.

So they knew her for a witch and were taking no chances.

But how alert were they? She let her eyelids flutter, parting them just enough to peer through her lashes. One of the mountaineers was sitting beside her with a warclub on his knee—but he wasn't looking at her, was instead laughing and raising a wooden mug in a toast to something someone else called out.

Allouette looked to the side and saw his friends—silhouettes around a campfire. She could dimly make out faces on the other side of the flames.

Now she bent her attention to trying to decipher their accent and let her endorphin level ebb so that she could concentrate a bit better. The headache increased, but it was nowhere nearly the crippling pain that had awakened her. Allowing for gutturals where there should have been H's and K's, for missing L's and TH's, and for some oddly distorted vowels, she deciphered their accent and realized they were saying:

"Aye, Zonploka will be greatly pleased with us, that's sure!"

"Well, he should be! The young wizard's lover? The lad will dare not move against us while we have her—and will keep his whole family at bay!"

"Aye, the High Warlock, the High Witch, and all their brood! Then, too, mind you, this one is a doughty witch in her own right."

"Not with that gag on her mouth, she's not! How'll a witch work a spell without speech, eh?"

Very well, actually, Allouette thought, but she wasn't about to let her captors know that espers didn't need to be able to talk to read thoughts, make objects move, make people think they saw things that weren't really there, or feel emotions they'd never known. In fact, the more helpless they thought she was, the greater her advantage.

So she lay still, listening to the mountaineers crow over their victory.

"Not just keeping the Crown's witches and wizards away!" one boasted. "If Zonploka is right, we'll be able to bid them clear the county of all the folk around these mountains, peasants and nobles alike!"

"Aye! Then we'll rule the lands our ancestors held!"

"We, and Zonploka's people," another reminded.

"True, but he only means to gather his army here. They'll not stay, they'll move out to conquer the land—but we'll hold the county! Zonploka has promised it!"

Some renegade sorcerer, then, who had promised them dominion for helping his treachery against the Crown and the people—and they expected him to keep his promise? Allouette could have pitied these poor naive peasants if it hadn't been for the pounding in her head.

But who, she wondered, was Zonploka?

There was no way to tell, and not enough information to work it out, though she did puzzle at the matter while she waited for the celebration to wind down and the mountaineers to fall asleep. She tried to project a thought to Gregory to reassure him she was well, but found the effort made her head ache worse and seemed to do no good. She would have to wait for the minor concussion to heal, then. She did manage to read the minds of the people near her and gained a good deal of information about their daily lives, including who lusted after whom and who had promised her favors to whom else, but she had to stop because even that slight effort increased her headache again.

So she lay still, working at lulling the headache into absence as, one by one, the mountaineers sought their beds of bracken. Some went two by two but were too thoroughly drunken to stay awake—and at last, Allouette was the only one conscious, hearing nothing but the breeze in the leaves and the noises of the small animals who inhabited the heights.

She reached out with a tendril of thought, exploring the lashings that held her hands. Yes, they were knots she knew. The effort wakened her headache again but this time she ignored it, making thong slide against thong as she lifted her head, opening her eyes to watch the knots untying themselves. When the leather fell away, she chafed her wrists to restore circulation, then flexed her fingers until the pins and needles had stopped. Finally she sat up—slowly, carefully, so as not to make the headache worse—and untied the thongs that bound her ankles. It took longer than telekinesis but didn't increase the pain in her head. Then she chafed her ankles, flexing her toes and making circles with her feet. She almost groaned aloud as the prickling began but clamped her jaw shut, waiting and massaging until she was sure her legs would bear her. Then, finally, she pushed herself to her feet and crept off into the night.

She would have made it and done no harm to anyone, but as she stepped over one man, he happened to turn in his sleep, tripping her. She fell heavily, then scrambled up—but a rough basso voice called, "Who moves?"

Allouette cursed; one sentry had stayed sober. She ran for the trees, but he saw her and ran after, shouting, "Waken! Catch her! Don't let her get away!"

Half the camp woke; ten of them made it to their feet and blundered after her in the dark, shouting and bellowing, for all the world like hounds on a scent.

Allouette kept stumbling toward the trees, but her legs still weren't working properly. When she heard the heavy thudding of feet behind her, she turned. The sentry shouted with triumph, swinging a warclub at her head. She pivoted, caught the arm and a handful of tunic, shoved out her hip, and threw him headlong into the bracken.

But it had delayed her long enough for the pack to catch her. A woman in the forefront swung her own warclub; Allouette blocked, but pain seared through her forearm. She caught the weapon with her other hand, twisted as she kicked the woman's feet out from under her, and turned to fend off another blow left-handed. She knocked it aside and recovered to crack the man's pate, but saw a quarterstaff swinging down at her right side and another warclub swinging from her left and knew with despair, even as she whirled aside from the staff and swung her own weapon to block the warclub, that they would bear her down by the weight of sheer numbers.

Then a double scream split the night, female voices howling in rage, and two furies leapt in among the mountaineers, one whirling a quarterstaff like a windmill, the other laying about her with a sword and smashing her shield into a bearded face.

Allouette froze for a second's disbelief, then realized that she still had a chance of escape and leaped into the fight with elation.

In minutes, the three women were back to back in a tight triangle. The mountaineers charged them *en masse*—once. Allouette felled one with her warclub, but another's fist cracked against her cheek. She staggered, the night suddenly filling with sparks, but through the roaring in her ears she could hear the furies' scream. When her vision cleared, she found herself staring at the woman who had struck her—now lying flat on the ground.

Another mountaineer bellowed; Allouette looked up, but the attacker was to her right. She gave a quick glance, saw a staff blur, heard it crack on the man's skull, and saw him falling. Three women screamed with rage on her left; Allouette turned to look and saw them charging her defender. She swung, hard and quick. Her club struck a shoulder and its owner staggered with a howl, clutching her hurt—but the other two fell back, their shields gouged with massive cuts.

Suddenly there was silence, the ring of mountaineers glaring at the women with hatred, looking for an opening, a weakness. Allouette cast a thought at a woman's ankle, tugging, but she still hadn't recovered from the blow that had knocked her out, and the mountaineer only glanced down in irritation.

Then one of the mountaineers' clubs swung to her left, hard, striking the cheek of the man beside him. "Owoo!" the man howled. "What did you do that for, Castya?"

"I didn't," the woman protested, "I only—"

But another man howled as a club struck his shoulder and a third bellowed as still another club struck a knee.

" 'Tis witchcraft!" a woman cried, her eyes huge. "Flee!"

They all turned and ran—except one hulking brute who snarled and waddled toward the three women, club swinging high—and higher and higher, jerking out of his hand, then tumbling end over end in front of his face. His eyes went round as platters and he turned and ran too, his own club chasing him.

"Enough, sister-to-be," one of Allouette's rescuers panted. "He will not come back."

Allouette recognized the voice. With foreboding, she turned to face her rescuers. "I . . . I must thank you . . ."

"Must you indeed!" Quicksilver cried. "Does that mean you would not if you did not have to?"

"Oh, don't badger the poor woman, Quicksilver!" Cordelia

said. "Can't you see that lump on her head? And the way her arm is hanging! Here, Allouette, let me see!" She stepped forward to take hold of Allouette's limp arm and bend it, moving her hand toward her shoulder gently, tentatively, slowly . . .

"There!" Allouette gasped.

Cordelia held the arm still, gazing off into space as her thoughts probed the bruise; then she nodded. "Only some little damage to the muscle and a swelling in the cartilage of the elbow. Hold still, Allouette." She gazed at the elbow.

Allouette caught the distinction—that Cordelia called her by name, but Quicksilver "sister-to-be." Still, what could their would-be assassin expect?

Cordelia released the arm and stepped back. "It will serve you now. Use it lightly if you can—the tissues must still do some healing of their own."

"I—I thank you," Allouette stammered. "How—how could you have so much compassion as to save me from those brutes?"

"We shall all be of the same family soon," Quicksilver said with a shrug, "and kin guard kin."

"So I shall," Allouette promised fervently.

"Why then, you owe us a life now," Quicksilver said with a smile, "or at least, your liberty."

"I owe you far more than that!"

"We shall collect in good time, I doubt not." Quicksilver looked around the campsite with a frown. "How came you here, and in such bondage?"

"Gregory and I learned from a peasant family that three ogres had come out of a most strange mist," Allouette explained.

"They were only of witch-moss, I hope?" Cordelia asked.

"Aye, and we turned them back into the jelly from which they'd come."

Quicksilver made a noise of disgust. "What a waste of a good chance for a fight!"

"Aye, but quicker, I am sure. So when they were undone,

you sought along their backtrail to discover the mist from which they'd come?"

"Aye, and blundered into a bog for our pains."

Quicksilver grinned.

Allouette blushed. "Your fiancés pulled us out."

Quicksilver and Cordelia exchanged a glance of surprise. "We have come faster than they, then."

"Either that, or they have gone astray in their search." Quicksilver frowned. "Could they not track by thought?"

"Not mine," said Allouette. "The knock on the head those mountaineers gave me has sorely diminished my powers."

Quicksilver looked up in surprise; then a calculating look came into her eye and Allouette shuddered, knowing that the woman had cause to want revenge—not as much cause as Cordelia, but enough.

" 'Tis also possible that these mountaineers may have taken you closer to our route than to the men's path," Cordelia mused. "You were unconscious, were you not?"

"Aye, for some hours."

"Time enough," Quicksilver said drily. Then her face darkened. "What use had they for you?"

"Only as a hostage," Allouette assured them. "Indeed, they drank so heavily that I doubt they could have managed anything else."

"Drank?" The former outlaw's eye kindled. "Did they talk while they were in their cups—perhaps to tell you why they had set upon you?"

"They did as they were bade," Allouette replied, "by a sorcerer named Zonploka."

Quicksilver frowned at Cordelia, who frowned back. "I have never heard that name."

"Nor I," Cordelia confessed.

" 'Tis strange to me, too," Allouette admitted, "but whoever he or she is, he has hoodwinked the mountaineers into thinking that they act for the good of their people. From what these raiders said, they wish to clear this county of peasants."

"Wherefore?" Quicksilver demanded.

"As a staging area for the sorcerer's army," Allouette replied. "When it marches off, the sorcerer has promised the valley to the mountaineers, who believe their ancestors held it."

Quicksilver shrugged. "That may be so; it would not be the first time that peaceful people have been driven out by warlike and learned to become warriors in their turn."

"Perhaps," said Cordelia, "but they are fools to think a conquering army will give up territory once they've gained it."

"That is so." Quicksilver turned to Allouette, and there was an edge to her voice. "You who were chieftain of spies and assassins—would you yield what you had gained?"

Anger surged in Allouette, but she contained it. "I am no such creature anymore—but villain or householder, I would fight to keep what is mine!"

"Right and proper," said Quicksilver, "but what if you had stolen it?"

" 'What if' indeed," Allouette asked, "O bandits' chieftain?"

Quicksilver gave her a toothy grin. "Never in a thousand years yield what I had gained!"

"Only a thousand?" Allouette retorted. Her stomach sank— she felt she was losing any chance of Quicksilver's forgiveness—but her pride wouldn't let her back down.

Quicksilver only shrugged. "A hundred would do. I would not live to see it. Let my children fight for what I'd gained!"

Allouette stared, amazed that the warrior hadn't loosed a torrent of insults. Then she recovered and said, "I do not doubt that the brood of so redoubtable a dam would fight for every inch."

"What if it were not rightfully theirs?" Cordelia asked quietly.

"Rightfully?" Quicksilver asked. "We speak of an army of conquest, lady! Wherefore would they speak of right or wrong?"

Allouette nodded. "To those who come in conquest, 'right' means only their self-interest."

Cordelia shuddered. "Alas, poor land—and poor moun-

taineers, who shall be so rudely betrayed! We must discover
who this Zonploka is, who has promised them and will betray
them!"

"Where shall we seek this foul sorcerer?" Allouette asked.

"Why, where you were bound ere they kidnapped you,"
Quicksilver answered, "in the mist that spawns monsters!
Come, let us find their trail."

"Where?" Cordelia spread her hands. "We cannot know if
they bore Allouette toward those mists, or far from their
track."

"We can," said Quicksilver, "if we capture one and ask
him." She caressed her sword's pommel. "Let us track these
mountaineers, ladies, and while we journey, think of arguments that might persuade them to yield up what they know."

Cordelia glanced at the sword hilt with a jaundiced eye.
"We shall, if you leave the persuading to us."

"But stand behind us as we ask," Allouette said with a
vindictive smile. "Our arguments may prove all the more
effective for your presence."

"So that it be our questions that be keen and not her
sword," Cordelia said quickly, then turned to scan the moun-
tainside and point toward a stunted tree. "As memory serves,
yonder they went."

Quicksilver glanced at the ground and the tracks of running feet, and nodded. "Your memory serves you well." She
put fingers to her lips and blew a shrill whistle. A neighing
answered them; two horses came trotting out of the trees.

Allouette stared. "How have I robbed you of your mounts
during battle?"

"Because surprise was more important than being
mounted," Quicksilver explained, "and our horses would
have drawn the mountaineers' attention. You shall have to
ride behind me, lady. Up and after them!"

"I could not impose so." Allouette wasn't at all happy
about sharing a horse with a woman who had doubts about
her, but told herself that surely it must be a good sign for
Quicksilver to trust the former spy behind her back. Nonetheless, she frowned in concentration for a moment.

A whinny that was surely filled with relief answered her, then galloping hoofbeats, and her own horse came pounding across the grass to her.

"She lost track of me among the mountaineers' scents," Allouette explained, "and I am only now recovered enough to summon her."

"Besides, you were somewhat distracted," Quicksilver said drily. "Well, then, damsel, mount and ride."

They set off uphill, and Allouette noticed with chagrin that the other women were careful to stay beside her, not letting her fall behind. She sighed and hoped it was out of concern for her wound.

After a few minutes, Allouette looked up at the sky with a frown.

"What troubles you?' Quicksilver demanded.

"That we travel southeast," Allouette said, "when the trail that I took with Gregory was northwest."

Quicksilver frowned, musing. "There is sense in that, if the mountaineers came from the place where they ambushed you."

"It is, is it not?" Allouette sighed. "Well, we must backtrack before we can turn and go forward again. I had hoped they had taken me back to their lair."

"Perhaps they had," Cordelia said, "but their lair lies near to where they ambushed you."

"Then why would they have brought me here?"

The three women were silent, looking at one another and at the scenery around them, trying to puzzle out the question. Then Cordelia hazarded a guess. "Could they have been taking you to meet their master in the mists?"

"Likely enough," Quicksilver snapped.

Allouette shuddered. "I must thank you even more for your kind rescue, damsels. I had rather not meet this Zonploka—nay, not until I know something more about him."

"Wise," Quicksilver acknowledged. "Well, let us follow their trail back to their lair if we must, and seize one who lags behind."

They set off again.

An hour later they came to a meadow, but one most thoroughly torn up in its center. Allouette looked about her as though scenting the winds. "It was here! It was here they set upon us!"

Quicksilver looked about, nodding. "Close enough to the trees for cover but with open space in which to fight. Their chieftain's not a complete fool, at least."

"But where," Cordelia asked, "are our men?"

The women looked about, puzzling over the matter. Then Quicksilver scowled at the ground and began to prowl the site of the skirmish. "There! 'Tis the mark of Geoffrey's boot—I would know it anywhere!"

"Gregory's should be much like it." Cordelia came to stand beside her. "We have all the same cobbler . . . There!" She pointed. "There stood Gregory, and from the flattened grass he struck well . . ."

"But Geoffrey stepped here behind him," Quicksilver said, "and struck another villain, like as not. A pox upon it! I can tell almost nothing from this fray!"

"The ground is too much chewed up," Cordelia agreed.

"Let us seek at its edge, then." Allouette began to prowl about the perimeter.

"A good thought." Quicksilver came to join her.

"Here the mountaineers fled." Cordelia pointed down at the ground. " 'Tis a trampled mire save two whose prints are deeper, and therefore clear."

"They must have been the ones who carried me!" Allouette scowled downward. "Smaller feet—here Gregory stood . . . but what mean these ovals in the grass?"

Quicksilver came to look. "Shins, lady. Your fiancé fell to his knees in his grief over your abduction."

Allouette looked up at her, startled, then down again to keep the glow within her from showing in her face. "Do you truly think so?"

"I doubt it not," Quicksilver assured her, then went back to prowling the edge of the morass. She stopped, pointing.

"The heels are deeper. Cordelia, are these your fiancé's boots?"

Cordelia came to look and nodded. "Even such does the royal cobbler fashion. But where is he going?"

"Hither and yon, I think," Quicksilver said, exasperated, "and here are Geoffrey's prints beside him. Let us trace their path."

"Gregory rose and came this way." Allouette stepped toward them, eyes on the ground. "Why, he came to join the others!"

"Now they all wander together," said Quicksilver, and so did the three women, moving in a triangle toward the trees.

Following the prints, they went in among the leaves. It was harder to follow the trail in the flickering shadows, but they managed, tracing its twists and turns until . . .

"They have come back to the meadow!" Cordelia cried.

"Odd indeed," Quicksilver said, frowning. "Even more, for they turn and go back in among the leaves."

They followed the men's footprints again. This time the winding route was longer, but its end was the same.

"The meadow again!" Quicksilver cried in exasperation. "Can they not keep their minds on one single point?"

Allouette said nothing, but her stomach sank, for the single point the men were presumably following was herself. The three were quiet for a few minutes, Allouette feeling her face set in the immobile mode that had hidden her feelings for so long, Quicksilver still prowling, scanning the ground as though the footprints could reveal the men's thoughts, Cordelia scowling about her in deep thought. Allouette finally remembered to seek out Gregory's thoughts, but she must not yet have recovered from the blow on the head, for she could find him nowhere. "Cordelia, would you seek for Gregory? I cannot yet hear with my mind."

"I have," Cordelia said, her scowl deepening, "and I find him not. 'Tis most perplexing."

"But wherefore would he not . . ." Allouette bit off the cry.

"Follow you?" Quicksilver asked. "He would, lady. The

lad is so besotted that he is a mooncalf studying to be a lap-pup. Be sure that if he lives, he seeks you."

Allouette looked down again, but too late to hide her blush, or her smile. "But if he sought me, why did he not find me?"

They were silent a moment longer, thinking the matter over, before Quicksilver delivered her verdict: "Something misled them."

"Aye," said Cordelia. "There could be no other explanation."

"But what?" asked Allouette, eyes wide in amazement.

CHAPTER
-5-

"What indeed?" Cordelia finally met her gaze.

"It could not be a will o' the wisp," Quicksilver said, "or any other sort of marsh-fire, for they would recognize such things and avoid them."

"Or banish them," Cordelia agreed. "No, something has clouded their minds quite thoroughly."

"What could so becloud a warlock's mind?" Quicksilver's brows drew down.

"Only a spell that they knew not of," Allouette answered.

Quicksilver gave her a wary look. "How could such a thing be done, lady?"

Allouette reddened, realizing that in Quicksilver's mind she was the authority on underhanded tricks, sneaky strategies, and hidden betrayals. Well, she deserved that—and the cure that Gwendylon had begun in her did not remove her knowledge. "Cast an enchantment on him while he is distracted," she said.

"You mean while Gregory sits in meditation?"

"No, even in that state he is aware of the world about

him," Allouette said impatiently. "It would have to be a charm laid upon him when he is in the midst of battle, or when he has discovered a new idea in study."

"Or when he has found a few minutes alone with you, I'll warrant," Quicksilver said.

Allouette paled. "You do not think that I would betray him now!"

"I do not," Quicksilver returned, "but I do think that you can distract him and hold his attention far better than anything save battle."

"Oh, study can—"

"He would far rather study your lips and eyes than any book," Cordelia said with asperity.

"Well . . . there's some truth to that." Allouette tried to hide her smile, then lifted her head and said sharply, "But if any sought to enchant him while I was with him, I would know it and turn upon them!"

Cordelia's head snapped up. "Do you say that you are not as riveted to him as he to you?"

"Even when we have time alone," Allouette countered, "his well-being is my prime concern."

Cordelia studied her a moment, then nodded. "I believe you—and that is a wholesale conversion indeed."

"Why, because I sought his downfall?" Allouette asked sardonically. "Believe me, lady, that is all the more reason why I am determined to ward him now!"

"I wish you all luck in doing so," Cordelia answered. "Truly, if the two of you are each intent on the other's well-being, it should be a thriving marriage."

Surprised, Allouette searched her face for signs of sarcasm or mockery, but there were none.

"I do not think, though," said Quicksilver, "that you were the cause of his distraction in this. Indeed, this confusion-spell was laid upon him as the moutaineers kidnapped you."

"Yes, that would hold his attention," Cordelia agreed. "As to Alain and Geoffrey, battle of any kind would suffice to distract them."

"So some enchanter has clouded their minds unbeknownst

and leads them about in circles," Quicksilver concluded.

"How certain a circle, think you?" Allouette asked. "Have we only to wait here ere they return once more?"

Quicksilver studied the ground. "The tracks are too old; they returned only twice, and the most recent was hours ago. No, whatever malicious spirit leads them, it has taken them farther into the wildwood."

An awful thought struck Allouette. "Quickly, let us follow! It may be they travel toward the mountaineers' home!"

The other two looked up, astonished. Then Quicksilver said, "That would be a good tactic, yes."

Cordelia's eyes were frightened, but she said, "If they are merely befuddled, not led . . ."

"They might still strike the mountaineers' trail and follow it!" Allouette cried. "Especially since they seek me!"

Cordelia paled, then nodded. "Yes, let us track them." She turned away with renewed purpose.

"Come, summon resolution!" Geoffrey clapped Gregory on the shoulder. "If you love the lass, trace their tracks and steal her back!"

Gregory's face hardened. He rose, taut and determined. "Even as you say. Come, let us follow in their wake."

He started forward, but Geoffrey caught his sleeve. "Softly, brother. They may be baiting a trap."

Gregory froze, then gave a single nod. "Lead on, sir knight."

Geoffrey took the lead. Alain, in prudence, fell in behind Gregory—if the scholar should do something rash, he intended to be handy to stop him.

Geoffrey led them in among the trees but within sight of the furrow the mountaineers had ploughed in the grass. Up the hillside they went, and the trees closed over the grassland.

Geoffrey stopped. "Ward me, gentlemen. I must walk in their steps now, for I shall not be able to see their tracks so far from the side."

"All should be well," Alain said, "so long as we go deliberately and with all due care. After all, they cannot ambush a telepath."

Geoffrey gazed ahead, eyes losing focus for a few seconds; then he nodded. "They still flee. They have not yet thought to surprise us."

"Not the ones whose thoughts you read," Alain reminded him. "There may be others who have learned to hide what they are thinking."

"That is somewhat sophisticated for a rough mountaineer," Geoffrey said, "but so is their manner of ambush, or we'd not have fallen prey to it. Well, we shall walk warily."

Gregory tried reading the kidnappers' thoughts too, and anger burned in his eyes when he heard them.

"Do not deny them some feeling of triumph, brother," Geoffrey said gently. "They shall not have it long."

"No, they shall not!" Gregory glared at the trees ahead as though he could see through them to the kidnappers.

Geoffrey looked down and walked forward, tracking their enemies. Uphill they went, through the trees, with Gregory and Alain vigilant and ready for the slightest sign of danger. Then the ground began to fall away. They walked downhill steadily, until the trees thinned.

"Now we come to a clearing!" Gregory drew his wand, eyes flashing.

"But why do their thoughts still seem to come from a distance?" Geoffrey wondered.

They crept forth from the trees and had their answer. Gregory stared about him, slack-jawed. "We are back where we were ambushed! How could they lay so false a trail so quickly?"

"Is it false?" Alain asked. "Listen to every thought, wizards, whether it be of earthworm, squirrel, or bird! If a woodsman can call like a jay, he may be able to think like one, too!"

"Well thought," Geoffrey said with surprised approval. Alain was the very soul of fairness, loyalty, and truth; he was steady as a rock, clear-headed in a crisis, and had an unimpeachable sense of judgment—but not much insight. Geoffrey hoped he was learning, although he had to admit Alain's qualities were far more important to the monarch he would one day be, than great intelligence.

Gregory looked very pensive for several minutes, then shook his head. "None are near."

"Then how did they lay a trail back here?" Geoffrey exploded. He hated being tricked.

They were still for a few minutes, looking at one another and trying to make sense of it. Then Alain said, "Was it truly them?"

"Who else could it have been?" Geoffrey asked with a frown.

"Some forest spirit?" Gregory gazed off into the woods. "It could be. I hear none, but magical creatures might guard their thoughts well."

"If they have them," Geoffrey said in disgust. "They may simply follow impulses."

"You mean some sprite has led us astray on a whim?" Alain looked skeptical.

"Puck would," Geoffrey pointed out.

"But he is our friend."

"Not above playing tricks on a comrade, though. Besides, there are several other kinds of supernatural beings who think it is the height of humor to watch mortals go astray—especially if those mortals are in some haste, for hurry is a concept the faerie-folk lack."

"Let us assume the worst and take it to be something of the sort," Alain proposed. "Follow those tracks again, Geoffrey, and we shall see if there is a body to go with those footprints."

They went off into the woods again, Geoffrey glancing keenly from the ground to the bushes and trunks around, alert for every slightest sign that someone had passed that way. He no longer watched for the path of a mass of people, but for the traces that a single being might have made in passing.

"How shall you distinguish between false tracks made by one sprite," Alain asked, "and true ones made by a dozen human feet?"

"There is no sure way," Geoffrey replied, "but the lone spirit might leave his own true track somewhere, which would not match the mortal ones—or have left a mark upon a tree trunk or broken a twig, in places mortals would not reach."

"Then too," said Gregory, "he might have been seen by a bird or fox or squirrel, so I shall read the mind of each as I come by."

"If the one who saw him is still near," Alain said, musing. "You cannot scan the mind of every dweller of this forest."

"There is that," Gregory admitted.

They followed Geoffrey deeper into the wood. This time, though, they noticed when they began to go downhill again.

"I have an unpleasant feeling about this," Alain said.

"And I a rather wrathful one," Geoffrey said, lips pressed thin.

"Let us press ahead quickly," Gregory urged. "If we go where we think, there is no need for caution."

"Our enemies would love to hear you say that!" Geoffrey answered, but he hurried forward too, sparing only glances for the tracks he followed.

They burst through the screen of leaves into the same churned-up clearing from which they had first come. Alain and Gregory listened with respect as Geoffrey set about cursing their unknown misguiding spirit with a vocabulary that was an eloquent testimony to the amount of time he had spent in the troopers' barracks, learning their modes of fighting.

When he ran down, Alain offered, "We know in which direction our attackers fled. Let us follow a landmark that lies in that quarter."

"Scarcely proof against a truly wily spirit," Geoffrey growled, "but I know no better way."

"It should serve," said Alain, "though a goblin that could lay a false trail would also prove capable of setting up a false landmark, and moving it subtly to lead us even more astray."

Gregory shook his head. "To make us think we see a mountain peak that is not really there would take substantial meddling with our minds. Distracted I may be, but I think I would detect such interference nonetheless."

Alain nodded. "Onward, then."

A third time, the trio set off to follow the original tracks of the mountaineers. Geoffrey pointed at a twisted rock on the summit of the slope. "Yon is our guide—like a monk with a hood."

Alain nodded judiciously. "Brother Boulder shall be our quarry, then. We march!"

Whatever their misguiding spirit was, it didn't succeed against determined line-of-sight navigation. An hour passed and they still had not come back to the clearing. On the other hand, they hadn't reached the crest yet, either—the land fell away in a gully, one that twisted and turned like a double-jointed snake, forming curves and oxbows. At the bottom, way down, they saw water purling.

"What a poxy place to put a river!" Geoffrey said, exasperated. "Has our misguider found a way to lay a barrier in our path?"

"No, this stream has been here many years," Alain said, "very many. See how it curves and twists?"

Geoffrey looked back over the course and nodded. "So many meanders mean years of water-flow—and it has cut thirty feet down into the soil."

" 'Tis an ancient river indeed," Gregory agreed.

"Well, there's no help for it—we shall have to climb down and find a ford."

"How did the mountaineers pass it?" Alain asked.

"Most likely by a bridge they know of, and we do not," Geoffrey answered, "or perhaps by climbing down, even as we do, but with slabs of rock placed as steps and camouflaged."

Alain nodded. "We could spend our last few hours of daylight seeking such a place. Well, down we go!"

It was a skidding and perilous descent, for the bank was steep; the river had cut its own ravine. They caught at saplings and low branches and tried to discover roots to use as footholds. More quickly than they would have wanted, but with only one or two falls, they came to the riverbank.

"Yonder is our crossing!" Geoffrey cried, pointing to a large raft moored to a tree. A cable was tied above it, stretching across the river and running through two large holes in the raft's railing. "It may be that this is the mountaineers' route, after all!"

"It would seem you have guessed better than you knew," Alain agreed. "Let us bring our horses aboard and shove off."

The horses weren't all that happy about such infirm footing, but they were well-trained war steeds, so they went. Gregory untied the painter while Alain and Geoffrey held fast to the cable. Gregory leaped aboard and prince and knight started hauling on the hawser.

"A novel idea, and a good one," Gregory said, nodding in pleasure. "The ride is quite smooth."

As soon as he had said it, they neared the middle of the river and the current caught the raft. Gregory and Alain shouted as the railing strained against the cable. Suddenly hauling was much more difficult.

Gregory went to the forward rail, peering out at the river. "Whence came such a sudden current?"

"From nearing the middle of the river, brother!" Geoffrey panted.

" 'Tis not so broad a stream as that," Gregory said. "It must have been . . ." He caught his breath, pointing, then managed to call out, "Hold! Freeze! Avaunt! Danger lies ahead!"

"What manner of danger?" Geoffrey turned, eyes alight at the prospect of action—and saw the circle of water in mid-river, a circle that expanded and deepened into a funnel even as they watched, pulling the waters toward it, pulling every bit of floating wood toward it—including the raft.

Suddenly the rude craft was straining against its cable.

"Surely many have survived this before!" Alain called over the roaring of the water.

"Not if this whirlpool comes solely for our benefit!" Geoffrey called back. "Pull, Alain! Back to shore!"

They hauled as hard as they could, muscles bulging with

the effort, but they might as well have been playing tug-of-war with a mountain; the raft stayed obstinately in midriver. Gregory ran to throw his weight against the current, pulling on the hawser with his new and powerful muscles, but even as he did, the whirlpool widened to its fullest diameter, its outer rim almost under the raft, and the roaring pressure strengthened. Gregory gave a quick glance down the funnel as it widened enough to show slimy mud at the bottom— and a bulb-bodied creature the size of a pony, with great buck teeth and burning eyes glaring up at them while its broad flat tail stirred the water to make the whirlpool and keep it formed. "Yonder is the spirit who has led us! 'Tis the afanc!"

Wood groaned from strain.

"Beware!" Geoffrey cried. "The whirlpool's pull may break the cable!"

But it wasn't the cable that broke—it was the railing. Wood burst apart with cracks like explosions and the raft surged toward the whirlpool. As they began to swing about it in a circle, the horses screamed, fighting to be free.

"Hold their heads!" Geoffrey cried in agony. "If they leap from here, they shall slide down the funnel and be drowned!"

"Peace, peace, my beauties," Alain soothed. He held all three reins tight in one hand and stroked the beasts' necks with the other. "We shall not capsize, for we have two powerful wizards with us. Endure in patience. There now, beasts so brave in battle cannot be afraid of a little water!"

On and on he went, and his soothing tone calmed the horses at least a little. They stopped fighting, but their eyes still rolled in fear.

Resolutely, Alain drew his sword. "Cold Iron is the bane of all creatures of faerie! If I can wound it badly enough to make it stop stirring the waters, we may live to swim to the surface."

"If we can strike it." Geoffrey, too, drew his sword, holding his horse's bridle with his left hand, eyes fixed to his enemy the afanc. "Creatures supernatural have ways of evading our blows."

" 'Tis so," Alain said heavily, then turned to Gregory. "You who have studied so much of faerie lore—can you not destroy this creature with your mind?"

"I have been willing it to dissolve," Gregory said, face taut with strain, "but some other power holds it bound in form." He raised his voice, shouting above the roar of the whirlpool. "Spirit of this river, hear! Come before us, we pray—appear! Your stream is invaded by a spirit impure! Banish it swiftly so your river endures!"

"But surely the afanc *is* the spirit of this river!" Alain cried in despair.

The raft tilted sharply and water cascaded down upon them. The horses screamed and fought the reins. The only thing that kept them on their feet was centripetal force.

"Aroint thee, malignant spirit!" cried a rusty but vibrant voice, and a woman broke through the wall of the whirlpool—an old woman, withered and wrinkled, hands hooked to claw the afanc. Her skin was olive-colored and her hair like silvered seaweed, floating about her head and shot with sparks. Her trailing green gown seemed to be made of river-weeds, and her eyes burned with anger. "Begone, monstrous creature! Get you hence! Away from my waters; pollute them no more with your pestilential presence!"

The afanc made a ratcheting noise, gathering itself to pounce—but the water-wraith sprang first, nails growing into claws even as she plummeted to the bottom of the funnel, claws that sank into the afanc's neck. It screamed and bit in a frenzy, whipping about, trying to shake the crone loose. Its huge incisors sank into her shoulder but she only laughed. "Can you hurt the water? Can you damage the foam? Forfend, foolish furball! Go away! Get you home!"

But the afanc kept trying to shake her loose, its whole body whipping back and forth. Its broad tail ceased to stir the waters, and with a roar the whirlpool fell in upon itself, burying wraith and monster both and drenching the men and their mounts. The horses' screams ended in gurgling, but their owners grabbed frantically for their nostrils, covering the velvet noses. The horses kicked out, but the raft rose beneath them, bearing them all back up to the surface. It popped into the sunshine, pitching from side to side. It was all the three could do to keep their feet. The horses tossed their heads, gulping air, and fought the reins frantically, hooves slipping on the sodden deck.

"Gently, O Prince of Horses, gently!" Geoffrey crooned. "The monster's buried in the tide; you have naught now to fear!"

"All is safe, they are gone!" Gregory assured his mount in what he hoped was a soothing tone. "The river-mother has ousted the afanc and we are safe."

"Aye, gallant warhorse, you have every cause for pride," Alain assured his steed. "You have borne up nobly, you have faced the river-demon with stalwart courage! Be at ease, be placid!"

Slowly the horses calmed, even though the waves rocked them, slowly subsiding, but moving them even more quickly than they had planned toward the far shore. The steeds were almost restored when the raft struck the riverbank, nearly jolting them off their feet. Hooves scrabbled and men clung frantically to reins, voices rising in assurance all over again. Quickly they led the horses off the raft and sagged against rocks and tree trunks, striving to catch their breath.

"I had thought we would certainly be drowned!" Gregory said in a tremulous voice.

"I, too," Alain seconded. "How did you know the afanc was not this river's true spirit, Gregory?"

"Because it so resembles a beaver, Alain," the younger brother said, "and beavers never stay overlong in any one river. They build their dams, eat all the fish their ponds catch, hibernate, waken, and move on."

"True," Geoffrey said thoughtfully. "They are visitors to any stream."

"Then too," Gregory said, "I suspect the spirits of every stream it visited chased it away whenever they found it, just as this one did."

"A point," Geoffrey said, frowning. "Therefore it would

be feign to attack anything living that came in or on the water, would it not?"

"There is sense in that," Alain said judiciously. "If the creature were supernatural, a surprise attack might win, and if it were mortal, it would be good to eat."

"What a charming beast!" Gregory said with a shudder.

"Let us be glad the water-woman was not beguiled." Geoffrey gave Gregory a narrow look. "I had not realized you knew the habits of beavers. How came you by such knowledge of game, O Scholar?"

Gregory smiled. "When I was a lad, I wished to learn all I could about everything, O Hunter. Do you not remember chiding me for spending long hours gazing at the river and whole days wandering the woodlands?"

"Truly, I do not remember saying it," Geoffrey said ruefully. "So that was study? And all these years I had thought you had gone off to brood!"

"To meditate, perhaps," Gregory said with a smile, "but not to brood." He glanced back at the water. "I had thought this stream was old, for it has many ox-bow curves—but I had not realized it was ancient!"

"Certainly its spirit was," Alain agreed, "but nonetheless powerful."

"Old or young, I bless that river-crone for safe deliverance." Geoffrey raised his voice. "Dame of the waters, we thank you for kind rescue!"

"May your stream always be pure," Alain called, "and your watershed well-forested!"

They watched the river, half expecting the water-wraith to rise from the stream to scold them for being so foolish as to take a raft that was far too convenient. The stream only flowed past them, though, still choppy, but with no sign of supernatural intervention.

"Do you think the afanc set the raft in place for us?" Alain asked, frowning.

"We should have realized that the mountaineers would not have left us the means of passage," Geoffrey said, chagrined.

"But the afanc had no hands!" Alain protested. "How

could it have bound the tree trunks together?"

They were silent, staring at one another for a few minutes. Then Geoffrey stated the logical conclusion: "It had help, of course."

"Surely," Gregory agreed. "If the mountaineers are willing to aid an invading army for the promise of land, why would not one of their number be willing to aid the afanc against us?"

"Only one?" Alain asked, frowning.

"A witch-moss crafter," Gregory explained, "for that raft was not built before the afanc sensed us nearing."

"Either that, or the mountaineers did use it and have for weeks or years," Geoffrey objected, "and the afanc needed only to push it back to the near shore in order to set its trap."

The three were silent again, testing the idea. Then Gregory asked, "How did it tie the mooring rope?"

Geoffrey frowned. "You do not think the beast was telekinetic, do you?"

"That it tied the knot with its mind?" Gregory smiled. "Why not? Some ancestral projective telepath did craft Puck with all his magical powers. Why could not his descendant make witch-moss into a monster that was itself an esper?"

"An esper making an esper!" Geoffrey shook his head. "I shall have to think that one over for some days, brother! But let us mount and ride on, for I do not relish the thought of spending the night by that stream."

"Nor I," Alain said with a shiver.

Thus they led their horses up out of the ravine and on to the top of the slope, looking warily about them every foot of the way.

"The swine!" Cordelia jammed her fists on her hips and glared at the raft on the far side of the river. "To leave their craft where we could not reach it!"

"Patience, good lady," Allouette advised. "Surely they do not know that you follow them . . ."

"Well, they should know!"

". . . and Gregory thinks he is following me," Allouette finished smoothly.

"There's some truth in that," Quicksilver allowed. "Not enough to excuse them, mind you, but some."

Never in her wildest imaginings had Allouette dreamed she would be the voice of reason.

"Still, it is no great feat to bring it back." Cordelia stared at the raft. After a moment, it lurched free of the bank and began to move toward them.

"How does it compare to a broomstick?" Quicksilver asked.

"Most unwieldy," Cordelia answered. "Still, you have given me a thought—perhaps we should fly."

"What, poor three of us, and three horses into the bargain? You would be worn out in minutes!"

Cordelia didn't argue; indeed, her brows drew down in a scowl of concentration, and she muttered, "Water's resistance is most maddening."

"And wearying." Quicksilver hiked up her skirts and waded into the river to catch the raft one-handed. "Aid me, Allouette!"

"I am here." Allouette caught the other corner-post and turned, plowing her way back to the bank, skirts held up in her other hand.

The raft touched the bank and Cordelia staggered as she loosed her mental hold. "I thank you, damsels! That took greater effort than I had thought it would."

"Board," Quicksilver said. "There is no reason for you to get wet with us."

"My enthusiasm for this quest is already dampened." Cordelia stepped aboard the raft, then turned to glare fiercely at the bank. "Board," she said between her teeth.

Allouette and Quicksilver stepped up to the bank again, then led the horses across to the boat. Both immediately sat, stretching out their legs to the sun.

"There is some advantage to their absence," Quicksilver said.

"Pooh, damsel! Surely Geoffrey has seen your legs before this!" Cordelia scolded.

"That he has," Quicksilver admitted, "but if he saw them now, we would cease to journey onward for some hours."

Cordelia gave Allouette a wink. "She does not mind boasting a bit, does she?"

Allouette smiled but lowered her gaze. "I was thinking much as she was myself."

"I too," Cordelia said, "but there is no reason to speak it aloud."

So trading verbal jabs, they drifted across the river and downstream until they bumped into the bank.

"I am dry now." Quicksilver stood in a single lithe movement, catching her horse's bridle. "Come, my lovely! You may have solid ground under your feet again."

The horse whinnied as though to say that was a very good idea and came with her onto the bank. Allouette and Cordelia followed with their mounts. Then Allouette dropped the reins and told her mare sternly, "Bide!" and went to tie the mooring-rope firmly around a tree trunk.

"What good is that?" Quicksilver asked. "Our men are on this side of the river now!"

"At least the raft will not go drifting downstream to be lost," Allouette said equably. "Besides, we may wish to return."

"There is that," Cordelia said. "Well! We have drifted downstream quite a way. Shall we not have to search for the men's trail?"

They mounted and rode along the bank, Quicksilver's gaze on the ground, Allouette watching the woods in case of danger, and Cordelia abstracted, mind searching for Alain's—a more difficult task than finding Gregory's or Geoffrey's, since the prince was only a latent telepath. "Odd that we cannot find their thoughts."

Quicksilver frowned. "If we cannot, they must be shielding themselves. What enemy do they fear who can read minds?"

Two experienced psis and one novice were silent a moment, contemplating the possible answers to that question and not liking them a bit. Quicksilver broke the silence by crying, "What happened here?"

Cordelia and Allouette looked down and gasped at the churned mud on the bank. "That raft certainly came to land with a great deal of force," Cordelia said.

The ground was plowed up sharply where the logs had jammed into the bank. The mud was riddled with hoof marks, but the boot prints were fewer and more centered.

Quicksilver dropped to one knee, studying the signs closely. "The horses were quite upset, prancing about—trying to break free, I would guess—but the men seem to have calmed them."

"What would so upset their steeds?" Allouette asked.

"Whatever it was, I hope it was not telepathic." Cordelia gave a nervous glance toward the river.

The other two women followed her gaze. "It seems tranquil enough now," Allouette said.

"What was it an hour ago?" Quicksilver returned. "Or was it longer than that?"

"Let us follow and see," Allouette proposed.

"And keep your thoughts to yourself," Quicksilver added.

Allouette's gaze snapped to her, affronted.

"I mean no insult," Quicksilver said, "only that if the men shield their minds, we should too. I'd rather not discover what stalks them by having it find us!"

"Oh." Allouette looked sheepish. "Your pardon, damsel. I had thought—"

"I was careless in my wording," Quicksilver said gruffly, "and it is I who should be asking pardon. Let us ride!"

They turned their horses and followed the trail into the woods.

Half an hour later, Cordelia reined in and looked at the trees about them. "Night comes on quickly and soon we shall not be able to see what obstacles lie in our path."

"I know a spell for light," Allouette offered.

"Do you not fear night-walkers?" Quicksilver asked with a frown.

Allouette barely managed to keep from saying that she

herself had been a greater danger than anything else that walked by night. Instead, "Not with two such doughty companions," she said.

Quicksilver eyed her askance. "Flattery, methinks."

"But nonetheless pleasant for all that," Cordelia said. "She has a point—one of us might be at risk, but together we can cope with any monster or hobgoblin I can think of."

"Provided they do not come in packs," Allouette qualified.

"Or that the packs are not too large." Quicksilver nodded. "Still, it is well thought, ladies. The men shall no doubt be wearied from whatever happened at that riverbank and will pitch camp for the night. If we keep riding, we should catch up with them before they sleep."

They were all silent a moment, each thinking about catching her lad before bedtime. Then Cordelia shook off the mood and said, "Press on!"

They turned back to business and set off after the men.

Before the twilight had quite ended, they came out of the forest into a wide lane, lined with low fieldstone walls on either side. Allouette stared at them and asked, "Who built these?"

"They certainly seem most strange in the midst of a wood," Cordelia agreed.

Quicksilver shook off the mood and said, "We forget betimes that there are farms all 'round every wood. Simply because ogres have come out of a mist over a field does not undo all the building folk have done over the years."

"But so high here in the mountains . . ."

"The mountaineers are not wild beasts, no matter their conduct to me," Allouette said. "Like as not they have fields planted wherever the ground is level enough—and where there are fields, they must build lanes for wagons. Let us follow this path and see where it goes."

They rode onward as the twilight failed. Finally Allouette scowled, concentrating, and a globe of light glimmered into life before them, casting just enough light to show them the next ten feet of road, albeit dimly.

Quicksilver gave her a sharp look. "Is that fox-fire yours, or a spirit's?"

"Only mine," Allouette assured her. " 'Tis only necessary to excite the molecules of air until they heat enough to give light."

"It will take some effort to keep it glowing, will it not?" Cordelia asked.

"Only a little." Allouette turned to her. "I can brighten it, if you wish."

"That would take more effort," Cordelia said, "and we may have hours yet to ride. We can see well enough."

They rode onward. Cordelia didn't tell the others that she had learned the same spell from her mother years before. She was quite content to let Allouette do her part.

Suddenly Quicksilver pulled up. "Hark!"

Allouette and Cordelia stopped their horses, listening. "Only nightbirds and crickets," Cordelia said. "What should I hear?"

"It has stopped now," Quicksilver said, frowning. "I heard a sort of brushing noise behind us."

"I heard nothing," Cordelia said, but doubtfully.

"Nor I." Allouette felt the first pricklings of fright, and her old response came instantly—simmering anger that anyone should beset her. "Let us ride on and listen as we go."

They rode ahead for several minutes until finally Allouette said, voice low, "I hear it! A brushing sound indeed, as though something scrapes against the stone wall behind us!"

"I hear with it the rattle of chains," Cordelia said, "but very faintly."

"Whoa." Quicksilver reined her horse to a stop as she spun to look behind her. Cordelia turned to look, too, but Allouette kept watch ahead, well aware that the sound could be a diversion. "What do you see, ladies?"

"Naught." Quicksilver turned back to the front. "Only shadowed trees and stone walls stretching behind us into deeper darkness. Let us ride on but hearken well."

They shook the reins and touched their horses' flanks with

their heels, moving ahead—and behind them, the sound began again: the whisk, whisk, whisk of something huge brushing against stone and, beneath it, the padding of great unseen
bare feet.

CHAPTER
-6-

Quicksilver spun in her saddle as though to catch whatever followed them by surprise. This time Allouette darted a quick glance backward too, but saw only blackness with the faint glimmering of stone walls at either side.

"It stops when we stop," Quicksilver reported.

"Ride on," Cordelia said, face hard.

They started forward again, and behind them, the brushing sound began once more—and the clanking of chains was clearly audible now. Faint it was indeed, but all three could hear it.

"Stalking is all well and good—as long as I am the stalker," Quicksilver said between her teeth. She pulled up, spinning in her saddle—and the sound, of course, also halted. "Whoever you are, avaunt and begone! Know that I am re-doubtable in my own right and will as soon run you through as look upon you!"

"Therefore will it not be seen," Allouette said, her voice trembling. "What monster is this that comes upon us?" She turned to Cordelia. "You, who were reared by a wizard and

a witch and have hobnobbed with elves and brownies all your
life—can you not say what follows us?"

"I have heard of a presence like this, that makes sounds
but is seen not," Cordelia said, her voice shaking. " 'Tis
called a barguest."

Allouette's breath hissed in, and Quicksilver drew her
sword. "What harm is in it?"

Cordelia said, "None in itself—but it is a forecaster of
death."

"Then let it forecast someone else's!" Quicksilver scowled
into the darkness behind her and cried, "Avaunt thee, barguest! Get thee gone!"

"Hold, I pray!" Allouette said in alarm. "It gives us no
hurt."

"No hurt!" Quicksilver rounded on her. "How can it forecast death and do no harm? Nay, I can forecast death, too—
with this omen here." She hefted her sword. "If the spirit
predicts our dying, it can only be because it causes death!"

"Not so," Allouette protested. "It has something of the
precognitive gift, that is all. We need only pay it no heed."

"No heed!" Quicksilver cried. "Perhaps you can walk a
nighttime road and truly ignore those sounds of chains, of
padding feet and furry sides brushing against stone—but I
cannot!"

"It will be unnerving," Cordelia agreed and turned to call
to the darkness behind them, "Show yourself, whatever you
are! Shame upon you for so frightening three weak young
women—and know that we are not so weak as we might
seem, for two of us can turn you completely to jelly! Appear
or be gone!"

Her concentration was so intense that it rocked Allouette
and even made Quicksilver's head snap back as though she'd
been slapped—so they should not have been surprised when
the darkness seemed to coalesce into a huge wooly black dog
the size of a calf with eyes like saucers, with triple irises—
a pupil inside a white ring, inside a blue ring which was
inside a red ring. Those eyes glowed balefully at the three

women as its lips writhed up in a snarl, revealing sharply pointed teeth that glowed in the night.

"Do not dare to challenge me!" Quicksilver snapped, brandishing her sword. "We'll have none of your dealing here! All three of us shall live many a year yet, and if you dare to contradict me, barguest, I shall prove it upon your body! Go on, get away, get you gone—or I shall loose my friends to tear you apart, nay, to make war between the cells of your body, so that your whole substance falls apart and oozes down into a puddle in the roadway, a heap of gelatinous quivering fungus that shall never again stalk poor travelers at night, let alone foretell the death of any being!"

Cordelia and Allouette stared at her, appalled. Her face was distorted with anger, bright red, her bosom heaving and her whole body trembling with the intensity of her rage as she stared furiously into the darkness.

The night was very quiet. Even the crickets seemed stunned to silence by Quicksilver's anger.

Then, almost furtively, the sounds began again—the brushing, the jingling of chains, the padding of huge feet— but moving away.

Cordelia and Allouette turned to stare into the darkness in shock.

The sounds faded and were gone. Quicksilver relaxed, sheathing her sword with a single nod of her head. "It knows better than to strive against Cold Iron in the hands of one determined."

Cordelia let out a long, shuddering breath. "I would not have believed it if I had not seen it—but I think, bold chieftain, that it was the sheer intensity of your anger that affrighted the beast. Certainly I felt you battering at my mind like a ram, and I was not even your target!"

"It knew I spoke no more than I was willing to do—or that you were," Quicksilver said evenly. "Oh, it was a fine game when it could pace behind us unseen and fill us with terror, but there is no pleasure in it when the prey becomes the hunter!"

"So it was only necessary to show resolution after all," Cordelia said, smiling.

"True resolution," Quicksilver insisted. "I was quite ready to set upon it with my sword, no matter the sharpness of those glowing teeth—and I trust you were just as willing to turn it back into the lump of fungus from which it was made!"

"Be sure of it." Cordelia shook her head as she turned to ride on. "I wish that all threats could be banished so easily."

"Most need a bit more persuading." Quicksilver kicked her mount into a walk beside Cordelia's. "Life has taught me that I must always be ready to fight. I can only rejoice that, with your brother, it is rarely necessary."

So they rode off into the night, discussing the young men they pursued—but Allouette rode behind them in silence, unable to rid herself of a nagging dread. If the barguest only predicted death, after all, banishing it would not prevent that death. She felt a chill that reminded her of her own mortality and hoped that the deadly forecast was not for herself or her companions, but only for their enemies.

Several hours later, they rode bleary-eyed and nodding into a clearing. Cordelia looked up at the stars and sighed. "The constellations have turned toward midnight, ladies. The men must be considerably farther ahead than we thought."

"They could be only a hundred yards from us," Quicksilver grumbled, "and we would never know it in the gloom under these trees."

"What other night-walkers might lurk among the leaves not even fifty feet away?" Allouette asked with a shudder.

"Well said." Cordelia dismounted and began to untie her tent and bedroll. "One haunting is enough for the night. By your leave, damsels, I'd rather sleep till dawn than wander." She paused to look up at her companions. "That's not to say, of course, that I shall not take first watch."

"No, I claim that privilege," Allouette said instantly. "I have learned Gregory's way of meditating in a trance that keeps him aware of the world about him, but gives as much rest as sleep. I shall take the first three hours."

Cordelia and Quicksilver exchanged a glance that quite clearly asked if they dared trust their former enemy to guard their slumber. Then, reluctantly, Quicksilver nodded, though her hand rested on her dagger-hilt as she turned toward her future kinswoman. "Thank you for the kind offer. I will accept it, for truthfully, I know not if I could keep my eyes open for even one more hour. Nay, do you take the watch with my thanks, lady."

"And mine," Cordelia seconded. Then she hauled the tent off her horse's rump. Before she started to set it up, though, she unsaddled and unbridled her horse and tied it to a tree on a long rein. She stroked the mare's neck, saying, "Do you graze now, my lovely, and sleep when you are filled." She knew she really should curry the poor thing but was too weary. With leaden limbs, she turned to help Allouette pitch the tent while Quicksilver laid the fire. "How far ahead are the men, think you?"

"An inch is as good a guess as a mile," Quicksilver said, exasperated. "Since they shield their thoughts, there is no way of telling."

Allouette pondered their reason for shielding and trembled with a shiver that was not due to the night's chill.

As sunset gave way to twilight and the men pitched camp, Alain asked, "Can you not cease shielding my thoughts now, Gregory? It must be wearying for you, and neither you nor Geoffrey has had any hint of a mind-reading monster near to us."

"It takes little more effort for me to blanket all three of us, than myself alone," Gregory said, "but perhaps you have the right of it. We certainly have had no hint of pook, hob-goblin, or spirk." He turned to Geoffrey. "What say you, brother?"

Geoffrey shrugged. "Why not chance it? If our thoughts bring forth monsters that lurk in ambush, so much the better; I had rather face them openly than wonder whether or not they await us."

Gregory nodded and let down his shields. Then he knelt, staring at the teepee of kindling and sticks, speeding up the vibrations of the molecules until a tendril of smoke arose. Seconds later, small flames began to lick through the gaps between sticks, and Gregory relaxed.

"Company," Geoffrey snapped.

Gregory and Alain looked up, startled to see a man lurking in the shadows at the edge of their clearing—but a most strange man indeed. He wore a green tunic and brown hose, like any forest dweller—but his hips tapered down on both sides into a single leg, massive and powerful.

Gregory rose slowly, tensed for fight or flight, even as he heard his companions' swords rasp loose from their scabbards.

"I think we had best shield our thoughts after all," Geoffrey said.

"My ward is in place already," Gregory told him, "and covers Alain's mind too."

The prince frowned at the apparition. "Who are you, and wherefore come you here?"

The stranger opened his mouth, but instead of words, he gave vent to a woeful wailing cry. It seemed to pierce right through the men's heads; they clapped their hands over their ears.

"Avaunt thee!" Gregory cried. "Get thee hence!"

He reinforced the command with a mental stab. The creature's shriek soared up the scale, hovering for a moment on the edge of the human hearing range and piercing even through their hands, waking pain from ear to ear. Then the pitch shot even higher and the men could hear nothing, even though its mouth was open—but in the distant woods, wolves began to howl.

"Cease, I bade thee!" Gregory snapped, eyes narrowing as his face reddened.

The strange creature winced with the pain of Gregory's mental stab and did close his mouth this time. Geoffrey and Alain advanced from opposite sides, blades on guard. The creature took the sensible course and turned to hop away into the recesses of the forest shadows.

Gregory stood, chest heaving, glaring after the apparition. As Geoffrey and Alain turned back to him, staring, he said, "We must be vigilant tonight. That monster will come back and will bring with him the wolves he has called."

"We shall meet them with the steel they deserve." But Alain was staring at Gregory as though he were himself something strange and weird. "Never before this night have I seen you angry, Gregory—and now twice in twelve hours!"

"Never before have I felt so pure a wave of malice as that creature wafted toward me," Gregory returned. "It thought to paralyze us with its wail and kill us easily." He glanced at Alain, abashed, then glanced away. "Forgive me, but I do grow wroth when I see an esper use its gifts for such fell purpose, upon those who cannot resist."

"Unluckily for him, he now found those who *could* resist," Alain said, "and luckily for me, I traveled with them. What would have happened if I had sojourned in this wood without your protection?"

"Why, it would have slain you," Geoffrey said. "I have read what Gregory did—that the creature kills for the malicious pleasure of the deed." He turned to his younger brother. "Nay, I pray it does come back—to meet our blades!"

"What was the hideous thing?" Alain asked.

"Ask the scholar." Geoffrey seemed nettled by having to pass the question. "Such creatures are rare enough that I have never seen one, let alone heard them spoken of."

" 'Tis called a Biasd Bheulach, Alain, and if we see it again, it will doubtless assume another guise," Gregory said.

Geoffrey looked up with a wolfish grin. "What guise does it favor?"

"It may appear as a beast of any kind, prowling about our campsite," Gregory told him, "though it favors the form of a greyhound more than any other. Its most dangerous appearance, though, is that of a very ordinary mortal man."

"Because the traveler does not know its danger until it pierces his ears with its screech?" Geoffrey nodded grimly.

"That would be most dangerous, yes—and most deceitful."

"Surely it will not bother us again," Alain protested, "now that it knows we can hurt it worse than it us, and knows we are wise to its ways."

"It does not know that last," Geoffrey said, "does it, brother?"

"It does not," Gregory confirmed, "and therefore will it test us more, most likely with its friends of tooth and claw— so I shall be true to my name as a most wary sentry. The first watch is mine."

Geoffrey shrugged. "If you wish, brother—though for some reason, I suspect I shall not sleep much this night."

None of them did, though the Biasd Bheulach did wait until they had eaten and lain down before it began its torments. No sooner had Alain and Geoffrey closed their eyes than a horrid whooping and shrieking sounded from the woods some distance away.

Alain sat bolt upright, hand on his sword. "What mayhem does it bring!"

"Naught," Geoffrey said, still lying on his side—but tense as a bridge cable. "It but seeks to frighten us."

"It has succeeded, then." Alain stared off into the forest with wide eyes. "Can you not make it stop, Gregory?"

Gregory, deep in his sentry's trance, sighed, "Should I?"

"Well asked," Geoffrey said. "As long as we hear its sounds, we know where it is."

Alain shuddered. "To have to listen to that all night long!"

Deep in the wood, a scream split the night, like that of a man pierced through with a sword.

"Did you truly think to sleep?" Geoffrey asked. "If so, I can arrange it—a soothing spell that shall yield a floating feeling to remove you from cares and lull you to sleep."

Alain actually considered the question for a few minutes before he shook his head. "A prince who would lead armies must keep a clear head at all times, most especially when danger threatens—and be able to ignore his weariness."

"Well answered." Geoffrey nodded. "I think I shall follow you in war."

A piercing cry echoed through the forest.

"Its sound is behind us!" Alain spun, trying to track the noise. "How can it move so quickly?"

"By being near and walking around us in a circle," Gregory breathed in a voice like the wind. "Hearken to its progress—it moves widdershins."

Alain turned slowly, following the source of the sound. It did indeed move from west to north to east.

"Is that its true place?"

"It could indeed be illusion," Geoffrey acknowledged. "Its shrieks make the whole forest ring, so you may be tracking an echo as easily as the Biasd Bheulach itself."

"How shall we know, then, from which direction it will attack?"

The piercing cries cut off.

"Blessed peace!" Alain sighed.

"Malicious, rather." Geoffrey's sword was halfway out of its scabbard in an instant. "When something that seeks to frighten us ceases to sound, beware attack!"

Something whined in the shadows.

"What comes?" Now it was Alain's sword that whisked free.

"A dog!" Geoffrey said with delight. "I should know that calling anywhere!" He sheathed his sword and knelt, holding out a hand and calling, "Come, poor thing! Be not afraid!"

The dog, if dog it were, whimpered in the shadows but stayed hidden.

"It fears people!" Geoffrey exclaimed. "How has it been mistreated?" He pulled a stick of dried beef from his pouch, broke off a piece, and held it out. "Come, fellow! Come taste! Nay, none here will hurt you—unless you should seek to bite the hand that feeds." He laughed softly, then called again, "Come!"

Into the firelight slunk the most mangy, decrepit old greyhound they had ever seen.

"There, now!" Geoffrey coaxed. "Come taste! It may be you will ward us from that which shrieks in the night, eh?"

"It may be it will not!" Alain cried. "Do you not remember

what Gregory said even now, Geoffrey? The Biasd Bheulach goes oft in the form of a greyhound!"

Geoffrey knelt stunned, staring in surprise—and in the instant of his amazement, the greyhound swelled to the size of a horse, its muzzle thickening into that of a mastiff and gaping wide, reaching for Geoffrey's head, huge enough to engulf it entire.

"Aroint thee!" Alain cried and leaped forward, sword thrusting upward past Geoffrey's head into that huge and putrid maw. He could tell by the sudden resistance that he had lanced flesh. The huge head reared up, slamming Alain back as the monster let loose a shriek that would have done credit to a steam engine.

By that time, Geoffrey had his sword out, face dark with fury. "Traitor! False friend! Would you take the form of man's greatest ally, then? Have at thee!" He leaped in to thrust at the dog's chest.

With a howl, the monster leaped backward, but the sword nicked flesh just before its huge paw sent Geoffrey flying. It screamed again—but even as it screamed, it made one more try at taking a bite out of Geoffrey. He rolled aside, though, and the huge jaws clashed shut only inches from his head. Then Geoffrey scrambled to his feet and leaped back in to thrust his sword into its nose.

The giant hound gave a most pitiful howl that would have drowned out the thunder itself as it whirled and fled back into the forest, leaving all three men with their hands clapped over their ears—and if it had turned back then, it would have been a proper race between the companions grabbing up their swords from the earth, and the Biasd Bheulach's teeth. Not knowing its opportunity, though, it only raced farther and farther away, its howls fading in the night until other canine voices answered it.

Gregory tensed. "Others . . . could they be other Biasd Bheulachs?"

"If they were, he would have brought them with him already," Geoffrey said. He plunged his sword into the earth, yanked it out, and plunged it in again. "Clean your blade,

Alain. There is no telling what manner of blood that creature possesses, or what it will do to our steel."

"Which certainly caused it pain enough." Alain stabbed the earth, too, then looked up at Gregory. "Will it come back, think you?"

"It will try again to cozen us," the scholar said, gaze abstracted once more. "Lose no sleep over it, though—it may be long ere it comes again."

"Sleep! As though my eyes could close!" Alain said, his voice shaky. "Nay, let us brew a cup or two, Geoffrey. I shall need its soothing heat and a bit of talk ere I can sleep again."

Geoffrey blew up the fire and sat down, holding his hands out to its warmth—but with his sword across his knees. "Only think what a fine story this will make to tell your grandchildren, Alain."

"Let us see to the children first," Alain said drily, sitting across from Geoffrey. "Nay, let us be sure of their mother before that."

Geoffrey frowned. "How now? Do you think you cannot trust my sister?"

"Trust her, yes," Alain said. "Be sure that she is so thoroughly mine that I never need to court her again? No."

"Well, of course." Geoffrey looked down at the flames. "A man can never take a woman for granted—even if it is she herself who has done the granting, for she might decide to take herself back at any time."

That easily, the conversation fell to discussing the finer points of their respective fiancées, which was soothing indeed—and led to swapping tales of their childhoods, so it was only a half-hour or so before Geoffrey stretched and said, "I could begin to think of sleep now."

"Think of food instead," pleaded a reedy voice from the darkness.

Alain tensed. Geoffrey leaped to his feet.

A wizened old man hobbled into the circle of firelight, one hand tucked inside his tunic, leaning heavily upon a cane and imploring them, "Think of the poor and the hungry, kind noblemen. Pity the humble!"

Geoffrey frowned. "How come you seeking alms at midnight?"

"Why, I cannot sleep for the pangs of hunger in my belly." The old fellow tottered, pleading, "Only a bit of bread!"

"Aye, of course!" Alain leaped to brace him up—just as Gregory's voice wafted to him. "Beware, Alain! He is the Biasd Bheulach in its most dangerous guise!"

The old man whirled with a snarl, the hidden hand whipping out of his tunic to reveal a single six-inch claw that plunged toward Alain's ribs.

Reflex took over and Alain whirled aside, left arm coming up to block the blow—and the huge claw slashed through cloth and skin. Blood flowed, staining the sleeve even as Geoffrey lunged. His sword pierced the old man's arm—old no longer, for he swelled even as he turned, mouth wide in a screech that pierced their brains—then suddenly stopped, though his jaws still stretched wide. His beard and hair were dark again, his body muscular, arm wrenching away from the blade and his huge claw slashing at Geoffrey.

Alain shouted even as he drew and lunged. His sword pierced the monster's shoulder; its mouth went even wider in agony, presumably emitting a shriek that went unheard. Then it turned away, crashing back into the woods. Only a few steps, and its screech tore through their heads again.

Prince and knight fell to their knees, dropping their swords and clapping their hands over their ears. When the screech had faded with distance, they uncovered tentatively, then lowered their hands with a sigh. Geoffrey asked, "You damped its voice with a counter-wave, did you not?"

"Even so," Gregory said with a voice like the breeze in the leaves. "The tone would have beaten upon your eardrums if his shrieking had not canceled it."

Alain frowned. "I must be associating with wizards too often. I almost understood that."

"You are quite able to understand wave mechanics," Geoffrey assured him, "but the study will not of itself lend you magic."

"Nonetheless," Gregory's voice breathed from his trance, "there is much you can do with it."

"You may teach it to me another time," Alain said in a strained voice. He turned, showing Gregory the bloody sleeve. "For now, wizard, I would appreciate your skill in medicine."

Gregory's eyes slowly widened. His hands trembled as his pulse rate began to increase and all his body's systems to accelerate. At last he stood up, came to Alain's side, and glared down at the wound.

"What does he, Geoffrey?" Alain asked through gritted teeth.

"He searches your blood for poisons," Geoffrey answered.

Alain gasped with pain.

"That is the flesh beginning to knit itself together." Geoffrey smiled. "He must have found that the wound is clean—that, or countered the poisons."

"There was only one," Gregory said, "like to a snake's venom. I broke the carbon chains apart, though, and rendered the substance harmless." He released Alain's arm. "There will be a small scar for some days. Shall I mend the sleeve, too?"

Alain stared down at the angry red welt on his skin. "No, thank you, Gregory. I think mending my hide will do."

"Then sit by the fire and speak of soothing things." Geoffrey suited the action to the word, then looked up in irritation. "Can that fellow not make less noise?"

"He has lost the fight, my friend," Alain said, smiling as he sat, "the fight, and his prey as well. Let us allow him the solace of venting his wrath upon the air."

"The air, aye. My ear, perhaps not." Geoffrey winced at a particularly loud howl. "The water boils. Shall you take that tea you wanted?"

"More than ever. What is the herb?"

"Chamomile, if we are to have any hope of sleep." Geoffrey poured powder into two cups, then added boiling water.

"Dare we sleep?" Alain asked, frowning. "Might not the Biasd Bheulach come upon us again?"

"It will not attack." Gregory resumed his seat, folding his legs. "It seeks easy game, not three men guarding one another's backs and ready to fight. If it can lure one of us off, though, it will."

"I am not about to leave the camp with that racket going on!"

"Then sleep," Geoffrey advised, "or at the least, lie down and think of pleasant things."

A horrendous scream made the tree trunks ring. Alain shuddered. "What thought could be so pleasant as to shield me from that pandemonium?"

"Cordelia," Geoffrey said succinctly.

Alain sat still for a moment, head cocked to one side. Then he sipped his tea and nodded. "I shall essay it."

Whether or not they really slept was debatable—but the two men did indeed lie down, though they tossed and turned from time to time, while Gregory brooded over the campsite like an enigmatic statue in his trance.

As the sky paled with the approach of dawn, the Biasd Bheulach's screams lessened until, with the first ray of sunlight, they ceased. Alain sat up, somewhat pale and definitely rumpled, but stoically silent. It was Geoffrey who pushed himself to his knees, groaning, "I feel as though I had not slept a wink!"

"Most likely you did not," Alain sympathized. He turned to their sentry. "Join the waking world again, Gregory."

Minutes passed; only people used to Gregory's trances would have noticed the flutter of the eyelids, the twitching fingers, the deepening breaths. Since Alain and Geoffrey did, it wasn't quite so much of a surprise when he lifted his head and said, "Let us break our fast."

"I shall brew herbs." Geoffrey knelt to toss kindling on the coals and blow them to flame under the camp kettle. Alain took out journeybread and salt beef.

Over breakfast, they discussed the events of the night.

They all agreed the Biasd Bheulach's screeches had taken on a definite note of frustration shortly before dawn and that the scream of terror that had brought Geoffrey and Alain upright, hands on their hilts, had indeed been its last real try at discomfiting them. So agreed, they drowned the campfire, buried the coals, saddled their horses, and set off along the forest trail.

"Are such spirits as these usually so persistent, Gregory?" Alain asked.

"They are," the scholar replied. "In truth, they are known to haunt a place until they have slain someone. Only then do they move on to seek new prey."

Alain shook his head, scowling. "Does that mean . . . since its cries have ceased . . ."

"Oh, no," Gregory assured him. " 'Tis only seen or heard at night. No, dawn sends it to hide." He was silent a minute or two, then said, "Mind you, that does not mean it did not slay anyone last night—but there is no particular reason to believe that it did."

"No, other than a hundred shrieks that could have been the death cry of any creature, human or animal!" Geoffrey said. "Still, I do not think it slew a hundred in one night."

"Have there always been so many murderous spirits in this land?" Alain asked.

"Not dwelling so closely together." Gregory frowned. "Indeed, this is a most unusual concentration."

"I would suspect enemy action," Geoffrey said, "but we have no reason to think there is an enemy nearby."

"Other than a most strange mist that leaves ogres behind when it lifts, no," Alain said. "I cannot help thinking that a bit unusual."

"What do you suspect?" Geoffrey challenged him. "Someone like Ari the music-rock maker, only considerably more sinister?"

Alain turned to stare at him. "What a horrible notion! And how well it fits!"

Geoffrey returned the stare, taken aback. Then he frowned

and started to say something—when Gregory let out a keening cry of distress.

They spun in their saddles to stare at him, but he was pointing ahead and to the side of the trail.

CHAPTER
-7-

Turning, they saw a man lying in the long grass—grass that was stained red, and a man who lay with one hand pressed to his side and another to his leg. His hands were red and his eyes stared, sightless; his features were frozen in a look of horror.

The three men dismounted, for the horses shied at the sight—and these were horses who were trained to ignore the scent of blood. The riders dropped the reins over their heads, dangling to the ground, for their mounts were trained to the sight as a signal not to wander. Then all three men came forward on foot, hands on their hilts. Gregory knelt by the man and gently pried his hands away from his body.

Alain let out a wordless cry of anger and Geoffrey's face turned to stone.

"Pierced," Gregory said, "as though by a single great claw."

"That last horrid cry we heard," Alain said, stiff-lipped, "the one of agony and terror that brought us upright. Do you suppose . . .?"

"I do indeed," Geoffrey agreed.

"I shall be revenged!" Alain cried, trembling. "I shall be revenged upon the monster who thus sets upon my people!"

"Do not take it so personally," Gregory advised.

"Why not? He would have slain me if he could!"

"If a peasant is pierced, his prince bleeds," Geoffrey explained to Gregory, "a good prince, at least." He turned back to Alain. "Let us discover who set the monster upon us before we seek to slay."

"Is there any doubt that the Biasd Bheulach did this deed?" Alain asked.

Gregory shook his head. "None. That single great claw that sought your heart pierced this man instead."

"Alack-a-day!" Alain buried his head in his hands. "He died in my place!"

"Be not so proud," Geoffrey told him. "If he had slain you here, he would have slain a peasant tomorrow, in some other parish."

"The thing thirsts for blood," Gregory agreed, "human blood, and it was not particular—it would have slain any of us if it could."

"Yes. Do not think it sought the life of a prince," Geoffrey concurred. "It was quite content to find a peasant, alone and unguarded."

"There is truth in that." Alain stood slowly, hand on his sword, glaring off into the forest. "Well, if I cannot slay the murderer, I can find and slay whoever set it loose. Let us take this poor fellow to the nearest church and see him buried, friends, then ride to seek his foe!"

Cordelia ladled porridge into the wooden bowls, saying almost indignantly, "I can scarcely believe the night passed with nothing to disturb us!"

"It is ever the way of it." Quicksilver looked grumpy in spite of the mug of tea whose vapors she was inhaling. She set it down to take the bowl Cordelia offered, saying, "Whenever a lass is prepared for a fight, it is never offered."

"Indeed," Allouette agreed. "Foes must ever creep upon

us unawares." Then she bit her lip as Cordelia and Quicksilver gave her quick glances and as quickly looked away,
studying their oatmeal. There was an awkward silence as all
three remembered that Allouette had indeed brought trouble
upon them when they least expected.

It only lasted a moment, though. Quicksilver tossed back
her hair and said, "Then it remains for us to seek out the
trouble that eludes us. Eat heartily, ladies, for we may have
hard riding this day."

Their fasts broken and their horses saddled, they rode off
on the trail of their fiancés.

"Let us hope we come upon them ere their enemies do,"
Allouette said fervently.

"Or only a few minutes thereafter," Quicksilver said.
"How think you, ladies? When we find them, shall we ride
just out of sight and stay alert for trouble, so that when it
comes upon them we may take it from behind?"

Allouette nodded. "A good plan."

"It would seem so," said Cordelia, "but let us find them
first."

"Not hard, for they are being quite careless about leaving
tracks." Quicksilver glanced at the ground to check the tracks
of the men, then stared. "They have suddenly become cautious!"

"What do you see?" Cordelia looked down with her and
frowned. "*I* see nothing."

"That is exactly what I see—nothing at all! No prints, no
traces, no tracks of horse or man!"

Allouette rode up beside them, staring with them at the
dirt. "Nothing? . . . No, nothing!"

"Not even brush marks where tracks have been swept
away." Quicksilver frowned. "Has my Geoffrey become
monstrously cautious of a sudden?"

"Such care is more Alain's way," said Cordelia, "but
would Geoffrey listen to him?"

"He might—if Gregory spoke in support of Alain," Allouette offered.

"There is some truth to that." Cordelia pursed her lips,

imagining the conversation between her brothers. "Still, Geoffrey is not given to acknowledging when Gregory has the right of an issue, unless it is one of scholarship."

"And tracking is not a matter of scholarship," Quicksilver said.

"But magic is," Allouette told her.

The women were silent for a moment, staring at one another in consternation. Finally Quicksilver said, "If their tracks have been whisked away by magic, they will not even know of it."

"Indeed not," said Allouette, "for they have no cause to look behind them."

"We are behind them!"

"But they do not know that," Cordelia reminded.

Quicksilver frowned. "A pretty puzzle this is! How are we to track them with no trace, and their thoughts shielded?"

They were silent again, looking at one another, thinking.

"They have been following this road so far," Allouette said. "There is no reason to think they would leave it."

"True." Quicksilver nodded. "Until we come to a fork in the road, at least. Let us ride, ladies."

"After all," said Cordelia, "if the road ends before we find them, we can always retrace our steps."

"I dislike the loss of time," Quicksilver said, fuming, "but there's little choice."

Allouette nodded and clucked to her horse. Side by side, the three women rode on down the lane between the stone walls. It was a very convenient lane, very comfortable to ride—and impossible to miss.

Down a slope it ran, then up another to a high ridge. At the top, they paused, looking down into a little bowl-shaped valley, only short grass on its side but at its bottom, an open meadow adorned with flowering trees. A brook meandered down its length.

"It is quite pretty," Allouette offered.

"It is indeed." Quicksilver scowled. "Why, then, do I feel that there is a pall of gloom hanging over it?"

"Well asked," Cordelia agreed.

Together they studied the valley, analyzing the cause for the bleakness they all felt. It was Allouette who put it into words. "There are no people there—no huts or cottages, no crops!"

"Nor even any sheep or deer." Quicksilver pondered the scene. "In truth, there is no sign of anything living, save trees, grass, and flowers."

"Why would folk not settle in so lovely a dale?" Allouette asked. "Why would they not farm it?"

Cordelia's face hardened. "This may be the danger we have felt approaching, ladies."

"And if there is no trail, the lads may well have ridden down into peril." Quicksilver kicked her heels against her mount's sides. "We must investigate at the least!"

They rode together down into the valley. The walls ceased but the track was still broad and level. The women were braced for trouble—so it was with amazement that Allouette turned to look to the side and cried, "It is Gregory! We have found them!"

Her companions turned to look, too, and Cordelia gave a glad cry. "It is Alain!"

"Nay, it is Geoffrey!" Quicksilver kicked her horse into a canter, crying, "Well met, my love!"

The other women rode quickly after her, toward the lone man who looked up at them in pleased surprise.

Quicksilver reined in, leaping off her horse and throwing her arms around his neck with a glad cry.

"Away, lady!" Cordelia cried in anger. "Would you have my prince for your own, then?" She dismounted and stalked toward Quicksilver and Alain.

Allouette dashed past her, crying, "Stand away from my Gregory! Is not his brother enough for you?"

"Brother?" Cordelia cried, scandalized. "I should say I know my brothers well enough, and Alain is surely neither of them!"

All three women fell silent. Quicksilver loosed her hold on the young man and stepped away, turning an appalled glance to her companions. "Do you not see Geoffrey?"

"I do not," Cordelia assured her. "It is Alain, by the troth he plighted me!"

"I see only Gregory!" Allouette protested.

"Nay, sweeting," Geoffrey said, "can you doubt me, then?" He slid his arm around Quicksilver's waist and stepped close. "Ah, you are so fair, so bright, the loveliest of Nature's wonders! Nay, it has been far too long since I have seen you, touched you, felt your breath on my cheek . . . my lips . . . nay, I shall die of famine if I have not your kiss . . ."

Quicksilver's gaze was drawn to his almost against her will. She stood rigid, finding herself unable to step away but unwilling to step toward her lover.

With good reason. "Will you not embrace me?" he mourned. "Ah, lack-a-day!" He released his hold and stepped toward Cordelia. "Fairest of the fair, surely you will greet me with love to answer my own!"

Cordelia trembled, unable to believe that the others could not see Alain as clearly as she—and as thoroughly unable to move as Quicksilver had been.

Alain stepped closer to her, caressing her cheek, tilting her face toward his own.

Cordelia managed to speak through lips that felt as though they were melting. "Alain . . . you were never wont to speak of love before others . . ."

"But *you* are before others," he said, gazing down with a look of such tender passion that she had to fight her own feelings to doubt him. "You are before all others, and are the sweetest blossom on the tree of life!" His lips lowered over her own.

"No!" Cordelia wrenched herself free, feeling as though the movement tore at her heartstrings. "I'll not kiss a man who but moments ago sought the lips of another!"

"Must I be left lorn?" Alain mourned, and impossibly turned from her toward Allouette. "The earth breathes where you walk, and its breath forms the greatest beauty in the land! Oh lady of wondrous form and fairest face, surely you will not turn from me as these others have done!"

"Oh Gregory, how could I deny you anything?" Allouette didn't step forward either, but her head tilted up, eyes half-closing, lips parting, full and moist . . .

"*Noooo!*" Cordelia remembered Allouette's attempts to seduce Alain, and all the rage and anger of those moments boiled up within her. She leaped forward, hands hooking to tear at the other woman.

Alain moved to place his body between them, breathing, "One kiss, only one kiss! For that do I starve, do I thirst, do I burn! Give me the honeyed moist sweetness of your lips, I pray!"

"He is mine!" Cordelia cried.

"Nay, mine!" Allouette spun to seize Quicksilver's sword, whipping it out of the scabbard—then froze, staring at the blade in her hand. "What am I *doing*?"

"You are coming to me!" Gregory held out his arms. "Forgo that whetted sliver and ponder my prayer! Ah, fair flower, you must not deny me!"

But the ringing of steel triggered Allouette's memories of knives in the dark, aimed toward the very women who now glared at her in loathing. It was like ice water in her face, waking her from a trance, and she turned her back on the young man, crying, "Deny you I shall, for you cannot be Gregory if you are Alain!"

"And cannot be Alain if you are Geoffrey!" Quicksilver snapped, reddening.

"He cannot be any of them!" Cordelia cried. "But how can he seem to be all three?"

"Because all women are beauties, and you three most of all!" Alain protested. "Does not each of you deserve your heart's desire?"

"*She* certainly seemed to think so." Quicksilver cast Allouette a venomous glare.

Allouette's gaze snapped up to the warrior woman and anger rose over the tide of self-loathing. Allouette demanded, "Have you nothing to say to the woman who steals your sword?"

The hot flush that spread over Quicksilver's cheeks told

her that she had struck home, for the sword is a warrior's pride and its loss a huge blow to self-esteem. Allouette braced herself for attack—but Quicksilver only set her fingers to her lips and blew a whistle so shrill that it made Allouette drop the sword to clap her hands over her ears— and Quicksilver snatched it up, point six inches from Allouette's throat. "Easily gained, more easily lost."

Geoffrey winced. "I am hard by, my sweet. You need not whistle me up."

Quicksilver felt as though she were a compass needle and Geoffrey a magnet trying to draw her away from her true course—but she kept her gaze turned away from his face, glaring at a magpie in a tree. "It is not you whom I summoned."

"Whom then?" Geoffrey stepped into her line of sight. "Surely you do not summon another man, you who are the very soul of loyalty, as true as you are lovely, as true as my love for you! Whom do you summon?"

Hoofbeats pounded up in answer and a horsehead interposed itself between Quicksilver and his face. She leaped up onto the mare's back with a feeling of relief, calling, "Mount, ladies! There is something wrong in this, for one single man cannot be all three of our loves! Mount and ride away!"

"Away?" Geoffrey mourned, stepping toward her, hands outstretched in supplication. "Ah, will you desert me, then? I, who hunger for you, who burn for you, who live only for the touch of your gentle hand, the taste of your sweet lips!"

Cordelia forced her head away. "You have right in this, for Alain would never speak of the touch of my hand or the taste of my lips in front of others!"

"Your hand and lips?" Allouette cried in indignation. "Wherefore should Gregory speak so of his sister? It was to me he spoke!"

"It was not Gregory, but Alain!"

"It was neither," Quicksilver said, her tone a whipcrack. "Mount and ride, ladies, for whatever sorcery's in this, it seeks to lure us to our dooms!"

Cordelia's head snapped back as though she'd been

slapped. She turned to her horse and mounted, trying hard to ignore Alain's blandishments, and turned her mare's head toward the slope down which they had ridden.

"Oh fairest of the fair, do not leave me lorn!" Alain called to her—and Geoffrey to Quicksilver, and Gregory to Allouette. Already standing in the stirrup, she wavered, turning back to look at his sweet, fair face, so strong yet so vulnerable . . .

"Mount, lady!" Quicksilver's voice seemed like cold water in Allouette's face. "Whatever it is, it is not your Gregory— nor my Geoffrey, nor Cordelia's Alain. Mount and ride for your life—and your love!"

Allouette hooked her right knee over the saddle horn and sat back, trembling, as she clucked to her mare. The sweet animal began to move away, back up the track, while Gregory called after her in despair, "Nay, do not leave me! The sun hides its face when you are gone, the night swallows me, clouds of fog enshroud me . . ."

"We must ride uphill!" Quicksilver said between her teeth. "We must ride, no matter what he says!"

"All gems lose their luster, all foods lose their savor, the very salt of the sea becomes flat and tasteless when you are gone from me! Oh, turn back, turn back, turn to me, bend to me, even if only for one last kiss!"

"Keep riding," Quicksilver grated. A haze of passion seemed to cloak her eyes, but still she bade her companions, "For your lives, ride uphill!"

"The stars fall from the sky, for your eyes *are* my stars, the bright beacons that guide me through life! If you take them away, how shall I know where to go? Nay, without those fair pole stars, I shall wander lost and lorn all my days!"

"Close your ears to him!" Cordelia tried to make it an angry command but was appalled to hear it emerge as a whimper. There was a strange churning inside her, a weakness in her limbs, but she said, "Heed him not, and ride on!" Then, out of the corner of her eye, she saw Alain again and let out a cry of despair.

"We have lost our way," Quicksilver ground out. "We have turned back toward him unwittingly! Pull right rein, ladies, right uphill again!"

"I do," Allouette said, her voice shaking, "but my mare will not answer! She tries to turn her head back toward him, and it is all I can do to hold her course straight ahead!"

"She, too, hears calls of love," Quicksilver groaned, "the mating calls of a most desirable stallion!"

"But none of our mares are in heat!" Cordelia protested.

"They are now, and Heaven help me, but I know how they feel! If we cannot turn them away, at least hold them on course!"

So across the slope of the little valley they rode, around and around its bowl in a circle with Geoffrey/Alain/Gregory/ the stallion at its center, turning to hold them with his gaze, calling out in a tone that turned them to jelly, "The grass dies when you cease to tread upon it, the leaves fall in sorrow, the very rivers cease to flow and lie stagnant and fetid through absence of the life that you lend them! Oh, come back, come back, for all of nature shall grow dry and sere without you!"

"Come back, and when he is done with us, something in us will die," Quicksilver groaned, "and that something is that which enables us to love our mates! Hold fast, ladies! Keep riding!"

"Aye, do," cried a shrill voice.

Her mare tugged at the reins, trying to turn downhill to the magical stallion, but a bird fell from the sky, fluttering madly right in front of the horse's eyes, and the mare shied away, whinnying its shock. Quicksilver fought to turn its head back uphill and succeeded in keeping the poor beast going straight ahead, across the slope. "Many thanks to that bird! But where did it come from?"

"*Krawk!* To advise you and your companions, chief of warriors!" The bird landed between the mare's ears. The horse tossed her head; the bird fluttered up briefly, then settled back. "Even a birdbrain could see that you need wise counsel to avoid that fellow below."

Blinking, Quicksilver saw that the winged one was the magpie who had been watching them from the tree. "We have seen for ourselves that we need to avoid him!"

"Aye, but not how or why," said the magpie.

"Tell us, I prithee!" Allouette begged. "What manner of creature is this, who can be all three of our fiancés at once?"

"A creature of faerie," the magpie answered, "for he is in truth a ganconer!"

Allouette and Cordelia gasped, but Quicksilver frowned. "What is a ganconer?"

"A cozener—a seducer." The magpie turned its head to the side, letting its beak loll open so that it seemed to smile. "Country maids call him the love-talker and full many of them has he persuaded to his bed, to their lifelong sorrow!"

"By lies and deceptions?" Quicksilver felt the anger begin to grow.

"By that, and some strange attraction he has over females who are so foolish as to bear their chicks inside them instead of laying eggs like decent folk," the bird answered.

"A ganconer—a love-talker!" Cordelia said with heart-rending dismay. She spun toward the young man in anger. "How many dairymaids and shepherdesses have you come upon alone and seduced, heartbreaker? How many will never know joy again or be able to truly love a living man because of your honeyed words and burning caresses?"

"Those caresses bring joy unbounded," Alain said to her, "and if no lass could delight in a mortal man after knowing me, it is because I have shown her such heights of ecstasy as no village swain could approach. Nay, come with me, lie with me, and you will know that your whole life has been worth this one brief hour with me!"

"And my whole life would have been mortgaged for those brief minutes!" Anger came to Cordelia's rescue. "How many women have you despoiled, how many lives ruined? But you have come upon bad luck today, love-talker, for you have encountered not one woman alone, but three allied in purpose!"

"And that purpose is now to avenge our sisters!" Memory

curved Allouette's hands into claws, memory of careless love; it brought those talons up to pounce upon the imposter in rage.

"Nay, would you turn upon me?" Gregory began to climb the hill toward her, arms still open and raised to embrace. *To caress,* some traitorous inner voice said, and she forced herself to look away as her anger melted in the heat of desire his voice kindled by its very intimacy as it came nearer and nearer.

Quicksilver trembled as Geoffrey came toward her, reaching up for her, pleading, "Put up thy sword, I beseech thee, sweeting, for naught should come between us."

"Geoffrey would meet steel with steel." Quicksilver tried to back her horse away, but the mare would not budge. "At the very least he would meet my blade with a stout staff and would knock the sword from my hand if he could." But some irresistible force dragged at her head, trying to turn her face toward him, for every fiber of her being cried out for her love. She fought the compulsion but it made her head turn nonetheless, slowly toward him, though her inner voice fairly shouted in alarm, clamoring, *Danger! Get away from him! Do not let him come near, or you will never be able to love a true man again!*

CHAPTER
-8-

As Quicksilver's head turned, though, the magpie came once again within her sight—but this time, its beak wasn't open in laughter; it was holding two large pellets. It hopped onto her wrist and dropped them in her palm. "Wool, damsel! Knots of wool pecked from the backs of the finest sheep! Stop your ears with it, for when you can no longer hear the love-talker, he will lose power over you and you will be free to escape him!"

With dragging hands, Quicksilver pushed the earplugs in—and the ganconer's voice dropped to a wobbling drone, scarcely audible at all through the pounding of her pulse.

The magpie grinned again, then was off in a burst of wings. In seconds it was back, hovering before Cordelia. Quicksilver turned to call, "Take the pellets and use them, for they will free us!"

The ganconer turned to Cordelia, beseeching, pleading, but she pushed the plugs into her ears and relief flooded her face. By that time the magpie was fluttering in front of Allouette, who took the plugs, applied them, and almost sagged as the pull on her lessened to a fraction of what it had been. She still burned for Gregory's touch, but the buzzing beneath the thudding of her pulse was certainly not his voice, and she was able to lean forward to cover her horse's ears so that it could follow Cordelia's uphill, plodding after Quicksilver and her mount, ears similarly muffled.

Behind them, a voice rose in an inhuman wail of loss and regret—and anger. The women and their mares ignored it, though, and rode on up the side of the bowl. They didn't even stop when they came to the valley's rim but rode on, out of the little valley so pretty and so sterile, and on into a high forest of pines and hemlocks.

Finally Quicksilver reined in and took the plugs from her ears. She looked about her but saw no wings. Nonetheless, she called out, "Many thanks, O Magpie! We shall owe you dearly for this!"

Cordelia was staring at the two little lumps in her hand and saying in desolate tones, "I feel as though I shall never see Alain again."

"Nor I Gregory." Tears ran down Allouette's cheeks.

"And I feel as though Geoffrey is lost to me forever," Quicksilver said, "but I know it is only the aftermath of the boiling emotions that monster stirred in us. Let us ride on, ladies, for our true loves still await us, and now more than ever must we catch them up!"

"Oh, for Alain to catch me up in his arms," Cordelia groaned.

"Then you must find those arms first! Ladies, let us ride!"

"Wait! Before we do . . ." Allouette rode up, her horse nose to nose with Quicksilver's. Her face was stiff, but she forced the words out. "I owe you a great apology. No matter the provocation, it was most despicable of me to steal your sword."

Quicksilver's face softened. "And most wrong of me to insult you for your past deeds, when you have proved so very loyal to your love—and to us." She reached out to catch Allouette's hand briefly. "Ride with me, damsel, for I daresay we shall learn to trust one another yet!"

"We had best do so," Cordelia said with a smile, "for we shall all be sisters-in-law, shall we not?"

"We shall most certainly," Quicksilver agreed, "so we had best learn to be also sisters in arms. Come, ladies, away, for our grooms await—though they know it not."

"We ride!" Allouette gave her a smile that, for a few brief moments, had nothing of suspicion or guilt in it.

So, side by side, they rode on through the woods, no longer in the broad walled lane but following a deer trail that they trusted much more.

Geoffrey, Alain, and Gregory rode through level ground that seemed flat as a board all the way to the horizon, where a few twisted trees stretched skeleton branches. On every side, dried bracken spread over the earth as far as they could see.

"What manner of place is this, dead as late autumn?" Alain asked, shivering. " 'Tis nearly summer!"

"Ask, rather, what power could have blasted it so," Geoffrey answered somberly. He turned to his younger brother. "What say you, O Scholar?"

"It reeks of sorcery," Gregory said, wrinkling his nose, "or of psi power misused, if you prefer to call it that."

"How would a warlock dry out a whole plain?" Alain asked. "How could he drain the water from it?"

"Or withhold it from coming in," Geoffrey offered. "Stop up the fountains with rockfalls and dam the streams."

They were all quiet for a few minutes, thinking of the afanc. The horses plodded on and crested a rise that was so gradual it hadn't shown—but Gregory looked up in surprise and said, "Houses!"

"Cottages, at least." Geoffrey frowned. "How could such level ground hide them so?"

They found out as they came to the crest. Below them, the land fell away into a small depression. Down its center ran a dry creek bed. A dozen yards from its banks stood a circle of thatch-roofed cottages.

Alain frowned. "This is wrong. I see not a cat nor a dog,

certainly none of the sheep who should be grazing on this common—and not a living soul!"

"Can this land have been dry long enough to drive the people away?" Geoffrey asked, frowning.

"Surely not," said Gregory, "when the land beyond this plain is green with spring."

"Spring . . ." Geoffrey lifted his head with a faraway gaze. "Could it have lain thus throughout the winter?"

"Perhaps, brother," said Gregory, "but the people would have melted snow for drink. They have not trooped away because of drought, not yet!"

"What else could have chased them?" Alain asked, perplexed.

A warbling howl answered him, predators hooting with bloodlust and delight.

The three companions spun about and saw dozens of pale-skinned, barelegged little monsters in hooded tunics spilling over the roofs of the cottages toward them, brandishing stone-bladed knives and spears. Under the cowls of their tunics their faces looked more like those of lizards than of humans. They were surely no more than two feet high, but their eyes glittered with the pleasure of the chase when the hunter knows that he is far stronger than the quarry.

"Hobyahs!" Gregory cried, paling.

"Alain, look behind us!" Geoffrey lugged out his sword.

Alain drew, too, wheeling his horse about. "More of them!"

"And to left and to right!" Gregory whisked his own blade out of the scabbard. "We are surrounded!"

With a gloating massed shriek, the hobyahs shot toward the companions on short little legs that moved so fast they were a blur.

"Back to back!" Geoffrey cried, and the three men swung their horses to form a triangle, heads facing outward. The howling horde descended upon them, and the men began slashing with their swords.

"Cold Iron!" the front row of hobyahs shrieked, and leaped back. Those behind them slammed into them, and in moments, they mounded up into a squirming ring surrounding the three warriors.

Alain took advantage of the lull to cry, "We have done you no harm! Why do you attack us?"

"Why, because you are meat!" cried half a dozen voices, and the others took it up in a chant: "Meat! Meat! Meat! Meat!" One or two plucked up their courage enough to leap forward.

Geoffrey sent them shying away with a slash of his blade. "We are meat with Cold Iron in our hands! Do you wish to warm it with your blood?"

"No, with yours!" a hobyah called back, and his comrades hooted approval.

"Take them apart!" Alain hissed at the warlock and the wizard, then raised his voice to call out again: "Surely you are not so vicious! Would you slay innocent people only from your hunger?"

"Why not?" called a dozen voices, and a single one answered their own question: "We ate all the villagers, didn't we?"

"Dissolve them!" Alain hissed.

"We do our best." Geoffrey's face was as strain-taut as Gregory's. "Some other mind holds them in form!"

Alain went back to distractions. "Assuredly you did not eat so many good and innocent folk!"

"Good indeed!' cried a hobyah. "Delicious, too!"

"Meat! Meat! Meat! Meat!" the whole horde chanted again, and began to move in on the companions.

Alain sliced at the nearest; it squealed and pulled back. Gregory and Geoffrey did the same on their own sides. The prince called, "There is no need to spill your blood on our swords!"

"No, but there is need to spill yours for our drink!" yet another hobyah cried, and to its fellows, "Seize them! Carry them off! They are meaty fellows and should last us two days!"

"Fasting is good for the soul," Geoffrey told them, whirling his sword for punctuation. "Hunger is better than death."

"Why do we linger?" one more hobyah called to its mates. "We can bury them beneath our mass! No matter how they slice and slash, some of us will tear their flesh!"

"But many of you will die, too!" Alain called. "Who will it be?" With lightning speed, he snatched up a hobyah and held it squirming and squealing before its mates. "Do you wish to be the first to die, little one?"

"You could not be so cruel!" the minimonster protested.

"Would you be any less so?" Alain tossed it back into the mob. "Which shall be next? Who shall be first to spit himself on my sword?"

"I have never seen your like in this land before!" cried Geoffrey. "From where did you come?"

"Where did your kind?" a hobyah retorted. "We know only that we awoke to life in hunger, and awaken so each morning!"

"Know you no word of magic that brought you to be?" Gregory asked.

"No, and if we did, we would certainly not tell our quarry!" yet one more hobyah answered. "But we do know a word to make you freeze with fear. Scream it, fellows!"

The whole mob answered with a massed shout: "Zonploka! Zonploka! Zonploka!"

"Somehow that wakes no terror in my breast," Alain called back.

But the shouting drowned out his voice as the knee-high horde began to tumble off roofs and advance on them again, much more slowly but also inexorably, chanting louder and louder, "Zonploka! Zonploka! Zonploka!" as though the word itself gave them power.

"What is a zonploka?" Gregory asked.

"What matter?" Geoffrey braced himself for the onslaught.

"It matters greatly," Gregory answered, "for if they can gain power through it, they can lose it, too." He raised his voice and, in the pauses between the hobyahs' shouts, gave a bellow of his own: "Akolpnoz! Akolpnoz! Akolpnoz!"

The throng of miniatures fell silent, frowning in puzzlement. "What is an akolpnoz?" one demanded.

"It is the opposite of a zonploka," Gregory called back, "and will cancel its power! With me, companions! Akolpnoz!"

"Akolpnoz! Akolpnoz! Akolpnoz!" Alain and Geoffrey chanted with him.

"Now, stop that!" one hobyah said peevishly, and the others stopped chanting to listen. "It won't work anyway!"

"If not, then why have you stopped your song?" Gregory countered. "Akolpnoz!"

"Akolpnoz! Akolpnoz! Akolpnoz!" his companions chanted with him.

"Don't listen!" A hobyah clapped his hands over his ears. "It might work as they say!"

All its mates covered their ears too—and the chanting fell into disarray, becoming a jumble of noise. The three companions raised their unified voice against it: "Akolpnoz! Akolpnoz! Akolpnoz!"

The hobyahs could no longer hear one another to decide what they should do. They began to mill about uncertainly, still shouting out their nonsense word.

"Now!" Alain cried, and advanced slashing about him, still chanting, "Akolpnoz! Akolpnoz! Akolpnoz!"

The hobyahs joined together again—in a massed shriek. Several of them leaped to scramble up over a rooftop and away. Several more saw them and turned to run—and in a minute, the whole horde had turned to flee, scrambling and howling away.

Alain let his sword fall to his side, beginning to shake. "By my troth, that was a near thing!"

"And you a most excellent commander!" Geoffrey said, eyes wide. "Whatever possessed you, Alain? I have never known you to act so decisively!"

The prince managed a smile. "No one else knew what to do, Geoffrey, so I did what came to me—any action was better than none. As it developed, the situation required only good judgment, for both strong arms and keen intelligence did little good."

Geoffrey nodded. "And that is what makes for a king,

though intelligence and strength of arms help greatly—and
your justice must be tempered by mercy."

"But I shall have Cordelia for compassion, insight, and
intelligence, and my brother Diarmid for genius with Gregory
to aid him—and yourself and Quicksilver for generals."
Alain gave him a shaky grin. "If I can evoke your support,
that is."

"You shall most surely have it," Geoffrey avowed, "for I
begin to see that you shall become a most excellent monarch!"

"Aye, and one worthy of our loyalty," Gregory said. "It
was fortunate these hobyahs had no great brains among them,
though."

"Nor any one true leader," Geoffrey seconded.

But Alain turned to Gregory, wide-eyed. "You mean saying their magic word backwards really had no effect?"

"Not of itself," Gregory told him, "no more than did
theirs—for both gained their strength from the hobyahs' belief in them, nothing more."

"So you saw that you could counter their nonsense word
with one of your own, and shake their belief in its power."
Alain nodded slowly. "Most ingenious, Gregory."

"Most desperate," Gregory corrected, his voice shaking at
last. "It was a ploy of desperation, a wild guess, nothing
more."

"Sheer bluff," Geoffrey interpreted, "but Alain and I did
not know that."

"Aye, so we carried it through with the authority that made
it work!" The prince grinned. "Well done, O Brain!"

"Good luck only," Gregory said darkly, "and I mistrust
luck deeply."

"As I mistrust these little monsters." Alain turned to scowl
at the houses around them. "They are fled, but how shall we
make sure they stay gone—and ensure they harm no other
folk?"

"The answer lies in this 'zonploka' they chanted," Gregory
told him, "but for the nonce, I shall craft a countermonster

from witch-moss, a ravening creature who has appetite only for hobyahs."

"Well and good," Geoffrey said slowly, "but what will it do when it has eaten every one of them?"

Gregory frowned in thought, but Alain said, "You shall make it hibernate until more hobyahs come, of course."

"A good thought." Gregory's tone was that of surprise; he wasn't used to Alain having ideas. "How if none ever come again, though?"

"Well, if it sleeps, you should have no trouble making it melt back into its original substance," Alain said, very practically. "Craft their Nemesis, Gregory. Then let us seek and be sure they spoke truly when they said they had eaten all the villagers."

Gregory looked up, astounded. "You mean they might have lied?"

"Why not?" Alain shrugged. "If we bluffed, might they not have too?"

Geoffrey gazed at the lip of the ravine in which the village sat. "All the more reason to be vigilant. Craft your hobyah-eater, brother." Then he stiffened. "Who comes?"

Alain and Gregory looked up in alarm, then relaxed as they saw that the silhouettes against the sky were quite human and dressed in peasant kirtles and dresses or tunics and hose. " 'Tis the villagers coming to see if their houses are safe," Alain said.

Gregory smiled. "It would seem you were right, Alain—the little monsters did lie, praise Heaven!"

"The hobyahs must have fled far and fast, for the villagers to be so bold as to even think of returning." Geoffrey's gaze lost focus for a minute; then he nodded. "The creatures are still running, still in a panic."

"How did they come to be, do you think?" Geoffrey asked.

Gregory shrugged. "I see no reason to think it is anything but the usual, brother."

"The usual" meant that someone in the village was a projective telepath but did not know it. He had imagined the little monsters, probably in the course of telling children a story, or dreamed of them. If he had told his fellows about the dream, other unwitting projectives might have reinforced his images—but the dream itself could have been enough. If, in the country nearby, there were any substantial amount of witch-moss, it would have shaped itself to those images and taken on as much life as the dream-images would have had. In the case of the hobyahs, that was entirely too much.

The villagers came down the slope and in among the houses slowly, warily, ready to run at the slightest sign of danger. One older woman came a little faster than the others, but with frequent glances back to make sure she wasn't too far ahead. She came up to the companions, or at least ten feet away, and asked in a hesitant voice, "If it please you, sirs, can you tell us—have the hobyahs gone away?"

"They have, good woman—gone far and fast," Alain assured her.

"How . . . how far?" asked one of the men.

Alain turned to Geoffrey. "How far would you say, Sir Geoffrey?"

The villagers' eyes widened at the "sir."

"Into the next county, at least," Geoffrey answered, "perhaps even the next duchy." He turned to the villagers. "Have they given you cause to fear them?"

"Great cause, Sir Knight!" the woman exclaimed.

One of the men added. "They ate Albin Plowman!"

"We must find his bones, that we may bury them." The woman's eyes filled with tears.

Alain's voice dropped to a gentle tone. "Did you know him well?"

"We all did," she sighed. "He was a good neighbor. Alas for his babes, for his wife and mother!"

"Alas indeed," Alain commiserated. "Who else did they harm?"

"None, for they crowded around his body and fought over it," another man said, hard-faced. "We fled while they quarreled."

"Wisely done," Alain said. "So he gave his life for you all, then."

"Well, not quite," the woman admitted. " 'We must make friends with them,' quoth he, 'so that they will be loath to hurt us.' "

"We called to him to come back to the safety of the house," a third man said miserably, "but he went on forward, calling to them that we were their friends and would aid them in gaining whatever they wished."

" 'We want meat,' they cried, 'red meat!' " said the old woman, voice thick with tears. "Then they all leaped upon him. One scream did he make, then was silent, and all we saw was the churning, thrashing heap of monsters, screaming and clawing at one another for pride of place at their grisly feast."

"Then we fled." The first man looked surly. "Could any blame us?"

"Not I," Alain assured them.

"Nor I." Geoffrey's face was grim. "I could blame them, though, and wish them just as vile an end as they gave your friend Albin."

"Alas! What could give them that?" the woman lamented.

"Will—will the hobyahs come back, think you?" a second woman asked.

"We cannot be sure," Alain told her, "but our wizard here . . ." He glanced at Gregory and found him gone. "Where is Gregory?"

"Yon." Geoffrey jerked his head toward a nearby woodlot.

Alain turned and saw the blue-robed young man standing with his hands lifted high, outspread toward the trees. The prince couldn't be sure, but he thought he saw several small gray mounds slithering out between the trunks and moving toward one another as they came.

Alain turned back to the villagers. "Our wizard has already set about making a guardian for you, a fierce-looking creature with a huge appetite for hobyahs."

"A wizard!" The woman shied away, stepping backward toward her friends—who looked ready to turn and run themselves. "A wizard making a monster?"

"He is a witch-moss crafter," Alain explained, "and will

make sure the creature is quite gentle to people, but will turn into a ravening appetite on legs when it sees a hobyah."

"I . . . I can only thank you, gentlemen and knights," the woman said hesitantly, "but we dare not come back to our homes with such a thing prowling the parish."

"The guardian will not hurt you." Alain glanced over his shoulder and saw that the mound of witch-moss had grown larger than Gregory, and was beginning to take on the form of something with at least four legs and a head—a very wide head. "Mind you, it will look like a thing out of nightmare, but to you and your children it will be mild as a lamb."

"But . . . but what will it do when it can find no hobyahs to eat?" the woman asked, staring at Gregory and the living sculpture whose shape was rapidly becoming more and more definite, and more and more horrible.

"It will fall asleep," Alain answered, "like a squirrel in winter."

"What . . . what will wake it?" asked one of the men, staring fearfully as the creature began to make a grating noise that gradually turned into a basso purring.

"Only the scent of more hobyahs," Alain assured it. He turned to look himself, and smiled. "See! Yonder it comes, and its crafter with it."

The tailor-made monster had the body of a giant leopard, but its head was twice as wide as its shoulders, shaped like two soup bowls set rim to rim—and where the rims met was a mouth that stretched all the way across. Its ears were each half the size of its head, round and cupped—but if they were the cups, its eyes were the saucers, with vertical pupils that could probably see very clearly by nothing more than starlight. Its nose was an egg half as wide as its mouth with huge nostrils.

The creature grinned, displaying a mouthful of sawteeth.

The villagers huddled away from it in terror—until Gregory reached up to scratch. The creature tilted its head upward so that his fingers could rub under its chin, and the purring became as loud as a cement mixer in love.

The people froze, staring in surprise.

Then the creature lay down and laid its chin on its paws, so that Gregory could scratch behind its ears. It closed its eyes in sheer pleasure.

"Perhaps it is nothing to fear after all," said the woman.

"Kitty!" cried three treble voices, and small feet pounded past the villagers in a tattoo as rapid as a drumroll. The villagers cried out in alarm and made a frantic dive for the children, but they reached Gregory and his creature first, where one proceeded to clamber up astride its back, another began to stroke its furry sides, and the third began to scratch at the corner of its jaw.

"Behind its ears," Gregory told the boy on its back. "It likes that almost as much as beneath its jaw."

The creature tilted its head up so that the child on the ground could rub its chin, or what passed for one. The boy on its back began to rub behind its ears as though it were a washboard, and he doing the laundry.

Gregory stepped away, smiling at his handiwork, then turned to the villagers. "Here is your guardian—your very own hobyah-hunter."

The adults stared, then crept forward step by step and, hesitantly, began to join the children in stroking their new pet.

"Are you sure it is safe for them?" Alain asked, frowning.

"Safer than a wall and a moat," Gregory assured him, "but it will take them a while to believe that."

They went on their way, the brothers eyeing the prince warily. Gregory's thought sounded in Geoffrey's mind: *When did Alain become intelligent?*

It must have been in him all along, Geoffrey answered, *but never had occasion to show itself until now.*

He has ever been a modest man—for a prince, Gregory admitted.

Self-effacing, almost, Geoffrey agreed. *Now, though, when circumstances are desperate, he does not hesitate to offer his ideas.*

Perhaps it is only that—knowing that his notions cannot

make things worse, and may save us all. Gregory didn't seem convinced, though.

Kill or cure, Geoffrey agreed, *save or die—and he has always been a man of good judgment.*

Now, it seems, judging when to speak and when to be silent. Gregory's eyes widened in surprise. *Why, it must have always been so! And the wisest course before, has been silence.*

His judgment only errs in his opinion of himself. Geoffrey sighed. *How shall we mend that, brother?*

That, Gregory thought judiciously, *I think we may leave to our sister.*

Let us hope he does not surprise her as he does us. Geoffrey's thought had a sardonic tinge. Then his eyes widened. *You do not suppose she already knows, do you?*

"What in good candor is that obscene thing?" Quicksilver stared at the roadblock ahead of them.

The women drew up their horses side by side, staring at a vast pulsating white mound that filled the whole lane.

"It would seem to be a mass of witch-moss," Cordelia said, "but what immense creature was it?"

"And who made it disintegrate into a mound of jelly?" Allouette asked.

There was no answer to either question, of course. The three women fought to hold their horses still—all three mounts were trying to shy away from the pulsating thing— and stared at the obstruction while they tried to work out what could have happened there.

"Dare we go closer?" Cordelia wondered.

"I fail to see any reason why we should not," Quicksilver returned. "If it is unformed, after all, it has no claws or teeth with which to do us harm." She touched her horse's flanks with her heels—but the mare dug in her hooves obstinately. Quicksilver frowned at her. "Nay, sweet horse! Go ahead!"

"Wait." Allouette raised a hand to touch her elbow.

Quicksilver whirled, a hot denunciation on her tongue, but Allouette was pointing ahead. "Another will test it for us."

Quicksilver turned back in time to see a squirrel dash across the road two feet in front of the mound.

CHAPTER
-9-

Quicker than the eye could see, a pseudopod shot out of the great jelly to swat the squirrel. There was one shocked squeal; then the little creature was completely enveloped in white protoplasm. The pseudopod drew back into the mound with a horrid sucking smack.

Allouette shuddered. "It is a Boneless!"

"It is quite clearly boneless." Quicksilver frowned. "What of it?"

"Nay, *a* Boneless!" Cordelia repeated. " 'Tis the name of the creature, not merely its state."

Quicksilver gazed at the mound through slitted eyes. "What is its nature?"

"Ravenous," Cordelia told her. "It will absorb anything living that comes near it, plant, animal, or human!"

"Then let us give it a wide berth." Quicksilver turned her horse, then hesitated. "But it will not stay where it is, will it?"

"Nay," Allouette confirmed. "We, at least, know what it is—but what will happen if a child comes upon it?"

Cordelia thought of the squirrel and shivered. "Dare we even let it stay upon this road?"

Allouette's eyes widened. "Look behind it!"

Looking, Cordelia and Quicksilver saw a trail shining for ten feet before it began to grow patchy with evaporation, then gradually ceased.

"It comes toward us," Quicksilver said with disgust.

"Slowly," Allouette qualified. "Nonetheless, it moves."

"We cannot have such a thing skating about the country-side," Cordelia said with decision, then glared at the Bone-less. It began to quiver, then spread out at the bottom, wider and wider as it sank into a puddle that spilled over the sides of the road into the grass.

"Well done," Quicksilver said.

"But not enough," Allouette amended. "Might it not pull itself back together?"

"Not if we divide it and give it other forms," Cordelia answered. "Will you join in the game?"

Allouette smiled. "Gladly."

Pieces began to break off the grayish-white puddle, pull themselves into balls, and go rolling off toward the roots of the roadside trees. There they stretched out thin, widened here and there, took on colors—and violets peeped over barky ridges, daffodils nodded in the shade, tulips opened their cups, roses bloomed, and more exotic flowers than had any business growing among oak and ash trees splashed gar-ish color through the wood.

Quicksilver forced herself to nonchalance while she watched, though the prickling of dread spread up her back-bone and across her neck and shoulders. She was a country girl who had been raised with the superstitions of her time and people, and living in constant contact with espers hadn't really changed that. Her mind knew that there was really nothing supernatural here, that these were only the tricks peo-ple with strong and rare talents could play—but her stomach knew nothing of the sort, and was trying to climb up into her gorge. She tried to shake off the feeling, telling herself that these "witches" were only young women like herself—

very much indeed, if Geoffrey was right about her having a touch of the gift of mind-reading herself—but her apprehensions refused to be banished. Soon the huge pancake had completely disappeared, the woodlot was ablaze with color and fragrant with perfume, and Cordelia nodded with satisfaction. "Well done."

"But too easily." Allouette frowned. "Why did not the fellow who crafted this Boneless resist our fragmenting of it?"

"Most likely he fled in fear of it," Quicksilver said. "After all, he did not know he had made it."

"There is truth in that," Cordelia told Allouette, "and it was very crudely fashioned, after all."

"Perhaps." Allouette scowled at the place the monstrosity had been, then gave herself a shake. "No, I am seeing enemies where there are none! Most likely I shall soon see specters in the shadows at noontime!"

Cordelia and Quicksilver exchanged a doubt-filled glance. Then the warrior turned back to the former assassin. "What do you suspect?"

"It is a foolish notion, I am sure," Allouette protested, "only an old habit of seeing enemies behind every bush, so that I should not be surprised if one of them were real."

"That can spoil your day, when there really are no enemies near," Cordelia admitted.

"But foes who really are there can spoil your day far worse!" Quicksilver said. "Indulge us, lady—share your fantasies. What manner of antagonist do you suspect?"

Allouette shrugged. "It only seems remarkable that we should come upon one after another of otherworldly creatures who are rare indeed, by all accounts."

"There is truth in that," Cordelia admitted.

"It may still be an accident," Quicksilver said, "but it would behoove us to assume it is not. How do you think these monsters came to be, damsel?"

"It would almost seem as though someone rides ahead of us crafting monsters," Allouette said hesitantly.

"There is some sense in that," Cordelia said, frowning,

"but if such a one does ride before us, why did he let us dismantle the Boneless so easily?"

"To lull our suspicions, of course," Quicksilver snapped.

Allouette shook her head. "My apprehension smacks of sickness. To suspect malice where there is none is to destroy all pleasure in life. This was a foolish notion. I should not have troubled you with it."

"It will do us no harm to bear the possibility in mind," Cordelia protested.

"And might do us great harm to ignore it, then discover it is true," Quicksilver said darkly. "Do not lose that habit of devious thought, Allouette—it may be the saving of us yet."

Allouette blinked, as surprised and pleased to hear Quicksilver call her by name, as she was affronted to be reminded that the warrior was still very much aware of Allouette's treacherous past. "I must keep the impulse under control, for it can destroy happiness to ever be suspecting enemies where there are none. Nonetheless, there is one other thing that does worry me . . ."

"Finish the thought!" Quicksilver demanded. "What else can you guess as to the cause of so many monsters in so short a space?"

Allouette sighed and asked, "Is it riding before or after our men?"

"Would it were so simple as an enemy riding ahead of us crafting monsters to waylay us!" Alain said with a sardonic smile. "Surely, though, you would read his thoughts if he were there."

"If he is so powerful an esper as to be able to do so," Gregory protested, "surely he could shield his thoughts so well that even Geoffrey and I could not hear them."

"It may be," said Alain, "but what of this 'zonploka' the hobyahs hailed? And the wall of mist from which the ogres came?"

" 'When several explanations present themselves, choose the simplest,' " Gregory quoted.

"Do not seek to shave him with Occam's Razor, brother,"

Geoffrey said, grinning. "I begin to realize that Alain's sense of judgment is not a matter of logic alone, but also of intuition."

"I do not think these matters through before I speak of them," Alain admitted. "It is simply clear to me that your notion of a rider ahead of us does not account for all we have seen and heard."

"Well, it was only a notion," Gregory said, miffed, "but you cannot deny the possibility of an intelligence behind this sequence of creatures."

"Nor do I," Alain said. "I simply doubt that it rides ahead of us."

"Where could it be, then?"

"Why, behind the wall of mist, brother." Geoffrey returned a cheerful grin for the daggers Gregory glared at him.

"The sun is low." Alain looked over his shoulder at the orange orb nearing the tops of the trees. "Where shall we pass this night?"

"Yon!" Geoffrey pointed at an orchard beside the road ahead. "Soft beds and fresh food both! How fortunate!"

"Suddenly I mistrust good fortune." Alain smiled, though.

"Oh, be not so dour, Alain! We have hard biscuits and beef jerky; now we shall have apples for dessert!" Geoffrey turned his mount off the road and in among the trees. "In truth, I am so hungry I shall start where I should end! But there is someone else more hungry, and who must be served first." He dismounted, unbuckled the bridle and took it off his mount's head, then reached up, plucked an apple, and held it out to his horse.

"Well thought!" Alain dismounted and unbridled his horse, too, then plucked an apple and offered it to the stallion. Gregory followed suit, plucking his horse's apple even as Geoffrey pulled a second off the tree and bit into it.

A swelling roar shook the whole orchard.

Geoffrey and Alain dropped the apples and spun, drawing their swords. Behind them, Gregory rested his hand on his hilt, but with an abstracted gaze, paying more attention with his mind than with his eyes.

The man who approached them looked like a tree come to life. His hair stood out in springy fronds, his jerkin and hose were rough and brown as bark, his fingers knobbly as twigs, his feet long and pointed as roots. He wore a crown of apple leaves that came down to frame his face like a beard. His mouth was a gash, his nose a burl; his eyes burned with anger as he stormed toward them, shaking his fist and bellowing, "Who are you who steal my apples?"

Geoffrey's answer was a wolfish grin, but Alain asked mildly, "Are you the farmer, then?"

"Farmer forsooth!" the man thundered. "He who planted these trees is dead and gone these fifty years! I am the Apple-Tree Man, who cares for limb and root and nurses the fruit from bud to ripeness!"

"Do you watch them fall and rot, then, too?"

"That I do, for such is the fullness of their destiny!"

"Is there no more?" Alain asked. "Surely they have grown in vain if none but you has ever scented their perfume, no one tasted of their pulp."

"Well said," Gregory agreed, though his voice seemed abstracted. "You made no protest when we fed them to our horses."

"That animals should eat when they are a-hungered, that is right and proper! That people should pluck more than they need is wasteful!"

"Come now, surely not." Alain frowned. "If people store the apples away to see them through the winter, that is no waste of your charges—and surely it is a nobler fate for a farmer to plant the seeds in the spring, than for them to rot away."

"Plant them? Will you do so?" the Apple-Tree Man demanded.

"No, but we shall take no more than will satisfy our hunger, either," Geoffrey answered. "Where is there more harm in our eating of them, than in our horses?"

"You do not carry the seeds away to begin another orchard, as the horses do!" the Apple-Tree Man exclaimed. "And you seek to take the fruit before its time!"

"If it is not fully ripe, it is quite close." Alain held up the apple he had taken. "Its color is full, though perhaps not quite so deep a red as it may become—and its aroma is rich and sweet." He held the apple under his nose, then breathed a sigh of delight.

"Still, I will not take what is not freely given." Geoffrey held the second apple out to his horse, who took it eagerly. He turned back to the Apple-Tree Man, spreading his hands wide to show they were empty. "Even so."

"I too." Alain held the apple out on his palm; his mount took it with relish.

"Well . . . I suppose the trees will not mind your eating of the fruit, if you promise to carry the seeds away as your horses do," the Apple-Tree Man grumbled. "Eat, then, for you seem to be men of good heart—but mind you, no more than you need!"

"Nor will we," Alain promised. "What say you, gentlemen?"

"One or two will satisfy me," Geoffrey said.

"I, too," Gregory agreed, "though my horse may seek more."

"He is welcome to them—they all are," the Apple-Tree Man grunted, "for such is the way of Nature. Eat, then, and sleep in peace—but mind you take the cores with you!" He whirled and went stamping off among the leaves, pausing now and then to examine a branch or a puckered apple.

Alain watched him go, muttering out of the side of his mouth, "Was he truly here fifty years ago, Gregory?"

"He thinks he was," the scholar answered, "and he has memories of those years—here and there."

"Bits and pieces, then?"

"Aye, with more holes than patches. Either he is what he seems and has very poor recollection, or whoever crafted him was careful to plant some scenes of his past."

"Can you test authenticity?"

"Not really," Gregory confessed. "One day walking among apple trees swelling with pride in their progress is quite like another. There are a few pictures of the farmer who planted this grove, at his work when young, then middle-aged, and at last limping about with a staff, smiling with pride at his handiwork full grown."

"Such could be manufactured," Geoffrey pointed out.

"Aye, but how should I tell that they were?"

"Is there nothing of his substance to tell you?"

Gregory shook his head. "There is no way to tell how old the witch-moss is, once it has been crafted into a being."

"But you are sure he is of witch-moss."

"Oh, aye. This is no ordinary man dressed up in a most elaborate costume, no. He is truly false."

"Or well and truly crafted," Geoffrey argued.

"True or false, he has told us all he can." Alain turned back to unsaddle his horse and take a curry comb from the saddle bag. "Perhaps he is really as old as he claims, for why would a monster-maker set him here astride our path?"

The brothers were silent a moment, thinking over the question as they unsaddled their horses. Then Geoffrey offered, "A temptation?"

"To what?" Alain asked. "To forgo the eating of apples?"

"No, to arrogance and injustice."

The prince was quiet, thinking. Gregory nodded with approval. "Well thought, brother. When the Apple-Tree Man came storming up, we might well have taken his outrage as attack and turned upon him."

"Run him through?" Geoffrey shuddered. "An unarmed old fellow whose only crime is care for his trees?"

"There are many who would have done such," Alain said grimly. "What harm could that arrogance have done to us, though?"

"It would have inclined us toward intolerance," Gregory told him, "and toward the unjust use of force."

"Becoming bullies, you mean." Alain scowled. "Hazardous indeed, if we are on a quest to defend the land from those who would take it unjustly and for no better reason than that they are brutal enough to succeed."

"Which means," Gregory said softly, "that they are not so strong as to be able to triumph by force of arms alone."

"No—they must corrupt folk here to become their allies in some fashion." Geoffrey smiled. "Why does that sound familiar?"

" 'Tis an old pattern," Gregory said. "The Saxons might never have taken England if King Vortigern had not invited them to come and aid him against his rival Uther."

"A legend only." But the prince clearly found it unsettling.

"Other kings have found it expedient to ask for soldiers from a neighbor," Geoffrey told him, "and found that when the war was done, the neighbor's army would not leave."

"I have heard of such." Alain's scowl was becoming darker and darker. "Some stayed to conquer. Others stayed only long enough to suck the lifeblood from the land, then marched triumphantly home, laden with spoils and captives."

"Lifeblood!" Gregory stared at him. "How very like a vampire—who cannot enter a dwelling unless he is invited!"

The three young men stared at one another in horror. Then Alain asked in a low voice, "Is that the purpose of these monsters, then? To demoralize the peasants until one of them seeks to curry favor by inviting in whatever sorcerer lurks in the fog?"

"A sorcerer who can send his thoughts into our land to craft witch-moss monsters," Gregory added, "but whose body cannot come without invitation?"

"His body, and his armies!" Geoffrey finished currying his horse and caressed the animal's neck thoughtfully. "I think we must find this cloud of fog and put an end to this eruption of monsters quickly."

"Quickly indeed, ere some greedy fool asks aid of the very ones who seek to slay him!" Alain shook his head. "I find myself yearning to travel onward this very night!"

"We cannot fight if we are tottering with fatigue and weak from hunger," Geoffrey objected. "Every soldier knows he must rest and eat while he can."

"So we shall, then." Alain sighed. "But can we rise with the mist and ride with the sunrise, my friends? We may not have much longer to seek!"

• • •

They did indeed ride as the sun was rising. The first two hours passed without incident; the countryside looked peaceful and prosperous, the fields of grain ripe and ready for harvest. Then they came upon a covey of quail and Geoffrey took out his sling. He fitted a stone into the cup and whirled it around his head, but even as he did, a fox pounced from the underbrush and the birds scattered.

"Blast!" Geoffrey resisted the temptation to do just that to the fox and caught the sling-pouch with his left hand. "Ten seconds more and we would have eaten fresh fowl for lunch!"

"How can it be fresh if it be foul?" Alain asked, amused.

Geoffrey stared at him, for he'd never heard Alain make a joke before. Then he recovered and cried, "A riddle! How say you, Gregory—can foul be fresh or fresh be foul?"

"So said Shakespeare." Gregory frowned. "No, that was fair and foul. May it be an apple that rots upon the tree?"

Geoffrey shook his head. "If it rots, it cannot be fresh even if it has not been picked." He cocked an eye at Alain. "I do not suppose you know the answer."

"Answer? Me?" Alain grinned. "I scarcely knew the question!"

So, chatting amiably about possible solutions to a paradox, they rode on through the morning. They found themselves riding uphill, so they weren't too surprised when the trees grew smaller and smaller until they ceased completely, and the plowed fields gave way to a broad rolling expanse of land covered with heather and bracken.

Gregory breathed deeply, tilting his face up to the sun. "So much room, so wide a sky! I had not realized how the forest and fields can press in on one."

"If you feel that way, brother, why did you build your ivory tower in the woods instead of out here on the moors?" Geoffrey asked.

"You know well—because I built where my site of power is. Besides"—Gregory grinned—"I would not want to dwell amid such a wide expanse of earth and sky forever."

Alain nodded. "It is lonely, and a man here would feel very much isolated."

" 'Tis very refreshing, though," Gregory said.

Geoffrey nodded. "A change, and a good one. We all need that now and again—and there could surely be no greater change from your forest, than these moors."

They rode across the uplands, studying everything they saw, for none of them had spent much time on the moors. Finally they came to a brook, and Geoffrey suggested, "Let us fill our waterskins."

"Let us indeed," Alain agreed, "for who knows how long it will be till we find open water again?"

"There is not very much of it, on these moors." Gregory dismounted, too, and came after Geoffrey as the older brother pulled the stopper and knelt on the bank, pushing the water-skin under—but before it was filled, Alain laid a hand on his shoulder. "Hist! Look up, but slowly."

Geoffrey whistled as he lifted the skin, pushed in the stopper, and just happened to glance across the brook—straight into the eyes of the stunted, large-headed man dressed in faded tan smock and leggins.

"What be you staring at?" the stranger growled.

He was worth the stare. It was hard to judge his height when he was sitting on his heels, but his legs didn't look to be very long at all, nor his arms either. His shoulders were broad—too broad for his size, though just right for his head. His face was deeply tanned, his moustache and beard dark brown, as was his frizzled hair. His mouth was wide, his nose large, and his eyes great and glowing, like a bull's.

"I might ask the same." Geoffrey felt the wolfish grin pulling at the corners of his mouth but fought it. "Indeed, you were staring at me even as I looked up."

"And well I might wish to study the loathly lads who trespass on my land!" the stranger said with simmering rage. "What! Have you no courtesy, no charity, but you must go tramping about my moors and crushing my bracken with your great iron-shod beasts? Have you no compassion, that you are scarcely come upon my moors but you must seek to slay my grouse?"

"I would say you grouse well enough without us," Geoffrey retorted, and when the man's face turned darker and darker, he added quickly, "It was the fox who seized the bird, not I—and who said the fowls were yours?"

"All things upon the moors are mine," the stranger bellowed, "even as I am theirs! I am grown out of the moors, I have the wide lands within me! I am the Brown Man of the Moors, as much of them as they are of me! How dare you seek to trample upon me with shoes of Cold Iron and think to slay my fox with your leaden pellet?"

"I withheld my bullet from the fox," Geoffrey said evenly, "even as I withhold my hand from you."

"Oh, you would seek to slay me too, would you?" the stranger roared. "Will nothing sate your appetite for slaughter?"

"I do like a bit of meat now and then." Geoffrey ignored his brother's frantic shushing motions. "From the look of you, you've dined on a hen or two yourself now and again."

The Brown Man leaped to his feet. "He lies who says so!"

Sure enough, he was short and square—too tall to be a dwarf, though it was his arms and legs that were short and his torso long. His limbs were thick with muscle, though, and Geoffrey looked willowy and frail in contrast.

"He slanders me who says I eat of meat!" the Brown Man stormed. "I dine only upon whortleberries, nuts, and apples!"

"How can a fellow sustain so much bulk as you have upon such a diet?" Geoffrey's words dripped sarcasm.

"Thus does a bull, and so do I!"

"A bull grazes constantly, all the day long," Geoffrey taunted. "Can you think of nothing but food?"

"Surely, Geoffrey, if the man says he eats only fodder, he does," Alain said nervously.

Geoffrey turned on him, shocked. "Surely you do not fear the fellow!"

"Surely I do not," Alain agreed, "but I understand what

he means when he says that he is of the land and the land of him."

Geoffrey stood frowning at him in thought while Gregory said, his voice low, "Even thus is a legitimate king. His ancestors fed from the land for generations; its elements are in his blood and bone."

"But not its fungus." Geoffrey turned back to the Brown Man. "So it comes once again to feeding, for thus are you made—of the substance of the land. No wonder you can think of nothing but food!"

"I think also of trespassers and murderers," the Brown Man said in an ominous rumble.

"A murderer you must be, then, for as I've said, your bulk requires meat," Geoffrey returned.

The Brown Man roared, "You would not dare insult me so if you stood upon this side of the river!"

Finally Geoffrey's wolfish grin broke loose, and he stepped toward the water.

CHAPTER
-10-

"Forfend!" Alain grasped his shoulder, then let go and dodged adroitly as Geoffrey's arm swung like a windmill to knock his hand away—but the prince caught his shoulder again and said, "If he feeds all day, what is that to you?"

"I do not call him liar," Geoffrey said evenly, "but people do not graze the livelong day, so I know he cannot live on naught but salad."

"Come home with me and see," the Brown Man sneered. "If you dare, come across this brook and see how you fare!"

Geoffrey stepped down into the stream.

"Brother, no!" Gregory caught his arm and, before Geoffrey could turn on him, said quickly, "You taught me when I was quite small that a man's a fool to take a dare and thereby let another steer him as he pleases!"

"I spoke of boyhood pranks then," Geoffrey said in a voice strained tight with self-control, "not a grown man's insult."

"Yet he will govern you as surely by those insults as a bully's taunts do manipulate a foolish boy! Come, brother, you are a man in his prime, and a knight!"

"And it is beneath a knight's dignity to stoop to brawling," Alain said.

"All excuses for cowardice!" the Brown Man jeered. "Cross the brook if you dare!"

Geoffrey froze with one foot in the water, his eyes narrowing. "The man who names me coward is too blatant in his aims."

Gregory sighed with relief, then frowned at a sudden thought. "You said you would not name him liar, but I shall—for he could not truly eat apples when the nearest orchard we have seen is so well guarded."

"What's this?" the Brown Man demanded, outraged. "It cannot be that some fellow has dared to steal my groves!"

"It most certainly can," Geoffrey said, gloating. "Indeed, the land seems to be bursting with guardian spirits in these latter days."

"Only I am rightful warden!"

"Of the moors," said Alain, "but the orchard we speak of stands where forest trees once towered, though fields of wheat and barley spread about it now."

The Brown Man fell silent, glowering.

" 'Tis the land of farms and farmers," Geoffrey said, "and no concern of yours."

"We should not have told him this, brother," Gregory said. "We should have let him go forth on another trip to that orchard all unknowing, and let him lock himself in combat with the Apple-Tree Man."

"The Apple-Tree Man?" The Brown Man's glower lightened to brooding. "I have heard him spoken of before."

"Enough to declare him your enemy?" Gregory asked, too innocently.

"Nay, my ally! And fool would I be to bait him into combat, for no matter who won, the world of trees and bushes would have one less guardian." The Brown Man eyed Geoffrey with reluctant respect. They could see how dearly the words cost him as he said, "I see you are brother to a wise man."

"The next best thing," Geoffrey said cheerfully.

"I shall greet the Apple-Tree Man with all courtesy, and offer him heather in place of his apples," the Brown Man decided. "Thus may we keep from coming to blows." He took a deep breath. "Loath though I am to admit it, I owe you lads a favor for telling me of him."

Geoffrey noticed that he hadn't said he was grateful and had certainly offered no hint of apology. "You shall owe us another, then, for I promise not to hunt any creature that moves till I have come off of your moors."

"That is not a favor—it is the course of discretion," the Brown Man snapped. "Know, belted knight, that if you had crossed that stream, my ravens would have fed upon your flesh and I would have enriched my moors with the dust of your bones!"

"If you could have," Geoffrey said, the wolfish grin now open and wide.

"He could have indeed," Gregory said low-voiced behind him.

"Know that the power of the moors is within me," the Brown Man informed him with no trace of boasting, "the life-force of ten thousand acres of bracken and heather, and all the creatures that feed upon them or make their homes within them! Do you truly think you could stand against such might?"

Geoffrey scowled and stood with every muscle tensed—but did not answer.

"Nonetheless, I would as lief not shed the blood of any creature, deserving or no," the Brown Man rumbled. "Nay, go your way, and come not again onto my moors with empty packs. Bring with you all the food you will need for your sojourn here."

"Why, so I have," Geoffrey answered, "dried beef and biscuit, and though I would have preferred fresh meat, I can do without."

"We shall indeed refrain from hunting until we have come down from your lands," Alain said. "Tell me, how long a journey have we till we have passed out of your domain?"

"Aye," said Gregory. "Where do these moors end?"

"Weary of them already, are you?" the Brown Man asked with a sour smile. "Well, you've a long and lonely road to travel yet, me buckos. Onward you go with the rising sun on your left hand, onward for two more days before you come to the end of my moors. Down a long slope you'll go then, to the shores of an icy lake—and when you see its waters, you'll think the moors a pleasant place, mark my words!" With a sinister laugh, he turned, stepped into the bracken, and was gone.

"Wait!" Geoffrey called. "Wherefore shall we rue that coming? Stay, spirit, and tell!"

Alain's hand fell on his shoulder. "Do not think to call him back, Geoffrey. It galls him to have to acknowledge a debt to us, no matter how slight, and he still rejoices in his revenge."

"Even if there is little reason," Gregory agreed. "There may be no cause to fear that lake—or for all we know, no lake at all."

"Quite so," said Alain. "The fellow seeks to steal our peace of mind, that is all."

Geoffrey turned back, frowning. "Telling a lie only to have us spend the next two days in apprehension? Aye, I can see that would be such revenge as he could allow himself even though he feels beholden."

"Call it that and nothing more," Gregory coaxed. "Come, dip some water from that stream and let us set to stewing some dried beef."

"That, at least, we do not have to hunt," Alain said with some irony.

As the three women rode through a sun-filled tunnel of leaves, Quicksilver asked, "Can you hear Alain's thoughts yet, Cordelia?"

"Nay," Cordelia answered, "nor those of my brothers. Can you, Allouette?"

Allouette frowned, shrugging to disguise a shiver of apprehension. "No, and never since we plighted our troth have

I been without awareness of his mind at the back of my own."

" 'Tis worrisome," Cordelia admitted, "but if Gregory and Geoffrey wish to shield their thoughts, I doubt not they can do it quite thoroughly. Indeed, Gregory could well shield all three by himself."

"I do not doubt it," Quicksilver said, "but I would expect a moment's slippage now and then—a thought or emotion let loose in a moment of excitement, or of danger."

"Let us hope it means they have come to no peril," Allouette said fervently.

"I shall hope so in truth," Quicksilver said, "but warriors develop instincts, and mine suspect the action of an enemy."

"How?" Cordelia frowned. "Can you mean someone other than our lads shields their minds from us?"

"Well thought!" Allouette wheeled toward them. "What more obvious for a foe to do, if he realizes how formidable a set of antagonists we could be if united?"

"Divide and conquer!" Cordelia cried. "Of course! But what manner of wizard would this be who could erect an invisible wall that bars their thoughts from ours?"

They looked at one another, shuddering at the thought of the kind of magical power the feat would take. Then Allouette scolded herself for being superstitious and said, "Merely a trickster who knows one prank that we do not."

"Well thought!" Quicksilver cried with relief. "He need not even be as strong as one of you ladies alone!"

" 'Tis well thought." Cordelia nodded. "Still, let us not lose sight of the chance that it is only their own shielding, for fear of some puissant mind-reader whom they approach."

"Or some sorcerer of vast powers indeed," Quicksilver said grimly. "I do not truly believe it—but a fool I would be not to be ready for the possibility."

"We must keep open minds on the subject," Cordelia agreed.

"Open minds, and an open landscape." Allouette smiled as they rode out of the woods into pastureland. "How bright the sunshine seems! But why is that milkmaid chasing her cow?"

They turned to follow her gaze and saw a young woman, pail in hand, closing in on a dappled cow who stood in a corner made by two hedges a hundred feet away from them. The milkmaid walked quickly, holding out a hand palm up.

"She speaks soothing words to the cow," Cordelia told them. "Can you hear her mind, Quicksilver?"

"I can," the warrior said, "but weariness drags at her thoughts. How long has she pursued the beast?"

The milkmaid stepped up to stroke the cow's neck, then her shoulders, then her side, moving steadily toward the udder—but as she knelt to prop her pail under the cow's teats, the beast lunged away, smacking the woman with her tail, and went gamboling over the field like a calf.

" 'Tis a most contrary cow," Quicksilver said with a frown.

The milkmaid's shoulders slumped; for a moment, she seemed about to sink to the ground in defeat—but she straightened, squared her shoulders, and started after the cow, her legs weighted with exhaustion.

"The beast has been leading her a merry chase for some hours," Cordelia said, "and will likely do so for hours more."

"Not if we can help it," Quicksilver said, "and we can! Ride, ladies, and catch the animal from front and sides!"

"Then it can only turn to run back to its mistress." Allouette nodded and kicked her horse into a canter.

The three women rode down on the cow. It saw them coming and veered to their right—but Allouette swung wide to head it off, and the beast turned back to try the other side.

Cordelia turned her horse to the left, circling away, then back toward the cow. It saw her, swung back, then stopped, nonplussed, to see Quicksilver bearing down. It lowed an objection, put down its head, and charged.

"This is most unbovine behavior!" Quicksilver drew her sword and leveled it at the cow's neck.

"No!" the milkmaid cried. "Spare my poor Dapple!"

The cow looked up at her words, saw the bright steel, and

gave a moo of disappointment. It slowed, tossing its head, and with a bang like that of a large firecracker, turned into a horse.

The three riders drew rein, staring. Then Cordelia cried, "That is not your Dapple, milkmaid, though it is a very clever counterfeit!"

" 'Tis a spirit, that's sure." Quicksilver kicked her horse again, holding her sword level. "Ride, ladies! Whatever it is, spirk or sprite, it must fear Cold Iron!"

They converged on the horse, a dancing roan, boxing it in, coming closer and closer. It could have turned and charged the milkmaid, but instead it gave another toss of its head and disappeared with another explosion—a bang that had echoes uncommonly like a horselaugh.

The milkmaid gave a cry of fear and dismay and sank to the ground.

"Quickly!" Cordelia cried. "She faints!"

Allouette was down off her horse in the instant, cradling the milkmaid's head in the crook of her arm, testing her pulse and peeling back one eyelid, then the other, to check the size of the pupils. She nodded to Cordelia. "She only sleeps."

The milkmaid's eyes fluttered; then she sat up. "What . . . where . . ."

"A moment's loss of consciousness, nothing more," Allouette assured her.

"No wonder, seeing a cow turn to a horse!" Quicksilver said.

"A horse!" The milkmaid clutched her head as memory came flooding back. "But where is my Dapple?"

"Eating acorns in the forest, as like as not," Cordelia said in a soothing tone. "Surely she shall seek you out, now that the horse has gone."

"That was no horse, but the Hedley Kow!" the milkmaid told them. "I have heard of it but hoped never to see it."

"So had we." Allouette exchanged a glance with her companions. "Surely there are shape-shifters enough in this land without that one."

"But the town of Hedley is far from here, is it not?" the

milkmaid asked. "I have only heard of it in minstrels' songs."

"So far away that I am not sure it is real," said Allouette. "It may be something the songsters made up to beguile an idle moment." But she exchanged another meaningful glance with Cordelia, then with Quicksilver.

They nodded their understanding: that the minstrel must have sung very recently and been a projective telepath who didn't know his own talents, or that someone else had crafted the creature deliberately.

"Surely it is a mischievous sprite," said Quicksilver, "but it has done you no harm, praise Heaven."

"Aye, only wasted some hours," Cordelia agreed.

"Most of the morning, I fear." The milkmaid sighed. "There is not so much harm in that, if I find my Dapple alive." She started to rise, wavered halfway up. Allouette caught one arm, Quicksilver the other, as Cordelia cast about quickly with her mind and read a cow's wordless satisfaction in the taste of acorns and leaves. She projected a "come hither" thought and, as the cow began to plod toward her, said, "I am sure she is alive, and only a little calling will bring her to you."

"I hope so indeed." The milkmaid stepped away from Allouette and Quicksilver. "I thank you, ladies, but I am stronger now. Dapple! Da-a-a-a-ple! Come, sweet cow!"

They let go, watching her anxiously. She took a tottering step, then steadied and started toward the woods. "Would she truly have gone among the trees?"

"I doubt not the Kow chased her there," Quicksilver said with a quick glance at Cordelia. Seeing her nod, she turned back to the milkmaid. " 'Tis the most convenient hiding place, after all."

They set out for the trees, their horses following, the milkmaid calling Dapple. They were halfway there when the heifer came ambling out into the meadow.

"My sweet Dapple!" The milkmaid ran to meet her, completely recovered. Quicksilver followed, carrying the pail, with Allouette and Cordelia close behind. The milkmaid threw her arms around the cow's neck. "I feared for you so! And, poor thing, your udder must be near to bursting!"

"It must indeed," Allouette agreed. "You set out to milk her at dawn, did you not?"

"Indeed." The milkmaid set the pail under the cow's udder.

"I shall hold her head for you." Allouette gripped Dapple's bridle.

When the pail was full and the cow looking distinctly relieved, the milkmaid offered them drinks, but they politely declined and mounted, turning their horses back toward the road. As they went, Cordelia asked, "Was she not overly concerned for that cow? It was not a babe nor even a kitten, after all."

"Nay—it was her livelihood." Allouette had grown up on a farm. "Think of it as her working capital."

Quicksilver nodded agreement—as a squire's daughter, she had seen how important livestock could be to peasants.

"I had not thought of that," Cordelia admitted. "If the Kow had slain Dapple, our milkmaid would have been poor indeed!"

"Still, I am sure she is genuinely fond of the beast," Allouette assured her.

"And most deservedly fearful of the Hedley Kow," Cordelia said fervently.

An explosion rocked the trail.

The horses shied and the women had to fight to keep them from bolting. When they looked up, they found themselves facing another horse—if one could call it that. Its ears were long and bristled at the ends, its head was like a giant plucked owl's, its legs rubbery and claw-footed, its tail like a bundle of broom. But it opened its beak to produce a very credible horselaugh and cried, "What fools you women must be!"

"How now, varlet?" Quicksilver asked in a dangerous voice. "What folly do you see?"

"The foolishness of antagonizing so powerful a spirit as I," the Kow said in menacing tones and padded toward them like a panther, every muscle in motion, its whole stance hinting at massive power waiting to be unleashed. "You have ruined my jest! All morning I led that lass astray, hours I spent to bring her to the point of hysterics when I transformed—but you made me spring the trap too soon, and worse! You were there to comfort her when she screamed!"

"Oh, how treacherous of us," Allouette said with dripping sarcasm. "Be warned, Kow—it may have been no mere chance that brought us to that place and time."

"Next you will have me believing in providence!"

"Is not the phrase 'Divine Providence'?" Cordelia asked.

"Speak not that word to me, nor none pertaining to it!" The Kow's neck stretched out to double its length as its beak opened, revealing a multitude of pointed teeth. "Foolish wenches, if I could not relish that creature's horror, I shall savor your flesh!"

Fear clawed its way up in all three women, even in the warrior Quicksilver, for this was no ordinary foe, no human or real animal but a strange and obscene thing of nightmare. But each of them had faced terrifying enemies before and all reacted as they had learned—with a fierce determination to defeat any attack.

"How ridiculous!" Allouette's counterattack was scorn. "Whoever heard of a beak with teeth!"

"Aye!" Cordelia picked up the idea instantly. "Are not things impossible called 'rare as hen's teeth'?"

"Impossible this creature is," Quicksilver agreed. "Cannot that beak tear as well as any eyetooth?"

"Do you say 'aye' to my tooth?" But the Kow's teeth dwindled on the instant and disappeared. It paced forward, reaching out. "Still, as you say, my beak is sharp enough to shred you!"

"Sharper than its owner, I doubt not," Allouette returned.

"But duller than my sword." Quicksilver drew. "My apologies, creature—it is not bronze."

The Kow eyed the sheen of Cold Iron with misgiving. Then its beak turned into a muzzle with lips that curved up in a grin. "Do you thirst, damsels?" And as they watched in horror, it grew an udder.

Cordelia turned to her companions, wrinkling her nose in disgust. "Why is it so obscene to see a horse with an udder?"

"If you can call that a horse," Allouette said with withering contempt. "I have never seen so bizarre a collection of parts in my life!"

"Have you never seen a man of parts?" the Kow returned. "Nay, I shall grow some if you wish."

"Thank you, no." Cordelia smiled, actually amused. "We all have men at home with all their parts, enough to last us all our lives."

The Kow frowned, clearly nonplussed. "Have you never learned it is rude to refuse a gift? Nay, taste of my milk!"

"I suspect this creature is beyond the pail," Cordelia told Quicksilver.

"Alas!" Allouette said to the Kow. "We appreciate the thought." She suspected that the Kow knew exactly how they appreciated what it was thinking. "Unfortunately, we have no bucket."

"If Fate is kind, you should indeed not seek to buck it," the Kow rejoined.

Cordelia kept her smile. "You do not claim that you are Fate, I hope."

"So should you hope indeed," the Kow returned. "Nay, make a bucket of bark so that you may taste of my milk!"

"A mammal has milk only because it has young to suckle," Cordelia pointed out. "Have you, then, given birth?"

"Any who know of me give me a wide berth indeed! What is this 'mammal' you speak of?"

"Why, any creature which suckles its young," Allouette explained.

The Kow frowned. "This is to say that a bird with webbed feet and a bill is a duck, but a duck is a bird with webbed feet and a bill!"

"The bill for thus baiting us will likely be too high for you to pay," Quicksilver said darkly.

"Then you would be well advised to duck when I say so!"

"It has the egg of an idea there," Cordelia admitted.

"No doubt that will make the creature brood upon it," Allouette answered.

"Be sure you would not wish to meet my brood," the Kow retorted.

"Are there more than one of you, then?" Cordelia asked in wide-eyed innocence. "I had thought you a singular creature."

"What, like the phoenix?" The Kow grinned again. "Would you have me disappear in a burst of flame, then?"

Allouette saw her chance and said with withering scorn, "As though you could!"

"Think you anything is beyond my scope?" the Kow demanded, affronted.

"I would not see you burnt to a cinder." Allouette backed her horse away, widening her eyes as though in fright.

"Behold what you fear, then!" the Kow cried triumphantly.

"Back, ladies," Quicksilver barked with sudden dread.

They all managed to back their horses a few paces away before the Kow, laughing hysterically, burst into a geyser of flames that ballooned out to singe the ground for thirty feet around before it died as quickly as it had bloomed, leaving only a mound of ashes behind.

Cordelia heaved a sigh of relief. "Most cleverly done, Allouette! You baited the creature to its own doom!"

Allouette flushed, pleased at the compliment and wondering if it betokened real acceptance.

Cordelia turned to Quicksilver. "How did you guess that it meant to burn us to char with itself, lady?"

"I would have to think somewhat to answer that." Quicksilver frowned. "Suddenly I knew what it meant to do—perhaps because it was too gleeful in its eagerness to demonstrate what Allouette had said it could not do, perhaps because its nature is mischief and malice . . . I cannot say for certain."

"Suffice it that her counsel saved our lives," Allouette said with heartfelt gratitude. "I thank you, warrior woman."

"And I you, dame of cleverness." Quicksilver gave her a smile. "Shall I play Achilles to your Odysseus, then?"

Allouette returned the smile. "As you please, so long as, together, we have defeated this Trojan horse."

"Who dares call me Trojan?" nickered a voice that seemed both distant and close.

CHAPTER
-11-

The voice seemed an echo of the Kow's neigh. A slight breeze must have moved across the trail, for the heap of ashes stirred.

"Beware, ladies!" Cordelia rode forward, glaring at the mound. "I shall see to it that it rises not!" The heap of ashes split into a dozen smaller piles that began to drift away from one another as though blown by all four winds at once.

"Nay, forfend!" the echo of the neighing voice protested. "How shall I reassemble if you scatter my substance?"

"But you are more likely to dissemble than to reassemble," Allouette pointed out.

"I prefer to take the creature in small doses." Quicksilver dismounted and knelt to scoop up a handful of dust. "The smaller the better."

"You need not take me at all!" the voice brayed. "I shall stay!"

With a doubtful voice, Allouette said, "In mischief you are too well versed."

"I shall refrain!"

"I fear his refrain may be worse than his verses," Allouette said to her companions.

"Let him take the shape of a singer, then," Quicksilver offered.

"I shall return in a form far more benign, I swear!" cried the neighing voice.

"I am sure you do, when you are thwarted," Cordelia told the Kow, "but I would have you spare our ears."

"So long as you will have me at all!"

"We will not," Quicksilver decided, "but we shall let you retain your substance if you swear that you shall only take form from happy thoughts and do all you can to aid mortal folk rather than plague them."

Allouette nodded. So did Cordelia, but she frowned at their powdered foe.

"Wherefore do I feel a sudden impulse to pounce upon all rats and mice?" the neighing voice wondered.

"It may be because you took an owl's head in your last form," Cordelia answered. "As a bird of wisdom who guards folk by night you may reconstitute yourself."

"Concentrate," Allouette advised, "but not till we are far from this place."

"I shall! I shall wait and re-form! Bless you, ladies! I shall sing your praises forevermore! I shall applaud you to the skies! I shall warble sweet notes of—"

"She said an owl, not a nightingale," Allouette reminded.

"A night owl I shall be then! If ever you return this way, remember there is one who owes you a favor."

The three women looked at one another in alarm. Then Allouette said, "The favor we would wish is that you treat all folk well, that you help rather than hinder."

"Whatever you wish! Oh, thank you for your kindness and mercy! *Merci!* Gramercy! Forever shall I extol your virtues!"

"You make it seem as though being good would be a chore," Allouette said, frowning. "There can be delight in giving aid."

"I shall patrol, guard, and warn!" the Kow averred. "As

an owl I shall guard this valley! All my life shall I hoot as I haunt this hollow!"

"May your life be a hoot and a hollow indeed, then," Allouette said. "Farewell, polymorph."

"Is that to be my name? Polly I shall be, then," the spirit cried, "and for you no more a fuss!"

"Polly Mor-a-phous?" Allouette smiled. "So let you be, then—and be sure we shall remember that favor!"

They rode away down the trail, glancing at one another but not saying a word until the leaves closed behind them and the strange deep warbling of a Kow learning to sing faded away. Then Allouette heaved a sigh and said, "The favor I'll remember—but I doubt I'll ever accept it!"

"It would not seem to be the sort of thing you could trust," Cordelia agreed. "Even with the best intentions, that creature's attempts to aid might go astray."

"They might rebound on us and redound to his discredit," Quicksilver said, then turned to Allouette. "But how is this, damsel? You might have been more accepting of the creature's repentance!"

"I wish I could have been," Allouette said ruefully, "but I was afraid to encourage its singing for fear the spirit might take to larking about."

"I see!" Quicksilver's eyes widened. "Worrisome indeed, for a lass whose name means 'skylark.' "

"I am perhaps unduly sensitive on the subject," Allouette agreed, "but since it has already set itself to becoming a blithe spirit—bird he never was before—I would have taken that sort of counterfeiting rather personally."

The sun was setting as Gregory, Alain, and Geoffrey rode down to the shore of a little lake. Their shoulders slumped, their heads sagged, and their horses' hooves dragged. "By my troth," Geoffrey sighed, "this has been a long day!"

"As well as a rather eventful one," Alain agreed.

Geoffrey almost fell off his horse and knelt to scoop some water from the lake. "Let us see if this water is sweet or brackish."

"Well thought," Gregory agreed, and dismounted to lead his horse down to the water. Alain was halfway there when a frantic bleating broke out all around them. Looking up in surprise, they saw a huge flock of sheep bearing down on them, too much in a panic to be afraid of the men.

"Shoo! Go back!" But Geoffrey was still on his knees as the wooly mob poured over him.

They nearly knocked Alain's horse out from under him, but he held the stallion by the reins and made shooing motions at the sheep, crying, "Avaunt! Retreat!"

They paid him not the slightest bit of attention, except to flow around him instead of over. Geoffrey, in front of his horse and still on his knees, was not so lucky; he went tumbling over as ram after ram and ewe after ewe leaped over him. When they had passed, he pushed himself up, staring after them. "Beshrew me, but I shall sleep soundly tonight!"

"Do not tell me you counted them!" Alain exclaimed.

"I missed some, I am sure—but I would estimate the herd to be ninety-eight strong, with one lamb."

"Six tenths of a sheep? Like as not it was," Geoffrey said, "though I would have thought them in a fever to run us down."

"Certainly a panic." Alain leaped down to help his friends up and batted at their clothes. "They have soiled you badly."

"As badly as they were frightened," Geoffrey said. "What could have thrown them into such a panic?"

A basso laugh answered him, echoing all around them—a senseless manic whooping. They stood stiffly, staring at one another as it faded.

"What manner of creature made that sound?" Geoffrey whispered.

"That one!" Gregory pointed.

They turned and saw, ploughing through the water along the shore of the lake, a huge bird, black all over, but with a metallic sheen, its back decorated with rows of white spots and with a white ring around a neck longer than a duck's, its foot-and-a-half of beak dark yellow and hooked like an eagle's, its huge eyes judging them as a replacement meal for the fugitive sheep. All in all, it was a very proper water bird—except that its body was at least eight feet long and its neck three, so its head was level with theirs as it glided toward them across the ripples.

A straggler sheep suddenly burst from a bush, galloping away from the shore.

Whooping with glee, the huge bird sprang from the water and waddled after the ram on webbed feet that sported thick sharp talons. Its legs seemed fairly short, but only in relation to its huge body, for it shot over the ground faster than the ram. The sheep swerved behind a copse and the bird swung after it.

Then, suddenly, there was silence.

The companions stared at one another. "Dare we go to look?" Gregory asked.

"Dare we not?" Geoffrey turned and ran toward the grove.

They stepped carefully and quietly between the trunks until, parting a final layer of leaves, they saw the giant bird gulping down a last bloody morsel. Of the ram there was nothing left.

Alain swallowed hard, then asked, "How name you such a bird, scholar?"

"It is a Boobrie," Gregory answered in a hushed voice. "I have read of such things but never thought them real."

"Perhaps it wasn't," said Geoffrey, "until now."

The Boobrie opened its beak and gave a cry of defiance. The men stared, for its call was a roar now, like that of a bull.

"The laugh must have been its mating call," Gregory said.

"Or a cry of delight at sighting dinner," Geoffrey said drily.

The Boobrie opened its beak again and emitted the whooping laugh as it waddled toward them.

Geoffrey and Alain drew their swords, but the Boobrie only roared the louder and waddled toward them—much faster than its short legs should have.

"Beware." Gregory's voice was oddly remote, his eyes glazed, even though he stared at the huge bird. "This is a thing of witch-moss, yes, but it has not been crafted to seem a faerie creature. It will not fear your swords."

"Then it can be carved by them. Let us attack from both sides, Alain, so it shall pause to decide which one of us to repulse."

"Indeed." Alain circled to the right.

Geoffrey circled to the left. The bird turned its head to look first at him, then at Alain, roaring in anger and bafflement.

"One of us, at least, shall end it with a sharp stroke across the neck," Alain said, determined.

"It shall not die so easily," Gregory sighed, "and those claws can do great damage ere death stills them. It is of such a terror I have dreamed—a nightmare creature, but one that could really live."

"Then take it apart!" Geoffrey said.

"I seek to," Gregory answered, "but something seeks just as strongly to hold it together."

Geoffrey's eyes widened. "Some secret sorcerer, watching even as we fight?"

"If he does, he watches from a great distance," Gregory answered. "I think it more likely a binding spell that lay quietly waiting for someone to try to dissolve the creature."

"A plague upon the magus who made it!" Geoffrey spat. "This was no work of a shepherd telling a tale to his mates, brother, but a well-planned work of a master crafter!"

The bird made up its mind and charged at Gregory, roaring.

"It knows the source of its greatest peril!" Alain shouted as he sprinted after. "Set upon it, Geoffrey!" He caught up with the Boobrie and swung his sword in a flat arc that would have bisected anything it met.

Geoffrey leaped in from the side, swinging and shouting, "Orange sauce!"

The bird jerked to a halt in sheer surprise, turning to gape at Geoffrey.

" 'Tis not a duck!" Alain protested.

The Boobrie's head pivoted to glare narrow-eyed at Alain.

"Duck yourself!" Geoffrey cried, and Alain did, just in time for the Boobrie's breast to slam into his shoulder as it charged. Its beakful of teeth closed on air instead of the throat for which it had aimed. From sheer reflex, Alain stabbed. "I spit thee, fowl!"

The Boobrie roared in rage and pain and curved its neck to bite at the nape of Alain's neck. He leaped back, though, pulled the sword free, and the poignard-teeth closed on the blade.

Geoffrey leaped up behind it and slashed—but he only sheared tail feathers, for the bird was turning to this new threat even as he swung. It lunged at Geoffrey, wings raised high, eight-feet-long clubs poised to strike.

Gregory jumped in, caught a wing tip, and threw his whole weight against it, shouting, "Savory! Sage! In a batter with wine!"

The Boobrie honked in dismay as it swung around him.

"Beware those teeth, Gregory!" Geoffrey cried, dashing in to protect his little brother—and a wing cracked into his head, knocking him to the ground.

"I am safe!" Gregory cried, releasing the wing-tip and leaping back. "Up, brother! Save yourself!"

There was no need to worry about Geoffrey, though. The Boobrie was charging Gregory now, blood in its eye, beakful of teeth reaching out, wings arched to strike.

"Drumsticks!" Alain cried, and dived to wrap his arms around one yard-long leg.

The Boobrie hooted, flapping its wings in a vain attempt to balance on one webbed foot. Then it tumbled; its foot twisted in Alain's grasp and the heel spur raked his chest. He ignored the pain and hung on, trying to clamber to his feet.

"Up, friend!" Geoffrey seized Alain's collar and hauled him upright. "Loose the beast and let it fly!"

The Boobrie was indeed struggling to get back on its webs. The young men backed warily away, swords at the ready, but something hooted out on the lake.

The Boobrie's head swung around.

The hooting turned into a burbling laugh.

The Boobrie roared in anger and ran heavily back toward the lake. It plunged into the water, leaving a few streaks of red in its wake, but gliding quite steadily nonetheless, answering the hooting mirth with its own chortling cry.

"How lucky for us that another Boobrie came to challenge it," Alain said shakily.

"There is none other, but this one shall circle the lake for hours trying to find it, growing steadily more and more maddened as it fails to discover what it seeks," Gregory said.

"I thought it was something of the kind." Geoffrey nodded. "How did you do it, brother? Ventriloquism?"

"Of a sort," Gregory acknowledged. "I studied the vibrations of its cry when first it called, so I knew how to modulate the air currents out over the water to make the sound of a challenger."

"Well done, if a bit tardily," Alain said.

"Tardily indeed!" Gregory tore open the prince's doublet. "Let me see how deep that wound is, and how much inclined to infection!"

"Oh, kill the bacteria with a thought," Geoffrey said crossly, glaring at the gouge in his thigh.

"As you do?" Gregory noted the direction of his gaze. "Well, knit the flesh back together, brother—or if you would like more objectivity, I shall do it for you. Are you angered from the pain, or because your hose are quite irretrievably stained?"

"Neither," Geoffrey groused. "I simply dislike losing—or in this case, not winning."

"Besides," Alain said through clenched teeth, "he was counting on roast fowl with all the trimmings. Have a care, Gregory! It may be deeper than it looks."

"The pain you feel is the wound closing," Gregory assured him. He stood up, watching the torn flesh flow back together as he made cell bond to cell. "This is easy enough to do. I wonder how our enemy made it so hard to render the Boobrie back into the fungus of which it was made."

"Perhaps it was simply the strength of its desire to live," Geoffrey suggested.

"It is certainly convenient to have a wizard along when I'm apt to be wounded," Alain said with a sigh of relief. He tested his wand. "I cannot see the slightest trace of a seam."

"He is a passable tailor," Geoffrey grunted. He looked up at another whooping laugh from the lake. "Are you certain there is no other male Boobrie about, brother?"

"Quite sure," Gregory answered, "because our Boobrie is a singular bird."

Geoffrey looked up, frowning. Then his eyes glazed as he gazed off toward the lake, his mind seeking thoughts like the Boobrie's. At last he nodded. "True enough. There are none others for miles about, at least."

"This part of the kingdom seems suddenly filled with monsters that have never appeared before," Alain said thoughtfully. "I suppose they must have now and again, though, or there would not be tales about them."

"Or is it because there are tales that they have come to be?" Geoffrey countered. He turned to Gregory. "Did you not say that this was just such a monster as haunted your dreams?"

"Not a dream exactly," Gregory explained, "but one among many in a scene that burst into Allouette's mind while she meditated. I shared it to leach some of the horror from it."

"And gained it yourself?" Geoffrey's voice held a new sort of respect for his little brother. "So you saw what she dreamed."

"This was the least of them," Gregory assured him. "Still, I could find it in me to wonder how it came from my dreams to this lake."

"Perchance through someone else's dream," Alain suggested.

"Wherefore would two dream the same nightmare?" Geoffrey asked.

They were all silent, looking at one another, knowing the thought they shared.

"It was no accident, was it?" Alain asked. "Someone planted those vile illusions in your minds."

"And if in ours, in how many other people's nightmares?" Geoffrey asked.

"Three, or a dozen, or a score." Gregory shrugged. "It matters not, as long as one of them was an esper who knew not his own strength."

"Then when he described the horrible bird to a listener, somewhere in the forest bits of witch-moss flowed together and took on the shape he saw in his mind's eye." Geoffrey nodded. "It is likely enough—but who placed that vision in so many minds?"

"It was someone beyond the mist," Alain said. "More than that, we cannot know."

Geoffrey shrugged. "We have been given a name; why not use it? Call that pusher of dreams 'Zonploka.' "

"It is as good a name as any, until we find the thing the word truly names." Alain nodded.

But Gregory frowned. "It is inexact and an invitation to error. What if, when we do find this Zonploka, it turns out not to be the dream-weaver—or perhaps not even human at all?"

Geoffrey tossed his head in exasperation. "*If* we discover the referent, we may need to seek a new term—or we may not; we may find that Zonploka is a man or woman, and the dream-caster indeed."

"And if it is not?"

"Why borrow trouble?" Alain asked. "Until we know better, let us assume it is Zonploka who sends these nightmares amongst us."

"The dream nightmares, or the ones that draw blood?" Geoffrey countered.

"Yes," Alain said. "Both, for if he sends the dreams knowing an esper shall speak of them, then he deliberately sends the monsters that grow from the words."

"Then I hope we find it so," Gregory sighed, "and do not seek so hard for a man who may not exist, that we look right past the true source of the trouble."

"We must keep open minds," Alain agreed, "and watch for every possible menace—must we not, soldier and knight?"

"We must be vigilant and wary, of course," Geoffrey agreed, "but if we do meet a man or woman named Zonploka, I for one shall shield my mind most shrewdly. Where now shall we seek him?"

"Where indeed?" Alain shrugged. "One direction is as good as another, and the road lies before us. Let us ride!"

The trees grew smaller and farther apart as the road wound upward. By midafternoon, the women began to hear a rushing sound in the distance. Allouette drew in her horse with a frown. "It is like to the noise of a flock of birds preparing to fly south."

"Strange." Quicksilver smiled. "I always thought such a flock sounded like a babbling brook."

"Brook or bird," Cordelia said, "let us chase the sound and see."

They left the path, angling eastward across the slope of the land toward the sound. It grew louder as they rode until they crossed a meadow and found themselves by a river— but one in full spate and choked with rapids. The water laughed and scolded, nagged and cried as it rushed around the boulders and fell over ledges. The women sat their horses, drinking in the sight and the sound, letting the spray on their faces refresh them.

"It is glorious, is it not?" asked Cordelia.

"It is indeed," said Allouette, but she turned with a frown and demanded, "Who is he?"

Cordelia and Quicksilver turned to follow her gaze and saw a man in a fur tunic sitting on a rock watching the water strike the boulders and roil on down the channel. There was something melancholy about him, something immensely sad as he sat watching the river. He wore the usual peasant's tunic and hose, but ones made of fur. His grizzled hair was cut evenly around his head.

"What is there about that fellow that makes me feel such sadness?" Allouette wondered.

The man looked up at the sound of her voice. He was middle-aged and round-faced, all his features seeming to droop—except his nose, which was too small, but the moustache beneath it more than made up for it. It was grizzled like his hair, very bushy, bristling out to hide his upper lip. His chin receded, scarcely visible. He was stocky and looked as though he should be slow in his movements.

"I see what you mean," Cordelia said softly. "Merely the look of him makes me feel the need to comfort."

The man's eyes widened, registering the sight of three beautiful young women, and he rose from his rock with a sinuous speed, a lithe economy of movement, that seemed to belie his age and appearance. He came toward them, hands rising in a plea. "I pray you, beauteous maidens, do not pass by!"

CHAPTER

-12-

"I fear that we must," Allouette said with gentle sympathy, "for we've young men waiting, and we must find them before they wander into trouble."

"Young men! What do young men know?" The ugly man was right beside her horse somehow; he had moved far more quickly than she had expected. "Age betokens experience! It takes maturity for a man to know how to read a woman's signs, to recognize her wants and needs and fulfill her wishes."

"You had best not be speaking of the wishes I think you mean," Quicksilver warned.

But the ugly fellow paid her no heed; all his attention was focused on Allouette. "Nay, maiden, stay awhile, and I shall show you such delights as never a young man could."

"I am no maiden," Allouette answered, beginning to be frightened but striving not to let it show—or to let it make her lash out. "I am no maiden, and my fiancé has already shown me all the delights I can stand."

Cordelia felt a perverse pride in her brother.

"All the delights you can think of." The ugly man's hands rose in supplication. "Nay, tarry with me, and learn far more exquisite notions than youth can know!"

"I wish no greater pleasure than the embrace of my betrothed." Allouette's voice hardened. "Foul are you to urge me to betray him! Forfend and farewell!" She turned her horse away.

But the ugly man caught her bridle, beseeching, "Only a little while, only an hour, only half! If I cannot teach you far more of desire than ever you have known in even so little time as that, turn aside from me and leave me evermore!" He reached out to touch her hand.

Allouette recoiled, for his flesh was cold and moist. "Forfend, forgo! I shall indeed leave you, and that without a minute's more converse!"

"Say congress, rather," the ugly fellow pleaded, "or even a kiss, only one! If that will not thaw the chill of your heart, then leave me indeed!" `

Allouette fought to conceal the revulsion that swept her at the thought of that bristly moustache against her skin and the cold moist flesh of those lips against her own. She let a little anger show. "Must I speak with cruelty, fellow? Loose my mare's reins and let me go, for I do not wish to visit harm upon you!"

"But your steed does not recoil from me," the ugly man pointed out. "Indeed, she welcomes my touch." To prove it, he stroked the animal's neck; her skin quivered. "See? She trembles with longing!"

"Or shivers with apprehension! Let go and stand off! Will you force me to be cruel?"

"You are so already, merely by denying me! O lady of beauty, O damsel of delight, pay heed! Suffer only one caress, and you shall crave more!"

"I should suffer indeed!" Allouette turned to her companions. "Ladies, will you not help me escape this importunate fellow?"

"He importunes you indeed." Cordelia studied the scene with brooding attention. "Off with you, old man! Cease your attentions when a lady shows she does not welcome them!"

"Ah, but she will if—"

"Away with you, she said!" Quicksilver sat tense and poised, her hand on her sword hilt. "We have no wish to be hurtful, but we will suffer your attentions no longer!"

"O paragon of loveliness, bid your friends ride on without you!" the ugly man implored.

"Be off!" Quicksilver drew her sword. "Or have you as strong a taste for steel as for women?"

The polished blade flashed sunlight into the ugly man's eyes. He cried out, covering his eyes in pain, and fell backward into the water.

"No! I will not have him die for dismissal!" Allouette kicked her horse forward toward the stream.

"Wait!" Cordelia seized her arm, pointing with the other hand. "See how he fares!"

The ugly man sank below the water. As the foam and the waves closed over his head, they could see his tunic tighten about him, saw his cross-garters dissolve and his legs fuse together, the fur leggings clinging to the flesh even as his feet broadened into the twin flukes of a tail. His thatch of grizzled hair darkened and seemed to flow downward over a skull that flowed into a powerful neck and shoulders; his mouth and nose bulged outward into a muzzle and the bushy moustache stretched into whiskers; the nubbin of nose turned black, and his arms shrank even as his hands grew and flattened into paddles. The seal shot back to the surface, balancing on its tail and turning to look back at them, calling out in one last mournful series of barks before it turned and plunged back into the roiling water, diving to twist and turn between the boulders as it raced away and shot glistening over a little waterfall, then disappeared in the foam.

"It was no true man," Cordelia whispered, "but a selkie."

Allouette began to tremble.

"It was a very handsome seal," Cordelia said tentatively.

"But a very ugly man," Quicksilver answered scornfully. "Come, ladies—let us ride."

• • •

"Surely we should stop to rest soon," Gregory protested. "Night is not a healthy time for travel when there are so many supernatural creatures about."

Geoffrey was nodding in his saddle, but at his brother's protest he shook himself back to some semblance of wakefulness. "Come, brother, what have we to fear? Whatever comes against us, surely Alain and I can hold it at bay while you disassemble it."

"Not if it is as tightly counterspelled as that last," Gregory said darkly.

"We have ridden the clock around," Alain reminded Geoffrey, "and we always pitch camp before dark. Why do we push ahead after sunset now?"

"After sunset? Well after sunset! In pitch darkness!" Gregory exclaimed. "What need?"

"Our encounters have made me wary of the darkness," Geoffrey confessed. "I wish stout walls about me this night, though I cannot say why. Only a little farther, gentlemen, and surely we shall come to a village!"

Ahead of them, a roar shook the night.

"I think a campfire would do well enough," Gregory said nervously.

"We must face our fears!" Geoffrey was fully alert now. "Onward! We must see what made that bellow!" He kicked his horse to gallop; the exhausted beast managed a valiant trot.

Gregory sighed as he and Alain picked up their own paces, clucking to their mounts as they tried to catch up with Geoffrey. They came abreast with him only because he paused at the top of a rise as another bellow shook the ground. "Yonder!" He pointed at the dots of light that made a semicircle ahead and below.

"What manner of sight is this?" Gregory wondered.

"It is the village your brother hoped for." Alain pointed at a tall shape glowing faintly in the moonlight. "That is a church, or I miss my guess."

"Aye, and there are cottages around a common," Gregory added.

Geoffrey frowned. "I see it now—and those little lights curve along one side of that circle."

The roar shook the trees about them; several dead branches fell.

"Curiosity consumes me," Alain confessed.

"And that roar has the sound of a monster seeking battle." Geoffrey grinned with anticipation. "Let us ride in and discover what it is."

They found a pathway and started down the slope. "Slowly," Alain cautioned. "There is no need to rush into danger."

Geoffrey's mouth tightened; he would have loved to do just that, but he held his peace, silently acknowledging that Alain had common sense on his side.

"Do my eyes deceive me, or has that half-circle of lights grown smaller?" Gregory asked.

Geoffrey studied the scene for a second, then nodded. "Your eyes show truly, brother. If there are people holding those lights, they are moving closer together."

"Ho! What have we here?" The prince drew his horse up.

Looking down, the brothers saw a man and a woman crouched by the roadside, one arm wrapped about each other, the others encircling a little boy and a little girl.

The roar sounded again. One of the children gave a cry of fear and the mother spoke soothing words, though her own voice trembled as twigs fell on her shoulders.

"Why hide you so far from your cottage?" Alain asked. "Be sure that if you fear for your safety, there are three swords here to guard you!"

"Swords will do little good against that monster," the woman moaned.

"What manner of monster is this?" Gregory said with keen interest.

"It is a ghost, Sir Knight," the man answered, "but it has taken the form of a bull."

Gregory stared. "Why would a human ghost so disguise itself?"

"In life, Bayurg was a most wicked man," the woman explained, and shuddered at the memory.

"He was a bully and a miser," the husband said bitterly, "who only did two good deeds in all his life, and many, many evil ones."

"He cozened the lord into giving him parts of the fields of each of his neighbors," said the wife, "and traded shoddy cloth for grain."

"And spoiled grain for good stout cloth," the man said darkly.

"He promised marriage to six different lasses," the woman said, "and when he had tasted their delights, he scorned each one. Four he got with child but would not give anything to their keeping. At last no woman would listen to his suit, so he went to take a seventh by force, but all the folk were watching him shrewdly by then and drove him away."

"He lied, he cheated, he swindled," the man said. "He stole tools and food and furniture and beat their owners if they sought to regain their goods."

"A most evil man indeed," Alain said, affronted. "What were the two good deeds he did?"

"He did give a worn-out cloak to a poor man," the wife said reluctantly, "and once, in a moment of weakness, gave a bit of bread and cheese to one of his children, for the boy was very hungry."

"But that was not enough to win him a place in Heaven," the husband said, "nor even in Purgatory, I suspect. He fell down dead in his forty-ninth year and the parson buried him, but none mourned him."

"So his two good deeds were enough to delay his exile to Hell," Gregory mused. "Why, though, do you think he could not gain Heaven or Purgatory?"

"Because his ghost came back," the wife said, and shuddered.

"It was doubtless to give him a chance to make amends for all the wrongs he had done," the husband said, "but he has only gone on as he did when alive. A bully he was, and as a bull he has returned, a giant bull who appears on the common in the dead of night. For weeks he will not come, and we will begin to relax when the sun sets—whereupon he will descend on us again, frightening any who dare walk abroad after dark, chasing them into rivers or mires, and bellowing so loudly on the common that he shakes the thatch off our roofs and makes the shutters bang so hard that they break."

The roar came again and a huge dead branch came crashing down a yard from Alain's horse. The stallion surged against the bit, but Alain held him and asked, "Have you not sent to your lord for help?"

"He would not believe his old flatterer would do ill," the man said bitterly, "and our friar sought to exorcise the monster, but the bull was too strong for him. It roared to drown out his words, then chased him into the church."

"We have had enough," the woman said, "more than enough, all we can take. We would flee the village outright, but Brother Anselm persuaded us to try one last measure."

"We have asked friars from eleven other villages to come and help put down the ghost for good." The husband nodded toward the lights below. "There they walk, each carrying a lighted candle, and we can hear their chorus of prayers in spite of all the bull's roaring."

"A most worthy undertaking!" Alain exchanged glances with Geoffrey, who grinned back and said, "And a most courageous! I would see the outcome."

"I too," Gregory agreed. "If there is anything I do not know about laying to rest a ghost, I will most eagerly learn it—and who knows? The dozen friars may yet need our aid."

"Thanks for the warning, good people," Alain said to the family, "but I believe we will ride into this danger nonetheless."

They could still hear the family groaning with fear when they were twenty feet away and picking up speed.

As they rode into the common, they saw that the half-circle had tightened, managing to ring the bull completely on three sides—and behind it rose the church. The bull towered over them, ten feet tall at least, bellowing and roaring and

pawing the earth. Now and again it charged a friar, but all
held their places in the circle with dogged determination,
candles high as they chanted their prayers loudly and stepped
forward, slowly but with great resolution. The bull turned
from one to another, about and about, still making its hideous
noise, confused and enraged as the circle tightened around
him.

"They push him toward the graveyard!" Geoffrey said.

"Of course—it is the place of the dead!" Gregory cried.
"But surely so wicked a spirit may not step on consecrated
ground without pain or danger of destruction!"

Nonetheless, the bull turned toward the cemetery—but
froze as it saw the dim, translucent forms rising from the
ground and gathering shoulder to shoulder to form a wall.

"The ghosts of those he cheated and despoiled!" Gregory
breathed. "It is ghost against ghost now, and they have the
strength of Right to brace them."

"And of numbers," Geoffrey agreed. "Surely the bull cannot venture into the graveyard now."

"True," Alain said, puzzled. "It cannot go backward, and
it cannot go forward for fear of the prayers and the blessed
light of the candles. How then do they mean to chase it
away?"

"I do not think they do," said Geoffrey grimly. "I think
they mean to lay it to rest once and for all."

"To force it to lie in its coffin and never come out?" Alain
asked, amazed.

"Something of the sort," Gregory said, studying the friars
and their roaring foe. "Let us see what they do."

Tighter and tighter the circle became, surrounding the bull
in a corral of lights. Its bellows stormed and threatened, but
still the ring closed in on it. At last, with an earthshaking
roar, the bull bolted toward the church door.

"It cannot go in!" Alain protested. "Not into a consecrated
place!"

"It is the church, or the ghosts whose yearning for revenge
burns white-hot," Gregory explained. "Which will hurt it
more?"

"The frying pan or the fire?" Geoffrey muttered.

The church shook with the bull's shout of agony, a long roll of sound that combined anger and pain so deeply that all three men shuddered. Even Geoffrey felt fear of that horrendous creature, but the friars strode with determination into the chapel.

"I must be there!" Gregory cried. "Who knows what the beast will do when it is cornered?"

"Nay," Geoffrey cried, "that is why you must not—"

Gregory disappeared with a small thundercrack.

"Oh, blast! What peril has he sent himself into this time?" Geoffrey turned to Alain. "Follow when you can!" And with another thundercrack he, too, disappeared, leaving Alain to decorate the evening air with some curses that any well-bred prince should not have known.

Gregory appeared inside the church with a thundercrack that was drowned out by the bull's most agonized roar. There were no pews, as in most medieval churches, so the floor was one wide expanse of flagstone with the bull in its center and two lines of friars striding with determination along the walls toward the altar, to protect the side and rear walls while a third spread out to block the doorway. They held their candles high and filled the church with the sound of prayer, somehow louder even than the bull's cries of pain and fury. It turned about and about, charging first one friar, then another, always repelled by the prayers. Finally it realized they were about to close the circle around it and charged the eastern wall, head down, horns stabbing out. It slammed headlong into the stone, rebounded, and wobbled back to the center, reeling and dizzy.

"It has cracked solid granite!"

Gregory looked up to see his brother beside him, pointing. His arrival, too, had been drowned out by the chanting and the bellowing. "Cracked, but not broken," he said. "This is a hallowed building, after all. It may hurt the bull sorely, but its wall is proof against the strength of his wickedness."

"And is stronger than he, it seems!" Geoffrey pointed. "See! It shrinks!"

Gregory looked, and sure enough, the bull was growing smaller. It must have realized its peril, though, for it sucked in a huge quantity of air, puffing itself up as well as it could.

Suddenly Gregory realized the bull's intent. "Beware!" he called to the friars. "The ghost means to—"

The bull let out all the air in one vast bellow, spinning as it did to sweep its breath over every single candle. The wave of frigid air snuffed out each one of the little lights. In the darkness, the friars cried out in consternation and the bull bellowed in triumph.

"Excite molecules!" Gregory snapped at his brother and stared into the darkness, visualizing tiny lights piercing its gloom.

"The very thing!" Geoffrey cried, and did the same.

One by one, the tiny flames rekindled, casting their glows over the faces of the friars. With joy, the clergymen began to chant again, and the bull bellowed in outrage—but his bellow slid up the scale, higher and higher as the friars stepped closer and closer. They were near enough now so that their candles illuminated the bull from every side, showing his shrinking; their horseshoe had finally become a ring, tightening around the monster as it grew smaller and smaller. The hymn rose up in joy and triumph as the creature dwindled, its baffled bellowing becoming a bleating, then a trilling, and finally a squeaking.

"Now, Brother Hendrik!" a friar cried, and one of his fellows stepped forward with a tinder box. He scooped up the tiny creature and snapped the lid shut.

Gregory and Geoffrey shouted with triumph. Another voice joined them; turning in surprise, they saw Alain standing near the door, cheering as lustily as they.

But the friars did not cheer, only sang a hymn of thanks to the Deity who had vanquished their enemy. Their song soared and ended, and the church lay silent a moment, its stone walls gilded by the light of the candle flames.

Then a squeaking came from the tinder box, a cricket chirp

that formed itself into words: "What will you do with me? Have mercy, I pray!"

"What mercy did you show to those who came within your power?" a friar demanded.

"You shall be served even as you served your fellows," another friar agreed.

"Do me this much, at least!" the tiny voice implored. "Bury this box under the bridge across the village stream, that I may be not completely alone!"

"Nay, fellow," the oldest friar said sternly. "We know the malice in your heart."

"And the powers even a tiny ghost may have," another graying friar agreed. "Most likely you would make every pregnant woman who crossed that bridge miscarry."

"Aye, and every cow and ewe, too," a third friar added.

The tinder box issued a frenzy of chirping that modulated into words. "A curse upon you for your suspicious minds!"

"If he would curse us, then we were right in our guessing his mischief," the oldest friar said with a grim smile. "Nay, villain, we shall wrap this box in lead and send it to the seacoast for a fisherman to take and sink as many fathoms deep as he can."

"Think of charity!" the box squeaked. "Would you doom me to eternity within this cramped and lightless space?"

"If it is not to your liking, you may go to the Afterworld and the reward your cruelty has earned you."

"Cruel as you, if you would doom me to damnation! You know that hellfire awaits me!"

"It is the fate you have chosen for yourself," the friar said severely, "by your mistreatment of your fellows while you lived."

Gregory stepped forward, one hand raised. "If I may intrude, holy brothers?"

The friars look up, startled. Then the oldest friar said slowly, "I wondered how our candles relit themselves. Well, if it is you who made them glow to life again, speak, for you have earned some voice in this matter, stranger or not."

"I thank you, men of grace." Gregory stared at the box,

fascinated. "Might you not sing the bull down smaller still, say to the size of a gnat, so that to him, his chamber is as spacious as a palace?"

The friars exchanged a look of surprise. "Aye," the eldest said slowly, "in charity's name, we might do that much."

"But to never again see light!" the box squeaked.

"Do not believe him," Gregory advised. "He is a ghost, after all, and can lighten his palace with his own glow."

"Curse you for knowing that!" the box squeaked.

"What," the friar cried, scandalized, "would you curse him who even now spoke up for you, who thought to make you so small that your chamber would seem a cavern? Nay, you are not worthy of such kindness after all!"

"No, no!" the bull squeaked. "I spoke rashly, I spoke in error! Nay, I revoke all curses I have laid! Only sing me smaller, men of virtue!"

"Would it were something other than force that could induce his remorse," the friar sighed, "but we can afford a morsel of charity after all. Brothers, let us sing."

Alain, Geoffrey, and Gregory left the church as they began. They paused a moment on the common to look back at the chapel, listening to the harmonies rising within.

"To look at it now, one would think only of peace and calm," Alain marveled.

"Aye," Geoffrey agreed. "Who could know of the cruelty and depth of malice of the creature, or the determination and courage it took to quell it?"

"It is enough that we know, and that harmony is restored to this village." Gregory looked up at the sky in wonder. "This has taken far longer than it seemed, friends. Dawn lightens the sky."

"Why, so it does," Alain said, astonished, then turned to mount his horse. "Somehow I have no great desire to sleep in this village, day or night. Since there will be light to show us our way, let us ride on a few miles more and pitch camp in some meadow."

"A good thought." Geoffrey swung up astride his stallion.

"Still, I cannot be sorry that we pressed on through darkness last night."

"Nor I," Gregory admitted. He set his foot in the stirrup and mounted. "Come, gentlemen, let us ride, for we can surely find a more secure place of rest than this."

Nonetheless, as they rode over the log bridge toward the forest, Geoffrey turned to his brother with a frown. "What are you smiling about now, Watchman?"

"Only thinking that word travels, and the friars have no reason to keep the events of this night secret," Gregory answered. "I doubt not that the folk of this village will be very cautious about crossing this bridge for some years to come."

"Have you any biscuit left, Cordelia?" Quicksilver asked. "Mine is gone, and I've only a few strips of jerky left."

"I've four biscuits but no dried beef." Cordelia handed hardtack to each of the women. "We shall keep one in reserve."

Hunger gnawed at Allouette's stomach—indeed, it growled at her in anger as she passed the biscuit back to Cordelia. "I thank you, damsel, but I can last some while longer. Perchance we shall find some nuts or berries."

"Or a rabbit who has tired of life?" Quicksilver asked. "Perhaps I shall hunt when we pitch camp, but skinning and roasting will delay us too long for the sharpness of my hunger."

"I shall subsist on the beauty that surrounds us." Allouette looked around at the trees to either side of the trail. "Surely these are old and venerable trunks! So tall, so massive!"

"I see some that are neither." Cordelia nodded toward a coppice, a patch of several dozen oak trees only a little more than a foot across. Then she looked down at the roots. "Why, they are growing from the stumps of trees fallen before them!"

They looked and saw that each of the young trees had a flat plane of wood beneath it, some only a foot high, some two feet—but eighteen inches wide or more, and each grew from the center of a three-foot-wide stump. Almost every one had another, smaller stump that had grown out of the side.

"Why, the oaks of this coppice have been cut three times!" Cordelia exclaimed. "These trees are the fourth generation!"

Allouette shivered. "There is something uncanny about this place, something weird, as though it waits to trap the unwary."

"Well might it hold a grudge against humankind, if each of its oaks has been chopped down three times!" Cordelia said with a laugh. "Nonetheless, you cannot deny that it is a pretty place."

"Oh yes, it is lovely," Allouette agreed, "perhaps because these trees spread so much smaller a canopy than the hoary old giants about them. They let more sunlight in—and look! The coppice is filled with bluebells!"

The small blue flowers did indeed fill the little grove so densely that they almost seemed to be a carpet. Among them the red tops of toadstools thrust up.

"How strange to see toadstools among flowers," Cordelia marveled, "and such large ones, too!"

"They seem almost jolly, almost festive," Allouette agreed.

"I wonder if they are good to eat?" Quicksilver pressed a hand over her rumbling stomach.

As if in answer, one of the toadstools rose upward. The three women gasped as they saw beneath it a gnarled and wrinkled face with a long red nose. Then the toadstool began to walk toward them.

CHAPTER
-13-

The "toadstool" proved to be no fungus but a man two feet tall and a foot wide, seeming to be mostly torso; his legs and arms were far shorter than most people's. His hands, though, held a platter of steaming roast beef with carrots and onions around it. "Are you a-hungered, then?" he asked in a rasping, guttural voice. "Nay, come into our coppice and dine!"

Cordelia inhaled the aroma with a sigh of longing and Allouette's mouth watered. "How very good of you!" she told the little man.

"Aye, of all of you." Quicksilver looked out over the coppice.

"All? What do you mean?" Allouette asked.

"Discuss it while we dine!" Cordelia moved her horse forward.

"Be not so quick." Quicksilver put out a hand to stop her. "Have you never heard that 'Fairie folks are in old oaks'?"

"Aye, but what has that to do with food?" Cordelia looked up at the leaves. "Truly, these trees are oaks, but what meaning is there in that?"

"It means that each of those 'toadstools' is truly the cap of one of the Wee Folk who haunt this grove," Quicksilver told her, "of one of the Oakmen."

Somehow the name sent a chill of apprehension through Cordelia and Allouette. "Is there truth in this?" Cordelia asked the little man.

He grinned, but it looked forced. "Even so! Meet all of your hosts!"

The red toadstools rose, and sure enough, each was the hat of a gnome with a long red nose, blue tunic, and tawny leggins. "Come in and dine!" they all cried in chorus.

"They have a most remarkable unity of opinion." Allouette's apprehension deepened.

"They also have food! Would you insult their hospitality?"

"Do not, we pray," said the Oakman. "See what other dishes we offer!"

Each of the Oakmen raised his arms, holding out a platter. Some had roast chicken with dressing, others a medley of steaming vegetables, others bowls of fresh fruit, some even candied sweets.

"Do not soldiers always dine when they can, for fear their next meal may be long in coming?" Cordelia asked Quicksilver.

"Only when they can trust the food," the warrior answered.

That gave Cordelia pause. "Oh . . . the tales I have heard of faerie food . . ."

Allouette's head snapped up, staring; everyone knew that if you ate the food of faerie folk, you placed yourself in their power. She had never realized how strongly those dishes might tempt a person to forget that.

"Slander, surely!" said the little man. "We are generous, that is all!"

"And very careful to guard your forest, from all I've heard." Quicksilver turned to her companions. "As I grew up, I was constantly in the greenwood exploring and gathering, damsels."

"And hunting," the Oakman snapped.

"And hunting," Quicksilver admitted with a frown at him,

then turned back to her friends. "Moreover, I lived in the forest four years while I was outlawed. I have learned something of the lore of the woodlands, and of the spirits who dwell there."

"What have you heard of us?" the Oakman demanded. "Nothing ill, I trust!"

"They who speak well of you, say that you guard the animals of the forest—nay, even the trees—with great zeal," Quicksilver told him. "Those who speak ill tell of the manner in which you punish those who hunt your beasts or fell your trees."

The Oakman's eyes sparked with anger, but he said, "What has that to do with the food we offer?"

"Aye." Cordelia edged her horse closer to the little man and his steaming platter. "What bother?"

"Why, look at their caps," Quicksilver said, "how they resemble toadstools—not mushrooms, but toadstools, poisonous fungi!"

Cordelia stared at the red caps, then darted a look of horror at the platter of roast beef. "You do not mean . . ."

"That their food is made of toadstools disguised by faerie magic? I do!"

"You would not poison us!" Allouette demanded, ashen-faced.

The Oakman stiffened with offended dignity. "Our food would certainly not kill you!"

"Not kill us, no," Cordelia said slowly, "but now that Quicksilver has opened my eyes to look at this coppice more clearly, I do notice something strange."

"What?" Allouette scanned the coppice closely. "I see naught."

"Look again—at the trees that do *not* grow from chopped stumps."

Allouette looked—and gasped. "I suppose . . . you might say they look . . ."

"Like people," Quicksilver finished for her. "Behold! That one holds up two branches, like arms showing empty hands—

see how the twigs are five in number? And the knots in the trunk—how like a face!"

"A face caught in horror," Quicksilver said, her voice hardening.

"And the fold in the trunk—like the legs of trousers! With roots shaped much like shoes!"

"But that one." Cordelia pointed. "Its fingers are hooked in threat, its face angry."

"Changed that one just in time, did you?" Quicksilver demanded.

"Mere daydreams!" The Oakman held up his platter. "Dine ere it chills!"

"Thank you, no." Cordelia moved her horse back a little. "I think it is time we rode onward."

"Nay, it is not!" The Oakman dropped his platter and whipped a bow from among the bluebells. He straightened, whipping an arrow from a quiver on his back and nocking it to the bowstring.

The other Oakmen scurried into the road with a sound like dry leaves blown by the wind. Turning, the three women saw they barred the trail quite effectively, with archers to either side, even high in the trees—and each held a bent bow or cocked crossbow aimed at them.

"Stand still," the Oakman advised. "You have heard of the perils of elf-shot, have you not?"

The three women froze, for they had indeed heard. A person struck with elf-shot fell down in convulsions. When he rose, he might be liable to have seizures for the rest of his life—or have one side of his face and body paralyzed.

"You heard rightly of our mission," the lead Oakman said, "that we protect the beasts of the forest, and the trees too, from the greed of mortal folk!"

"I hunt only when I hunger." Out of the corner of her eye, Quicksilver saw the abstracted looks that came over the faces of her companions. "As to wood, I take only fallen branches, or cut down trees that have already died."

"So you say," the little man challenged. "What proof can you offer?"

"Does it matter?" Quicksilver did her best to sound bored as she rested her hand on the hilt of her sword. "We have not come to this wood to dwell here, after all. We are only passing through it, on our way to search for monsters such as ogres, who break down living trees simply because they are in their way—or afancs, who gnaw them down to make dams in your rivers!"

The little folk shuddered. "Spare the trees from so slow a death!" one groaned.

"Are there truly such spirits abroad?" the leader asked, his visage darkening.

"There are indeed," Quicksilver told them. "We have met others like them. Some sorcerer has loosed them upon us, and we go to seek and fight them."

A crafty look came over the Oakman's face. "Three gentle damsels such as yourselves? How could you stand against creatures of terror and ferocity?"

"I bear Cold Iron in the steel of my sword." Quicksilver started to draw it, but every bow in the company instantly shifted to aim at her. She froze.

"But our true weapon," Cordelia said, "is magic."

"Magic?" the Oakman said with a sour smile. "What manner of spells can you wield that would discomfit an ogre?"

"Something like this." Cordelia glared at the bare earth of the trail; it erupted into flame. The Oakmen shouted in panic and crowded away, but the fire died as quickly as it had started. "I kindled it on bare earth," Cordelia explained, "for I've no wish to let my blaze devour your trees."

The Oakmen stared, the whites of their eyes showing as they shifted their aim to her.

Quicksilver smiled, knowing that she could draw her sword before they could shift aim back to her.

"Believe me, she can kindle flame more quickly than you can loose," Allouette told them. "She might die, but your forest would burn for weeks."

The crossbows swung toward her; the leader scowled. "Would you truly do such a thing?"

"To your forest, no," Allouette said, "perhaps not even to

an ogre. I might, however, do this." She wrenched with her mind, and a tree branch swung down to slam against the bare earth of the trail, only a yard in front of the Oakman. He jumped back, shaken, as the branch swung back up. "How," he asked in a husky voice, "can you so move the forest?"

"Because the trees know I am their friend," Allouette said simply, "and that, in my own way, I seek to protect them as surely as do you yourself."

Quicksilver cast her a glance of admiration.

The bows lowered on the instant. "It must be so," the lead Oakman said, "for neither beech nor birch would heed one who sought its doom. Oak and elm both know their enemies and would smite them."

"We are friends to the forest," Cordelia said, "not its enemies."

"Go, then, to fight the forest's foes!" the Oakman said, and his people backed away to the sides of the trail, bowing. "There is a spring half a mile down the trail, and on its banks grow wild strawberries and blackberries."

"It runs through a hazelnut grove," said another gnome, "and the nuts are ripe and falling."

"I thank you, friends," Cordelia said slowly, "but if there is to be a truce between humankind and the forest, we cannot leave without our own."

Quicksilver gave her a look that clearly said, *Don't push it!* Allouette cast her an appalled glance that sobered even as she stared; she nodded judiciously.

"These are enemies of the forest!" the Oakman said angrily. "If we loose them, they shall attack our trees with axes, just as they did when they came to our coppice!"

"But you have buried their axe-heads and rotted the handles," Cordelia pointed out. "As to their intentions, have no fear—most of them, I am sure, will never dare come near you again. Those who do will not dare defy two witches and a swordswoman."

The Oakman looked doubtful, but he said only, "It will take some time."

"We can wait an hour or so," Cordelia answered.

"Or so," the Oakman echoed, looking grim. "Very well, lady, you may have your criminals—but one move wrong from any of them, and be sure our barbs shall pierce their skulls."

Two hours later, the women rode behind half a dozen dazed peasants who stumbled down the path, casting fearful looks at every tree they passed.

"Strange that four of them chose to remain as trees," Cordelia said, troubled.

"Try not to think about it," Allouette advised.

Cordelia glanced at the grimness of her face and drew her own conclusions. She turned back to watch the trail with a shudder.

They rode in silence a few minutes longer; then Allouette thawed enough to offer, by way of explanation, "You can never know how glad I am to have met your brother."

"Are we closer to the coast than we know?" Alain asked.

Geoffrey followed the direction of his gaze. "What would make you think . . . why, what is that beast doing here?"

"That beast" was a shaggy pony, scarcely half the size of Geoffrey's warhorse. His coat looked to be very rough indeed, and he was festooned with seaweed.

"Let us look somewhat closer." Gregory kicked his horse into a trot.

"No, wait . . ." Alain said, overcome with a sudden sense of misgiving, but the brothers were already halfway to the pony. Alain sighed and rode after.

Geoffrey and Gregory rode up on either side of the shaggy pony, but Geoffrey dismounted fifteen feet away and walked forward, fishing a piece of carrot from his pocket and holding it out on his palm.

Both horses tossed their heads, snorting, and Gregory swerved to catch the reins of his brother's mount. "How is this, Geoffrey? Our horses do not like this little fellow!"

"Jealousy, I doubt not." Geoffrey held out the carrot, his voice smooth and gentle. "Here, then, fellow, take and taste, and know me for a friend."

The pony blew through his nostrils and shifted uncertainly.

"Nay, take it!" Geoffrey urged. "I shall not seek to harm you."

"Nor to ride you," Alain prompted.

Geoffrey cast him a black look.

"We have not the time to tame a fourth horse, Geoffrey," Alain said imperturbably, "nor the need for one."

"I fear that is true," Geoffrey sighed, and turned back to the pony. "Well, then, fellow, let us only greet one another in friendly fashion, as befits fellow wayfarers."

The pony stepped forward warily, sniffed at the carrot, then wrapped it in mobile lips and carried it back to its teeth. It was gone in two grinds and a swallow.

"Very good." Geoffrey smiled. "Perhaps on another journey, we shall meet again and become traveling companions."

"Why should you think I am a traveler?" the pony asked in a gravelly voice.

All three men stared. The horses danced, not liking what they saw and heard.

Geoffrey recovered first and spoke as though a talking horse were the most natural thing in the world. "Why, because you are decked in seaweed, which certainly grows nowhere nearby—so you must have come from the coast."

"And quickly, too," Gregory added, "for your kelp is neither withered nor dry."

"You mark what you see," the gravelly voice said in an approving tone, "and make sense of it as few mortals do. Well, then, make sense of this."

His form softened, melted, and flowed.

The horses reared, screaming; Alain and Gregory had all they could do to hold them down, but they quieted as the pony's substance steadied into a new form—that of an old man with long white hair and beard that had seaweed plaited in with it. He wore only a seaweed kilt, and his skin, though loose and wrinkled, overlay muscles that were still thick and rolling. "You are kind to a lonely stray," he said, "and good hearts deserve rewards."

"I—I like all horses." Geoffrey looked as though he were

about to make an exception. He glanced up and down the almost naked man and added, "I expect no reward, nor do I see that you have any to give."

"What I shall give you is knowledge, which takes no space to carry save a moiety of brain," said the old man. "I shall tell you this: Beware the Whirlpool of Mist."

"I thank you." Geoffrey frowned. "Where shall we find it?"

"Over the river," the old man answered, "in the mornings and in the evenings. Do not enter it, and whatever you do, ask no one to come from it."

"We shall not," Alain said gravely, although he hadn't the faintest notion of humoring a crazy man. "What, though, if those we do not invite should pull us in?"

"They cannot," the old man said firmly, "but if you feel you must enter, bear Cold Iron with you."

"I always do," Geoffrey said automatically, "or at least steel." He touched his sword hilt.

The old man glanced at it and nodded with approval even as he took a few steps backward. "Steel is Cold Iron made more pure and alloyed with the core of life. Bear it well and wisely—and be glad to come away alive; take no booty with you."

"Booty?" Geoffrey frowned. "I despise soldiers who loot. What manner of booty mean you?"

"Living booty," the old man said, backing farther away. "Enemies."

"What enemies?" Alain demanded, pressing forward.

But the old man's form fluxed and flowed again; the horses reared, and all three men had all they could do to keep them from bolting. When they settled, the companions turned to look at the old man but saw only the small, shaggy pony festooned with seaweed, galloping away from them.

"I do not blame the horses," Alain said in a shaky voice. "A sight like that makes me wish to bolt, too."

The women elected to ride at night, though their eyelids were leaden and their shoulders drooped with weariness.

"Why do I feel so urgent a need to press onward?" Cordelia wondered aloud.

"Oh, I did not mean to let my anxiety leak out to disturb you!" Allouette said in chagrin.

Quicksilver managed an ironic smile. "Why do you think yourself so important as to be the psi who sets these feelings going, lass? Might not Cordelia be the source?"

"Or even yourself," Cordelia reminded.

Quicksilver shook her head with certainty. "I am nowhere nearly so powerful an esper as either of you, and certainly not so skilled. My strengths lie in other areas."

"If it is not us, then someone ahead is sorely troubled," Allouette said, frowning.

"That," Cordelia allowed, "or perhaps someone is intending a deed that makes all of us apprehensive." She turned to Quicksilver. "Do not deny that you feel it, too."

"Oh, I do indeed feel it," the warrior said, "a sense of impending doom. I am strong enough for that, after all—but not to send out such emotion."

The breeze shifted toward them, and the three women stiffened as they heard a faint and distant sound of chanting blown toward them.

"What in Heaven's name is that?" Cordelia gasped.

"If it is in any name, it is not of Heaven," Allouette said grimly. "Come, ladies! Ride more quickly!"

Adrenaline shoved weariness aside as the three women cantered down the moonlit road. The trees loomed to either hand, dark and threatening masses, deepening their sense of danger even as the emotion behind the chanting became stronger. It was savage, hungry, brimming with anticipation of some fell deed, and the three companions had to force themselves, and their horses, to keep riding toward it.

They burst out of the woods into the edge of a little valley, a hollow in the rolling land before them—and at the bottom of that hollow burned a fire with something turning on a spit over the flames. Dozens of men and women cavorted around it, chanting in a language the women had never heard—and in their center, around the fire, lay the charred bodies of a score of cats.

"It is the Taghairm!" Allouette gasped. "It is the ceremony for summoning a demon!"

CHAPTER

-14-

Face thunderous, Quicksilver rode down into the hollow. Cordelia stared in dismay, then rode after her, crying, "No, lady! Do not interrupt until we know their purpose!"

"I shall find it out," Quicksilver called back, and leaned down to seize the shoulder of a woman who sat at the edge of the crowd, watching. She spun the woman around, demanding, "Speak, wretch! What do your people seek here?"

The woman looked up at her with glazed, excited eyes, a few flecks of foam on her lips. Slowly she focused on the warrior's face but didn't seem surprised to see her; she was beyond shock or delight, well on her way to mob mania. "We honor the monsters who have haunted our dreams," she told them. "If we offer them food and drink by our fire, surely they will favor us and spare us in the conquest they have told us they will visit upon all the land."

"Offer hospitality?" Quicksilver cried. "Cat's paw! Cat's paws and dupes, all your people! The ogres and horrors will come in when you ask them, aye—but they will not *leave* when you bid them, and at their pleasure they shall wreak havoc among you!"

"Nay!" The woman's eyes cleared a bit as fear rose. "Surely they will spare those who appease them!"

"Spare you? Fool!" Quicksilver took her by the shoulders and gave her a shake. "The only favor they will show is to conquer you first—conquer, aye, and likely enslave, torture, or devour you!"

"Surely not," the woman pleaded, tears in her eyes. "Surely they will be kind to their friends!"

"We cannot be friends to them, only victims!" Quicksilver spun toward her companions. "Quickly! We must stop this obscene ceremony!"

"Indeed we must." Allouette spurred her horse and rode down toward the bonfire while Quicksilver was still remounting. Cordelia rode after her and Quicksilver brought up the rear, mouthing imprecations.

A cat yowled with fear and pain as two men held up the spit to which it was tied; another man lifted a bloody knife over it. Allouette swerved her horse and the mare's shoulder slammed into the men, sending them sprawling. The cat yowled as it fell, but Quicksilver swerved, leaning down from her saddle to slice through the rope that held it bound. The cat ran for safety, a ginger blur in the firelight.

"Villain!" one of the cat holders cried, struggling to his feet. "You have ruined it all!"

"Nay, she has not!" The knife holder sat up, pointing across the fire. "See! She was too late! Big Ears has come!"

Above the fire, smoke was gathering into a ghostly form— a giant cat with huge tufted ears, each as high and wide as the creature's head. Lying Sphinx-like in midair with its tail waving, it seemed as tall as a woman's shoulder. Its purr was a rasp, its eyes glowing coals.

The people froze, staring. Even Cordelia and Quicksilver felt hollow with fear, and Allouette, staring up at the spirit, had to summon up white-hot anger to counter her panic.

The apparition opened its mouth, showing far more and far longer teeth than any true feline owned. "Do not let them stop you, Friends of Zonploka! Persevere! Continue the Tag-hairm! Pay no heed to the voices of cowardice!"

"Cowardice?" Quicksilver jolted out of her trance. "Vile creature, if you were flesh and blood, you would answer to me for that insult!" Her sword flashed forth.

Big Ears turned and grinned down at her, drops of saliva glinting in the firelight. "Eagerly will I look forward to that encounter, tender morsel."

"Morsel!" Quicksilver cried, outraged. "You shall find me more than you can chew, I promise you!"

"I shall remember your promise." Big Ears turned to the villagers. "As I will remember your treachery, if you turn away from me now. Keep on with the Taghairm, for if you do not, another village shall—and my masters, who are far more terrible than myself, will remember your perfidy and descend upon you to pillage and torture and slay!"

The crowd moaned in terror.

The man with the knife turned on Allouette, shouting, "See what you have done! Would you make us monsters' meat, then?" He spun to the crowd. "Hearken not to these women and their squeamish ways! Harden your hearts to do what must be done!" He whirled, kicking one spit off the fire and catching up another. "Big Ears, come for good guesting! Our village is yours! Is it not, neighbors?"

"It is!" the crowd answered with one single shout.

"Big Ears, come!" the man shouted, then repeated it again and again. The crowd took it up, making it a chant: "Big Ears, come! Big Ears, come!"

"You seal your own doom!" Allouette cried, but their voices drowned her out.

"It wants you only for toys!" Cordelia shrieked, but even her shrilling couldn't penetrate their chants.

"Big Ears, come! Big Ears, come!"

As they chanted, the giant cat grew more and more solid. Quicksilver turned to face it, sword in hand, bracing her mare for a charge.

"Big Ears, come! Big Ears, come!"

"I accept!" Big Ears yowled in triumph. It leaped down to the ground, its eyes wild and wicked, its teeth showing in a greedy grin.

The people shouted approval—and as they were still cheering, the monster turned and pounced on the man with the knife, crying, "Learn how your cats felt!"

The crowd screamed, some turning away sickened, some riveted to the sight in horror.

Big Ears lifted its huge head from its gruesome meal, blood dripping from its fangs. "Fools, to host one who thirsts for your blood!"

"But we invited you, we praised you!" one of the cat holders cried in terror. "Will you not favor us for that?"

"Favor indeed," Big Ears said, flashing its teeth, "for you shall be the first to be plundered and murdered. Know how my master Zonploka honors you by this favor, for your deaths shall be quick! But he cannot yet come to visit you, nor any more of his host of warriors. Continue the ceremony, fools, or you will die slowly and in agony instead of quickly and cleanly."

The people moaned, crowding away from the grisly creature.

"Do not listen!" Cordelia shouted. "Do not believe the monster! It is your emotions it desires, not your bodies! It will drink in your fear and your pain! It kills and tortures only to arouse them! Turn away from this thing of evil!"

"Aye, turn away," Allouette cried, "for it has no power but that which you give it by your fear!"

"You have lived too long, interfering wench!" Big Ears spat, and crouched to pounce on her. "Disrupt my Taghairm, would you? Seek to deny me entrance to your world? For that you shall be next, you fat and juicy tidbit!"

"Fat? How dare you!" Allouette cried, outraged. "Suffer the fate you would visit upon me!" She narrowed her eyes in a glare.

Big Ears twisted around, a sudden pain in its belly. "How dare you, impertinent woman?" it gasped. "Learn now what pain is!" It gathered itself to pounce.

"Nay!" Quicksilver cried, and her horse darted between them. "She is ours and not for you!"

Allouette stared, suddenly limp with amazement.

"She is ours indeed, and who seeks to touch her does so at great peril!" Cordelia sent her horse galloping in, then reared, hooves poised to strike at the monster.

Big Ears yowled and leaped, claws flashing out to rake across the horse's belly. It screamed and fell, flailing. Cordelia struggled to rise, but her leg was pinned beneath the animal's weight.

"I shall dine on you at leisure," the monster sneered, and turned to Quicksilver. "First I shall snap up this one, who thinks herself tough but is only a tender morsel."

"This morsel shall stick in your craw!" Quicksilver shouted, and stabbed. "Taste Cold Iron, O Greedy One!"

The sword lanced the creature's tongue and it shrieked, leaping away. "Cold Iron! For that you shall die most miserably!"

"She shall die not at all!" Cordelia glared at the monster.

Big Ears howled with pain. "What . . . what is this?" it panted, and turned toward the pinned woman, eyes wide with confusion. "You cannot! How can so slight a one as you cause me pain?"

"Suffice it that I can!" Cordelia shouted, pointing a finger.

Big Ears caterwauled again, then shot through the air, a blurred arc descending on the woman, screaming, "Die, and my pain dies with you!"

"Nay, it lives as long as I do!" Allouette shook herself out of her trance and hit the monster with every jot of the welter of emotions that boiled within her—guilt, shame, amazement, confusion, and the sudden fierce urge to protect the women she had thought were her enemies.

Big Ears twisted in midair, screaming with sudden pain. Its back slammed down on the dead horse and Cordelia cried out in pain.

The sound seemed to pierce Allouette from side to side. She glared at the creature, thinking of tearing, of ripping, of giant crab claws slashing and shredding within. Big Ears howled in agony, curling around its pain, and Quicksilver stabbed again and again, crying, "Leave this carrion to me!

Cordelia and I shall hold it while you banish it! Speak to the people, lady! Lead!"

Allouette stared in surprise a moment, then turned away with determination. Surely a bandit chieftain knew what she spoke of when it came to leading a mob. "People of mine own kind!" Allouette spread her hands towards the crowd, crying, "It is for you to undo what you have done! What you have brought here, you can send away! The door you have opened, you can close again!"

The cringing people froze in amazement.

"Think of your anger and pain!" Allouette exhorted them. "Think of your anger at this creature's betrayal! Do you want it and its kind here among you?"

"No!" "No, no, of course not!" "Send it away, lady, send it away!"

"It is for you to send it away, for it is you who brought it in!" Allouette scolded. "What, would you have me clean up your mess for you? Well, then, I shall!" She spun to glare at the fallen feline, caterwauling and lashing out at Quicksilver, who was somehow never where its claws struck, but whose sword found its hide again and again. Pinned beneath it and the horse, Cordelia nonetheless jabbed her fingers deep into its fur to touch its flesh, pouring all her own pain into it.

Allouette held up her hands, palms out, fingers spread, and called out, "Get thee hence! Flee, creature, fly! Get thee back to thine own place and never come nigh!" She turned back to the people, gesturing for their voices. "Get thee hence!"

They stared at this outlandish Fury, amazed. One or two of them mumbled, "Get thee hence!"

"Louder!" Allouette cried. "All of you!"

"Get thee hence!" more people cried.

"Louder yet! I can scarcely hear you!"

"Get thee hence!" they all called.

"Louder and stronger!" Allouette demanded. "So much louder that this fell cat's master Zonploka shall hear you in his own realm!"

"Nay, dare not to call out!" Big Ears screamed, galvanized

by the name of its master. "I shall rend you, I shall tear you, I shall terrorize you like—"

Quicksilver rammed her point into its neck and the monster broke off to howl as its whole body convulsed in agony from Cordelia's channeled pain.

"It cannot equal two weak maidens in power!" Allouette cried, stretching the truth a little. "Fear it not! Send it home!" She turned to face the monster again, calling, "Get thee hence!"

"Get thee hence!" the people shouted.

"Flee and fly!"

"Flee and fly!"

"Get thee gone to thine own place!"

"Get thee gone to thine own place!"

"And never come nigh!"

"And never come nigh!"

"Get thee hence!" Allouette called, beginning the chant once more, and the people echoed her. Line by line, chanting more and more loudly, shouting, bellowing, they followed her, advancing step by step on the very monster they had summoned then feared, and before whom they had cowered. Their shouts were almost loud enough to cover Big Ears' howls of agony as, little by little, it began to become translucent again, fading to fogginess, then only an outline of itself, before finally fading completely from sight.

The people fell silent, amazed and astounded by what they had done—and heard, dim and distant, the giant cat's yowling anger, then sudden howl of pain.

Allouette stared, realizing that the battle was done, fought and won, by the sheer strength of the emotion she had poured out into the people and felt crashing back upon her—and feeling the first tremors of exhaustion. She thrust it away, though, knowing the importance of appearances to the morale of those she commanded. She turned to them, declaring, "It has found its master again, and claims its reward."

"But what if it comes back?" one woman wailed.

A stifled groan sounded behind her and Allouette whirled and ran to Cordelia.

The peasant followed, demanding, "Tell us, lady! What if it comes back?"

"Then you had best hope there are ladies like us here to defend you," Allouette said between her teeth, "and there will not be, if you let her drown in her own pain! Six of you, come lift this poor dead horse off this woman who has held the monster at bay whilst we sent it packing!"

Half a dozen villagers came on the run and lifted the horse enough so that Allouette and Quicksilver could drag Cordelia free. She burst into tears.

"There now, sister, I know," Quicksilver soothed. "It is agony, yes, but we shall soon have it mended." She cast Allouette a wild, lost look.

Allouette nodded with all the assurance she could muster and tried to ignore the weariness creeping up on her.

"It is not the pain," Cordelia said through her tears, "though that is horrendous."

Allouette stared. "What, then?"

"Her horse," Quicksilver said.

"Aye, my poor, sweet mare!" Cordelia gasped. "So loyal, so fierce to defend, so gentle—and she had not even borne a foal!"

"Aye, it is a great pity," Allouette agreed, "but I have greater concern for you, who defended me. Hold your breath and set your teeth, for I must see if the bone is broken."

"It is, I know," Cordelia moaned.

"Hold her tightly," Allouette directed Quicksilver, then began to probe Cordelia's leg. Cordelia screamed once, then set her teeth. Quicksilver held her by the shoulders and squeezed her hand in reassurance.

"The knee is whole, thank Heaven," Allouette said. "But here . . ."

Cordelia screamed again.

"Lady, do you know this much healing?" a peasant asked nervously.

"This much and more," Allouette assured her, for part of her training as a field agent had been first aid and rough-and-ready surgery. She braced herself for one last trial, then had a happy thought and turned to stare into Cordelia's eyes. The other woman stared back, startled, and Allouette used the moment to send a probe deep into her hindbrain and trigger the sleep reflex. Cordelia's eyes rolled up; she went limp.

"What have you done?" Quicksilver demanded, aghast.

"Put her to sleep, nothing more," Allouette assured her. "Call it nature's anesthetic." Then she turned to straighten the broken pieces of bone with her hands while, with telekinesis, she matched them up like a jigsaw puzzle. Then, satisfied that the break was restored to its proper position, she probed and encouraged, pouring her own waning energy into Cordelia's fibula, making it grow, making calcium flow and harden. Finally she took her hands away and let out a shaky breath. "It is mended."

"If so, it is the quickest healing I've ever seen," Quicksilver said, staring.

"Ask her." Allouette turned to gaze at Cordelia's sleeping face. Eyelids fluttered and opened, and the woman looked back at her, bemused and amazed. "What . . . where . . ."

"You are in a valley where peasants performed the Taghairm," Quicksilver reminded her.

Memory came flooding back. "Aye, and we banished the monster they had summoned!" Cordelia's gaze snapped down to her leg. "But my poor mare . . . I was trapped . . ."

"How feels your leg now?" Allouette asked.

"As it always has." Cordelia sat up and probed her own flesh in amazement. "Is it whole?"

"As far as I can tell," Allouette said. "Test it."

"Not so soon!" Quicksilver said angrily, but Allouette nodded inexorably and Cordelia gathered her feet under her, frowning. She leaned on the arm of a protesting Quicksilver and rose in spite of the protests. Allouette was quick to take her other arm and brace her as, very carefully, she put her weight on the healed leg, first a little, then more, then all, then began to walk, eyes wide in amazement. "It is a wonder, lady! My mother herself could not have done better."

"I am pleased to see you walk," Allouette said simply.

"As pleased as I am by my own steps," Cordelia said fervently, and turned to embrace her.

Allouette went stiff with surprise, then relaxed in wonder and let her own arms come up to return the embrace. She drew back, blinking at Quicksilver, who was grinning from ear to ear and saying, "I thank you, lady."

"Aye, we are glad indeed to see the lady healed!" cried a peasant. "But what of the monster, lady? How shall you protect us from it?"

But Allouette had reached the limit of her endurance. With a long shuddering sigh, she fell senseless to the ground.

"What has befallen her?" the peasant asked in alarm.

"Exhaustion, nothing more." Cordelia knelt beside Allouette. "She expended a great deal of energy in fighting the monster you summoned, and more in healing me."

The peasant's face darkened at the reminder of their guilt, but Cordelia paid no attention, merely laid one hand on Allouette's brow and the other on her breastbone. "A gift for a gift—energy to replace some of that which she lent me for her healing."

Quicksilver nodded. "We shall all sleep early this night— or perhaps even this day."

Cordelia frowned intently, her gaze on Allouette's face. After a minute, her patient's eyelids flickered, then opened. Allouette looked about her, frowning, letting memories surface, then turned to Cordelia with a radiant smile. "I thank you, lady. You have restored me."

"Even as you did for me," Cordelia answered with an affectionate smile of her own. "Rise, companion in arms. We have not yet laid this enemy to rest."

"Have you not?" the peasant cried with alarm. "Lady, if you have not laid this fell spirit, what shall we do when it comes again?"

"Oh, they have laid Big Ears to rest," Quicksilver told her, "but not its masters. Indeed, they may send it against you again—and a hundred more like it, if you dare seek to summon them."

"We shall not! But what if Big Ears seeks to come back without our asking?"

"Do not let it," Cordelia said simply.

"How can we keep it away?"

"Do not perform the Taghairm," Quicksilver said with great practicality.

Cordelia nodded. "We think these creatures cannot enter without being asked to come; they can only send the puppets they make out of the witch-moss of our own world."

A man stepped up beside the woman, frowning. "Then it is enough that we not perform this ritual again?"

"No, more is needed," Cordelia answered. "The core of the Taghairm is cruelty, after all, and any viciousness you show to one another is invitation enough to an evil spirit."

The woman pursed her lips. "So if we are cruel to no one, the monster cannot come among us?"

"Even so." Cordelia nodded. "Indeed, if you truly wish to keep such monsters away, be friendly and helpful to one another; be merciful even to the animals you slay for food. Be kind and gentle to all and you shall close up even the smallest hole by which such a monster can come among you."

The people stared at one another, amazed and thoughtful.

"Then let kindness begin with these three who have saved us," the peasant woman said with sudden determination. "The lady has lost her horse in our defense; let us give her another, and a cart to carry the other lady who has spent so much of her strength for us."

The villagers looked startled, then chorused agreement.

"Darby, your cart would be big enough," one of the men said.

"My cart? Then how shall I bring my goods to market?" Darby protested.

"We shall build you another," a second man said, "new and sound—but the lady needs wheels now."

"No, no, friends," Allouette protested—but the hand that she raised felt heavy as lead. "I—I shall manage quite well with my horse."

"With *my* horse," the woman insisted, "three years old, and as sweet a filly as you will find in the land. It may be she shall not do for a warhorse, but she shall pull your cart with a right good will."

"But she is your livelihood!" Allouette protested. "I cannot take—"

Cordelia's hand on her arm stopped her. "We may send the beast back when we have found a new mount for me," she told Allouette, "with a present to thank the woman and her neighbors."

Allouette looked up, saw Cordelia's smile, and understood—it was a chance to give something to the peasants without making them feel it was charity, and to give them a chance to begin practicing the kindness that would stop at least one door through which the real monsters might enter. She returned the smile slowly, then turned back to the peasants. "I would dearly love to lie down while I travel," she admitted. "Thank you for your kindness, friends. We shall appreciate the loan of your horse and cart, appreciate it most strongly."

The people cheered.

So, half an hour later, a stolid little mare pulled a cart between two tall horses. Allouette lay back, half-sitting, against a cushion of pine boughs and looked up at Cordelia. "Thank you for interceding, lady. It would have been most rude of me to refuse their gift—but I could not bear the thought of such poor folk losing goods of such great worth to them."

"Or of their regretting their generosity later," Cordelia agreed. "It was the least I could do for one who spared me the pain of a broken leg—especially if it had not healed straightly."

"I am glad I could make some return for your kindness." Allouette looked down, blushing. "Indeed, I—I was quite overwhelmed by your protecting of me—me, who was your enemy, who sought to steal your lovers and heap humiliation upon you!"

"That is in the past now." Quicksilver's tone was unusually gentle as she reached down to take Allouette's hand.

"Aye." Cordelia took her other hand. "We are comrades in arms, and you have proven yourself so this day."

Tears poured down Allouette's cheeks. "Your kindness stabs me to the heart! I deserve it not!"

"So that is what made you so fierce in our defense!" Quicksilver cried. "Lady, did you feel you needed to prove worthy of our friendship?"

"I did, and ever shall!"

"There is no need," Cordelia said gently, "for you have shown yourself to be a most valiant friend this day, shown that our interests are yours now."

"And yours are ours," Quicksilver agreed. "I for one believe that I am far safer with you beside me to aid in the fight, than if I stand alone."

"You . . . you trust me, then?" Allouette asked with wide and wondering eyes.

"I do," Quicksilver answered, "for you have proved trustworthy this day."

"Indeed." Cordelia smiled. "If you had meant us any harm, lady, you had only to turn and ride away, leaving us to battle the monster by ourselves."

"But you have been kind to me! In spite of all I have done to you and your fiancés, all I tried to do, you have guarded my back on this venture and fought by my side!"

"Exactly," Cordelia said, smiling. "It is today that matters now, not last month or last year. Recover your strength, lady, for it is our shield and our dagger, and we would be sorely weakened by the loss of you."

"After all," Quicksilver said, all business again, "we may have sent Big Ears packing, but its masters will surely send against us another monster more horrible still."

Allouette shuddered but said, "You do not think it was made of witch-moss, then?"

"No, oddly." Cordelia frowned. "I tried to take it apart, but there was no response at all. Whatever its substance, it is as impervious to thought as real flesh and blood."

The three women were silent, each coming to the logical

conclusion but not wanting to say it. It was Quicksilver who faced it first. "If it is real, we do not simply face some telekinetic crafter who seeks to make his own army of horrors."

Allouette frowned up at them. "You do not think the mists that disgorged the first of these monsters actually hide the gateway to some other world, do you?"

"If so," Quicksilver said grimly, "it is a world impoverished, for its creatures are most hungry for our riches."

"Or for our blood and bones," Cordelia said darkly, "unless Big Ears' threat was pure cruelty."

"Greed or hunger, it matters not," said Quicksilver. "All we need to know is that they seek to despoil Gramarye, slay or enslave its people, and take the land for themselves."

"Yes," said Cordelia, "and there are espers among them, reaching through the portal to this world with their minds and crafting witch-moss monsters to frighten the people."

"What use is there in such a campaign of terror?" Quicksilver asked. "It will only make our people fight with greater ferocity."

"Not all, warrior," Cordelia said darkly. "See what it has done to this one village—terrified them so badly that they have not only lost the will to fight, but even seek to befriend the monsters at any cost in hopes of appeasing them!"

Quicksilver's nose wrinkled with disgust. "As though they would be appeased by an offer of hospitality!"

"Aye," said Cordelia,

"Offer hospitality?" Allouette cried. "*That* is the reason for the sendings!"

Quicksilver and Cordelia turned to stare at her. "How is that?"

"Have you never heard that vampires cannot enter a house unless they are invited?" Allouette asked.

"True," Cordelia said slowly, "but we have seen no vampires among them."

"Even so, these spirits must suffer the same limitation," Allouette explained.

"But our folk need not know they extend the invitation,"

Quicksilver objected. "They need only do evil deeds; that is all the invitation Zonploka needs."

"Is not this killing and roasting of so many poor helpless creatures evil enough?" Allouette countered. "It is not as though they were slain for food or clothing or any other useful purpose, after all! They were slain only out of wanton cruelty! Nay, the masters of these evil monsters seek not to enter a mere house, but our whole world!"

"But if that is so," said Cordelia, shocked, "our stopping this village's Taghairm is surely only a pebble in a gravel pit!"

"Meaning that some other village will take up where these have left off." Quicksilver's brows drew down, glowering.

"Aye!" Allouette cried. "Surely every villager in Gramarye is dreaming these nightmares, and every knight and lord too!"

"You have the right of it," Cordelia agreed. "Other villages will try to curry favor with the invaders by performing the Taghairm or some other ritual to invite them in."

Allouette shuddered and spoke with iron resolution. "We must find some way to seal this portal for good and all, ladies, and that right quickly, before some fool tears it off its hinges, unable ever to close it again!"

Quicksilver and Cordelia stared at her, suddenly seeing not the gentle and reticent companion of their journey, but once again the Chief Agent who had commanded a small army of spies and assassins. Then Quicksilver grinned. "I rejoice that you are on our side now, lady! Aye, let us seek the mists that hide this portal and bind it with stout bars of Cold Iron that shall never be opened again!"

They set off down the woodland path with renewed determination—but Quicksilver pulled up her horse with a look of alarm and held up a hand to halt her companions.

"What worries you?" Cordelia asked, then realized the answer. "The birds are silent!"

"Someone lies in ambush nearby," Quicksilver hissed.

"It is there!" Allouette pointed, eyes wide. "See how that bush shakes ever so slightly?"

"Aye, and not a breath of wind stirring." Quicksilver drew her sword. "Whoever seeks to surprise us shall have a most unpleasant shock of his own."

But Cordelia was gazing off into space wide-eyed, with the vacant look that meant a telepathic reconnaissance. She held up a hand. "No, warrior! It is—"

But she was too late. With a banshee howl, Quicksilver charged the underbrush, slashing with her sword and crying, "Who bears arms against me shall lose them!"

CHAPTER
-15-

Another blade shot up from the trees to parry her blow as its owner called, "Alas, lady, for then could I not embrace you!"

Quicksilver froze, sword high against his, staring into the grinning face of her beloved. But the grin softened into a wondering smile as Geoffrey moved his horse close enough to turn the sword bind into a *corps a corps,* left arm encircling Quicksilver's waist, lips claiming hers.

Cordelia stared in surprise, then looked a little miffed. "Shall she have such bounty, and I none?"

"Never!" said another voice.

Turning wide-eyed, she saw Alain riding out of the grove to catch her up in his arms.

Gregory, however, was more circumspect. He rode up to bring his horse next to the cart where Allouette reclined. He asked gravely, "Beloved, how fare you?"

"Nearly starved," Allouette answered in a suddenly throaty voice, "starved for the feel of your arm about me!"

"And I near to die of a thirst that only your lips can assuage," Gregory whispered, and leaned down to drink deeply.

Finally each couple broke apart and, with glances of longing, nonetheless turned to the others. "Dearly though I would love to seek a bower with my beloved," Geoffrey said, "I fear there may not be time for us to indulge in the joy of meeting."

"And great it is," Quicksilver said, squeezing his hand. "I would never have thought I could be so delighted by your touch when we have only been parted three days!"

"Ah, but it was three days filled with danger," Allouette pointed out.

"It was indeed." Geoffrey turned to her, all concern. "But what dangers have you suffered, my flower?"

Quicksilver smiled, amused. "Nothing that the three of us together could not deal with, kind sir. Cordelia and I were somewhat affronted by your gadding off to adventure without us, so we took horse and followed your trail."

"It gave out in the swamp, I doubt not," Geoffrey said, already looking worried.

"It did, so we cast about for a trail of thought and read Allouette's awakening with a splitting headache. As her memories returned, I discovered she had been kidnapped, so we rode toward her thoughts and soon found the mountaineers' trail . . ."

"My deepest thanks, sister and warrior," Gregory said with heartfelt emotion.

Allouette squeezed his hand and said, "They burst out of the forest like avenging Furies and freed me in minutes. We rode away, but discovered a barguest hard upon our trail . . ."

"A barguest!" Alain paled.

"It was no true predictor, but a sham that was easily chased," Cordelia assured him, then went on to give details.

So for the next half hour, each trio told of the monsters they had encountered. The men were outraged by the ganconer's imitation of them, and Gregory said nothing when hearing of the selkie's advances but seemed to swell with the intensity of his anger. Allouette, fairly glowing, only touched his hand, turning the sunshine of her smile upon him, and most of the anger seemed to drain away.

The women were horrified in their turn by the men's adventures; Quicksilver held tightly to Geoffrey's hand, as though to remind herself that he was there, alive, and well, as he told of their encounter with the afanc. When they had each brought their account up to that current hour, they sat staring at one another—somewhere during the narration they had all dismounted and sat on the ground in a circle. Then Alain took a breath and said, "None of us thinks that such a plague of monsters can be coincidence."

"Never, surely!" Cordelia answered. "And both parties have heard of the monsters' masters, and of Zonploka."

"But who—or what—is Zonploka?" Gregory asked. "A group of evil sorcerers? One evil sorcerer? A place? An army?"

"Not an army," Quicksilver replied, "for one told you that it commanded armies."

"A person, then, and Zonploka is a name." Alain nodded. "But are these monsters of his making, or his minions'?"

"That matters not," Cordelia told him, "any more than it would matter whether you could say, if you commanded a general to march against a rebel lord, that the battle that ensued would be his doing more than yours."

Alain shuddered. "I hope I shall never have to do such a thing! But each of my ancestors has in his turn, even my mother! Thank Heaven she had my father's support, and that of your parents!"

"As you shall have ours," Geoffrey assured him, "beginning with this current matter."

"I thank you, my friends." Alain beamed around at them, then frowned. "Yet should I send for that army now?"

"What could they do?" Allouette shrugged. "There is not even a squadron of monsters for them to fight, let alone an army."

"But the peasants have dreamed of a foul and fell army about to march through the mists!"

"Definitely a portal to another world," Gregory said,

scowling, and turned to Allouette. "But you say they cannot come unless they are invited?"

"Aye," she answered, "and this Zonploka, or his minions, are sending dreams and cobbling nightmares of witch-moss, to affright the peasants into rituals of just such invitation."

"Or to turning upon one another with cruelty that is as good as an invitation." Gregory nodded heavily. "You had the right of it in that, chieftain."

Quicksilver nodded thanks, unsure whether her old bandit title was a compliment or not.

"Then how can we stop the plague of monsters?" Cordelia asked.

"The answer is plain, though we do not wish it," Allouette said reluctantly. "We must stop the crafters who make them."

"But Zonploka will only recruit more crafters," Cordelia objected.

"Thus we come to it," Geoffrey said grimly, "as we all really knew we must, sooner or later."

"Aye," Alain agreed. "The only cure is to stop Zonploka."

Cordelia looked up at him, surprised that he had thought the matter through for himself.

"He has been a man of surprises on this quest, our prince," Geoffrey told her with a wry smile. "He has the right of it, too. If we wait for Zonploka to bring the war to us, it will be too late—certainly too late to prevent great loss of life."

"If his army is anything like the nightmares he sends, it will also be too late to defend ourselves," Gregory said grimly.

"Well enough, then," said Alain. "Where shall we find this Zonploka? And how shall we fight him?"

"We came to the river and saw nothing," Gregory said slowly, "but we did not wait for evening."

"Or morning!" Allouette cried. "Of course! It is not that the mist hides the portal—it *is* the portal!"

"Then let us go back to the river, camp there, and wait for dawn," Alain proposed. "How, though, shall we fight so powerful a sorcerer, aye, and one with lesser magicians at his command?"

"By magic." Gregory tuned to Allouette. "We must ponder long and hard, my love, to discover some spells that may counteract the worst Zonploka may throw at us."

"First we should ponder what magics he may work against us," Allouette said.

"Aye, and what manner of soldiers we shall confront," Alain said to Geoffrey, "for surely he shall be well guarded."

"We faced a giant cat that was well nigh a demon," Cordelia said with a shudder, "and you faced a giant and blood-thirsty beaver."

"I should not wish to confront a barguest if it sought to wreak death, not merely foretell it," Quicksilver said with a frown, "and there may be worse there." She turned to Geoffrey. "How shall we meet them?"

"Back to back," he answered, grinning, "serving as one another's shields, as we have done before."

She gazed into his eyes a minute before she smiled.

"If we need to fight, that is surely the way," Alain agreed. "Still, it would do no harm to discuss the issue with the sorcerer first."

"Oh, aye," Geoffrey scoffed, "give him time to call up a small army to bait us."

"Yet we might find other places better suited to his interest, and save fighting for all of us," Alain pointed out, and grinned as Geoffrey subsided muttering. "I know, my friend, that you do not desire to avoid a fight—but I must ask myself how many people would die in it."

"Surely you do not think Zonploka can be talked into abandoning this conquest," Geoffrey objected.

"Why not, if we can show him it will cost him gravely in soldiers and gear, and can find him another place that will cost nothing?"

"Would you send him to murder some other folk, then sir?" Cordelia cried. "Fie, fie!"

"Exactly, my lady." Alain inclined his head toward her. "His monsters would be a plague in any land—but on this world of Gramarye, only this great island has been made fit for human folk to live on."

The other three stared at him, beginning to understand. "The rest of the planet is desert and swamp," said Gregory. "Who shall you send his monsters to raven—the dinosaurs, or the giant insects?"

"Are the deserts truly filled with giant insects?" Alain asked, interested.

"Giant insects, small reptiles, and many varieties of snakes," Gregory answered.

"Not large enough to satisfy his monsters, I would guess," Alain said regretfully. "No, I suspect he would rather have the swamps, that his bloodthirsty minions may feast upon dinosaurs."

"He would rather have Gramarye," Quicksilver pointed out, "for our folk are more likely to be easy meat than a tyrannosaurus."

"Not for creatures that fear Cold Iron," Alain reminded her. "Indeed, even if they do not, a score of giant cats such as this Big Ears you speak of will find even a tyrannosaurus less dangerous than fifty determined yeomen with bows and pikes."

"I am not sure our people would be the tougher meal," Geoffrey said judiciously, "but they would cost the monsters many lives, I agree."

"Many lives!" Quicksilver protested. "They will run in panic at first sight of the creatures!"

"Only the first time they see them," Geoffrey reminded her, "and perhaps not even then, if we warn them well enough ahead of time."

"And of course," Allouette said, "any who are made of witch-moss shall melt even as they advance." She caught Gregory's hand again. "There are some among us who can see to that."

"What of those who are flesh and blood?" Cordelia asked. "Shall *we* run in fright when we see them?"

"There is not a one of us is not well braced for horrors now," Quicksilver opined. "Terrified we may be, but we shall attack all the harder for that."

"Are we agreed, then?" Alain looked around at the little group.

They all nodded their heads, saying, "Aye."

"Take the fight to the enemy." Quicksilver said.

"Enough, then." Geoffrey stood up. "We ride!"

They had to camp for the night—in separate tents, and what each of the three couples did or did not do was nobody else's business, especially if, as Alain had so far insisted, he and Cordelia had agreed to wait for the more intense delights until they were properly wedded—and royal weddings take a long time to plan and execute. But they were up before the first gray light began to filter into the darkness and reached the riverbank when the sky was bright and the sun still only a rosy forethought in the east. Sure enough, mist hovered above the water, filling the banks of the river and spilling over.

"I had not thought there would be so much!" Cordelia looked to left and to right, seeing the fog stretch out to the limit of sight on either hand. "Where within this nebulous kingdom is their portal?"

"Yonder." Allouette pointed, though her eyes had the far-away look of one who listened more with her mind than with her ears. They had left the cart behind, and she was riding the little mare.

"Yonder it is," said Alain, and turned his horse upstream. Cordelia hurried to catch up with him and the others fell in behind. She, too, began to look abstracted, as did her brothers, concentrating on the thoughts that seemed to stem from someplace upstream. Quicksilver glanced at them, nettled, for her own telepathy had not yet developed to be able to detect what they did.

Then their faces began to twist with disgust and horror, and she no longer envied them.

Soon after, the thoughts hit her with an impact that made her shudder; she recoiled from the intensity of the malevolence. She tried to assure herself that the bloodlust and longing to drink emotions of fear and agony were only her interpretation of alien concepts, but she didn't believe it for a minute.

"Yonder." Allouette halted the mare in the midst of a river meadow and pointed toward a knot of mist that was floating closer and closer to shore.

Geoffrey's lips stretched back from his teeth in a wolfish grin as he drew his sword and said, "Set on, and let them drink no emotions of ours but anger and ferocity!"

"Not even that!" Gregory cried, alarmed. "Give them any emotion, brother, and they have a hold on you already!"

Geoffrey turned, frowning. "Why, how is that?"

"Fear begets anger," Gregory counseled. "So does hurt— and ferocity is first cousin to bloodlust. Nay, brother, if we would defeat this crew, we must march against them with tranquil minds and hearts."

Geoffrey glowered at him, unable to refute the idea.

"There is truth in what he says," Alain said quietly. "Our master of arms taught us that anger slows the arm of a swordsman." He looked around at his companions. "Take a few minutes, friends, to let your emotions ebb and peace of heart and calmness of soul replace them."

With varying degrees of unwillingness, they complied; they all knew the basic techniques of meditation. Slowly, though, even Geoffrey and Quicksilver felt their excitement fade into calm self-assurance, and something more—all six began to be aware of a bond between them, a tie of kinship, for Cordelia, Geoffrey, and Gregory were siblings, and through them Allouette and Quicksilver were quickly becoming sisters, more thoroughly than the mere title of in-law which they would soon gain, and Alain, too, was becoming their brother-in-law in more than name.

Finally Alain looked up with a sunny smile, glanced from one to another and said, "Sisters and brothers, let us go forth to meet our enemy."

They smiled their agreement and turned to follow Geoffrey into the knot of mist.

They felt terror clawing its way up inside as their horses balked at the riverbank; they urged the beasts forward nonetheless. Geoffrey's horse slipped down on one forehoof and neighed in protest, then stopped in surprise. He spoke softly, urging the stallion forward, and the warhorse stepped into the mist, nostrils flaring.

Seeing that nothing had misfallen the first horse, the others followed, and their riders with them, trying to ignore the fear that chilled them. They drew their swords—except for Cordelia and Allouette, who held only daggers but readied their most powerful thought-blasts, even as they resolved to always bear longer blades in the future.

The mist closed about them, swirling and opaque—but carrying sound all the more quickly for its thickness: a chittering, a grumbling, a growling, a sucking, and a rumbling. The riders pushed forward, swords raised, suspense stretching razor-thin—then found the mist clearing as their horses stepped onto a gravelly beach. They stopped a minute, staring in wonder at the blasted landscape before them—gravel stretching away to become hard-packed earth, sere and dry, to left and right—but before them stood a cliff face with a cavemouth yawning lightless.

Flanking it on either side were the afanc, the Boneless, the barguest, and Big Ears and, behind them, the huge shambling figures of two ogres, male and female.

"I see it now!" Gregory cried. "Those we melted were of witch-moss, but they were copies of real creatures who dwell within this land!"

"Say 'monsters' as you intended," the Big Ears purred, "for we are every bit as perilous as you thought—and you shall not melt us here, for we are flesh and blood!"

"Where is 'here'?" Alain asked.

Quicksilver, Cordelia, and Geoffrey stared at him, appalled that he would parley—but Gregory and Allouette fought smiles, recognizing the wisdom of delay while they pondered their course of action.

"You are in the land of Trahison," the giant cat told them, "before the stronghold of the sorcerer Zonploka. Lay down your weapons and give up all thoughts of struggle, for Zonploka cannot be beaten."

"His minions could be," Alain said, looking grave but fearless. "We know, for we bested copies of some of you, and"—looking directly into Big Ears' slitted pupils—"in some cases, it seems, the originals."

"Only on your ground," the creature spat. "Now, though, you are on ours!"

"I doubt that you are any stronger for it," said Allouette, "since the life has been leached from this land. It has no more strength to lend you."

"Strength enough, foolish morsel, as you shall soon discover!"

" 'Morsel'? " Cordelia frowned. "Do you not mean 'mortal'?"

"I mean what I say!" The cat arched its back and spat, "Death to the weaklings!"

Geoffrey and Gregory each exchanged a glance with their fiancées, then disappeared with a double bang, echoed off the cliff face a second later by another double bang.

"See how your brave young men desert you!" Big Ears sneered.

But the women and the prince only glared defiance, for they saw Geoffrey and Gregory clinging to the cliff face one-handed just behind the ogres' heads, their swords swinging high.

"Lie down," Big Ears advised, "so that your deaths may be quick!" Then it sprang.

Both women leaped aside. Big Ears twisted in midair trying to follow first one, then the other, and landed in an ungraceful sprawl with a yowl of outrage. It spun toward Quicksilver—but the warrior had leaped back in and thrust her sword deep into the creature's maw. Big Ears screamed with pain and Quicksilver yanked her hand back out; her blade cleared the creature's fangs by an inch as its jaws clashed shut, leaking blood.

The afanc chittered with maddened passion and charged toward Quicksilver—but Cordelia glared at it, and its teeth crumbled to powder even as it opened its jaws to bite the warrior. It spun with a shriek of rage, swinging its huge flat tail like a club. It hit Quicksilver with a smack, sending her flying.

Big Ears yowled and leaped—but only a yard; weakened, it could only plod toward the fallen woman as the afanc reared, walking forward on its haunches, thick sharp claws reaching out for Cordelia. The barguest barked furiously and charged, racing Big Ears for Quicksilver. The giant cat spun, spitting, and raked the dog's side with razor-sharp claws. The barguest yelped with pain but buried its fangs in Big Ears's throat. The cat brought up its rear legs to rip at the dog's stomach.

Quicksilver pushed herself upright, shaking her head to clear it.

The Boneless suddenly shot toward Allouette on a chute of slime, pseudopods growing out of its mass to reach for her. Allouette darted toward Quicksilver and her sword, but the Boneless swerved to follow her.

Alain darted in to stab the giant beaver in the belly.

"Alain, no!" Cordelia cried and raced forward just as Alain leaped back; the two collided and fell in a graceless heap. Doubled over with pain and only able to hiss its rage, the afanc nevertheless slashed at them with its claws before it toppled and fell dead upon them.

The ogres, seeing three of their number fallen, roared and shambled forward—but heavy weights hit their necks and shoulders; they stumbled and fell, and Geoffrey and Gregory leaped clear just in time to keep from being pinned beneath them.

Alain heaved with all his might, managing to push himself to his hands and knees, levering the bulk of the dead afanc a foot off the ground. "Quickly, my love," he groaned, "roll clear!"

Cordelia did, then scrambled upright, shook her head to clear it, and stared at the dead afanc. The carcass lifted itself six more inches of its own accord, on a cushion of her thoughts. "Now you," she said, teeth gritted with strain. "Out."

Bellowing with fury, the ogres pushed themselves up—

just enough for the two young men to lunge, swords piercing hearts. They leaped back, but not quickly enough; huge fists swung, slamming into them and knocking them together. They fell but shoved against each other even as they did, pushing themselves tottering to their feet—and saw the ogres' hands falling, their eyes glazing, then their bodies slamming onto the rocky ground like fallen trees. Red stains spread out from each.

Gregory stared, awed by what he had done.

"Forget that female and see to your own!" Geoffrey cried.

Gregory's head snapped up; he saw Geoffrey running toward Quicksilver who, with Allouette beside her, stood facing a huge, white, gelatinous mound. With a cry of horror, he dashed toward the Boneless.

Then he skidded to a stop, staring at the creature's bottom edge as it inched forward over the still-kicking corpses of barguest and giant cat.

"Walk warily," Allouette advised him. "The thing absorbs anything it touches."

Gregory gave it a wide berth indeed as he went to embrace his fiancée.

"Are you well?" Geoffrey demanded of Alain and Cordelia, who were holding each other up. They blinked, dazed, and nodded. Geoffrey grunted with satisfaction and dashed past them to Quicksilver.

"I am well, doughty warrior," she assured him. He skidded to a stop and hugged her to him left-handed, his right hand still holding his sword on guard—as was hers.

Gregory had his arm around Allouette's waist as they backed away from the Boneless. "Think you there is any reason to interrupt its meal?"

"Not really," she answered, "though it will bear watching. Still, I see no reason to stop it from finishing what we have begun."

"Someone must clear away the dead," Gregory agreed, but he shuddered at the manner in which it was being done. Then he realized that Allouette was trembling, too, and turned to embrace her. She let herself go limp in his arms, let the trembling take hold of her, then gradually slacken and cease. Finally she looked up, to see him beaming down at her with pride. She blinked, nonplussed, then straightened a little, bringing her face closer to his; their lips touched in a kiss, touched and stayed.

Finally the shaking stopped and the three couples withdrew from kissing and turned to blink at one anther in amazement. Alain put words to it. "We are alive," he said in tones of wonder.

"And not much the worse for wear," Quicksilver agreed.

"Cold Iron seems to weaken these creatures as badly as it did their witch-moss doubles," Gregory concluded.

"It must indeed," Cordelia said, "for how else could six quite human people prevail against such ferocious monsters?"

"There is, then, some reason to feel we may match wits with their master." Alain turned somberly to the cavemouth. "Let us see what lies within."

"Aye, let us," Cordelia agreed.

Hands linked and gaining strength from one another, they detoured carefully around the Boneless, still intent on its hideous meal, and stepped into the gloom of the rocky portal. The others followed with similar caution.

The rocky walls narrowed as they went farther in until they found themselves in a twisting downward passage. The first twist cut off the light.

"Hold, I pray you." Cordelia pulled Alain to a stop, held her palm out flat, and thought hard of racing molecules. A dot glowed to life above her palm, glowed and grew till it was a large rotating globe, casting light all about them.

Alain sucked in his breath. "Lady, you shall never cease to amaze me!"

"I hope that shall prove true, sir," she said with a heavy-lidded smile, then turned to start walking downward again. "Let us see what lies below."

Step by step they traced the downward spiral, wary of booby traps and enemies, but nothing stayed them. Tension mounted as they crept farther and farther below, tighter and tighter until Allouette thought she would scream.

Suddenly, though, the tunnel opened out into a cavern, pillared with stalagmites and stalactites joined, lit by lamps hammered into the walls—jets, rather, tapping into fissures of natural gas. They gave a yellow glow to the huge chamber, focusing on the center—a dais holding a giant chair, almost a throne. Within it sat a tall, skinny, horse-faced man clad in blood-red robes with a high pointed hat, bright vindictive eyes under lowering brows, an aquiline nose, and a smile of smug satisfaction.

"Welcome to my parlor," the sorcerer purred. "Call me Zonploka."

CHAPTER
-16-

"You would have us *call* you Zonploka?" Cordelia asked. "Then it is not your real name. Are you afraid we will use it to work magic against you?"

Zonploka only answered, "Be sure you shall not leave this cave alive."

"I am not sure of it at all." Geoffrey fondled the hilt of his sword. "Your creatures seem to be quite as allergic to Cold Iron as the spirits of our world. Wherefore, though, have you sent them among us?"

"Why, to weaken you for the assault of my armies," Zonploka answered, still grinning. "These you have met are only a few of my host. There are hundreds of monsters, and after them shall come thousands of soldiers, each eager for loot, for the joys of conquest, and for land that he may rule to his own liking—which, I assure you, shall not be yours."

"They shall not come," Alain said, frowning, "for there was more to the assault of your vanguard than terrorizing the people, was there not? You may not enter unless we invite you."

"True," said Zonploka, "but some fool of a peasant is bound to finish the Taghairm as the dreams I've sent have shown him—and he will do that soon, for you few who have realized my stratagem have come here into my stronghold and shall not go out again!" He threw back his head and laughed.

The companions exchanged a glance, saw the anger and grim resolution in one another's eyes, and knew that the sorcerer was wrong—that they would go back into their own world no matter how many men and monsters Zonploka sent to stop them. Still, it was folly to let an enemy know their strength, so Alain turned back to the sorcerer and asked, "What will you do once the portal is open to you?"

"Why, send my vanguard of monsters and my army of cavalry and footmen, of course," Zonploka said, grinning. "They shall despoil the land even as you have said—and rule it all according to my dictates. I shall be king of your land even as I am king of my own!"

"King of stony desert and waterless wasteland," Geoffrey said, flint-faced, "king of a land with no life. How came your domain to be so sterile, sorcerer?"

Zonploka only grinned the wider, toying with his wand. "It is mute testimony to my power, foolish child."

"Mute indeed." Allouette's voice shook with anger. "No wonder you want our world, for you have blasted your own! What sustains this army of which you speak? What do they eat and drink?"

"The last of the cattle who used to live here, of course." Zonploka's grin turned feral. "Flesh for food and blood for drink—but they are few who are left, and growing fewer."

"When you say 'cattle,' do you speak of cows or of people?" Cordelia demanded, trying to throttle her rage.

"Yes," Zonploka answered her, "for once they are conquered, there is no difference. All are our beasts of burden and our meat."

"And thus shall Gramarye be within months of their coming," Gregory said grimly.

"Why?" Alain demanded. "Why would you wreak such

devastation, allowing your monsters to come out into Gramarye and destroy everything they find? By what right would you slay a whole land?"

"Why, by the right of might," Zonploka answered impatiently. "Is not that obvious, youngling? If I can seize the land and slaughter the people, surely it is right for me to do so!"

"It is anything but right," Alain contradicted. "The king is there to protect the people, not despoil them."

"Foolish innocent!" Zonploka sneered. "The king makes the nobles yield him men and money, and they in their turn exploit the people, forcing them to labor for their lord's gain!"

"There are some such," Alain admitted, "but they are base and vile creatures who ignore the obligations of nobility."

"They respect the rule of nature!" Zonploka spat. "This is the natural order of things, that the strong should prey upon the weak! You must conquer all you can to prevent a rival from rising—stamp him out before he can gain enough strength to conquer you!"

"So when you learned of this portal to our world, you saw at once that you must conquer us before we conquered you," Alain concluded.

"Conquer me! Fools!" said Zonploka with a mocking laugh. "Do you truly think you can stand against my monsters? Against my human armies? Be mindful that horrible though they are, they obey me only because I am more horrible still!"

"You have seen very little of our world," Gregory demurred.

"What I have seen is most amusing in its weakness. Do you know how I learned of you? By a rock! A rock a plowman discovered in a meadow, one that gave out a strange sort of thumping with a thrumming that your kind, I suppose, call music! He brought it to me, hoping to curry favor, and I knew it was nothing that had ever been in this land, nor was likely to be."

"Too pleasant," Allouette inferred. "Too soft."

"Soft indeed, and I never before had seen a stone that yielded to the touch! I knew that whatever land had given it birth must be a soft land indeed, and one ripe for the plucking! I made the peasant lead me to the spot where he had found it. From there I cast about with my magic until I found the gateway to your realm, small and inconspicuous though it was, and only visible when the mist rose from the river and gathered about it in a knot."

"Yet you found you could not pass through it," Gregory guessed.

"Nay, for it was tiny, scarcely big enough to admit an imp; it was sheer blind chance that the rock had flown through it! But I brought my magical slaves, shackling their powers to mine, and made that portal expand marvelously!"

"He speaks of espers he has enslaved," Allouette said, her face hard. Her companions turned very grim, too—Zonploka had chained their own kind.

"But," said Gregory, "even when the gate was wide open, you found you could not pass."

"No, not until I heard the plowman mutter a wish for another rock whose sounds would lighten his labors, let him forget his toil—and lo! Another stone flew through! Thereby I knew that I would have to manipulate your folk into inviting me, and they proved most easy to mold to the task!" He laughed.

"Terrorize, you mean." Alain fought to keep his face neutral. "You found that thought could pass through the gate, so you crafted monsters out of witch-moss in our land and sent them to destroy anything they found, naming you as their author, so that folk would fear you and seek to appease you."

"Aye, and creating so much chaos that your folk would long for order, any order at any price! Oh, they were quite easy to turn!"

"Poor folk, simple folk who knew no better," Alain interpreted. "So you sent them dreams of the Taghairm, and when some among them do manage to complete the ritual, you shall send an army of monsters into our land, to lay it waste and raise terror in the hearts of our people, terror and despair?"

"Aye, and thus shall they learn that they can never prevail against my forces! Foolish lad, not to know the natural order of things! Nay, if your like seeks to defend these fools, I am bound to conquer all!"

"What, with monsters who can do naught but destroy?"

"Nay, with my army of human warriors, who can rule as well as plunder, force folk to work as well as come to the slaughter," Zonploka retorted.

Allouette shuddered at the thought of the deeds those soldiers might wreak, to make people hop to do their bidding. "We have heard enough, Highness!"

"Aye," said Gregory, "enough to know that the gateway is not something this sorcerer made, but a natural phenomenon."

Zonploka frowned. "What nonsense do you speak?"

"Only words you have not heard before," Alain assured him. "Still, Gregory, it would seem the portal is susceptible to manipulation by your sort of magic, or his chained magicians could not have made it widen."

"Agreed," Gregory said. "We have learned enough." He turned and went back into the helical tunnel.

"Halt, impudent insect!" Zonploka snapped. "I have not given you leave to go!"

"Then we had best go leave." Alain turned to follow Gregory. "Ladies, Sir Knight, let us march."

They fell into place behind him as Zonploka ranted, "I bid you stop! I bid you halt! I bid you return and bow!" He stood and stabbed a finger at the prince.

Alain's belly clenched as though he had been struck with a mace; he doubled over but kept staggering toward the tunnel. Cordelia cried out in outrage and spun to glare at Zonploka. The sorcerer slammed back against his throne, eyes wide in shock, and Alain straightened up and strode swiftly toward the tunnel. "Quickly, my friends. He has resources other than himself!"

Sure enough, as they stepped within the tunnel they felt

as though they had suddenly stepped into a morass of molasses. They had to struggle to move their legs, barely managing to shuffle slowly forward—but Gregory linked hands with Allouette and the morass disappeared as suddenly as it had come. The companions staggered with relief, then steadied to a quick walk.

"Go swiftly!' Geoffrey called. He squirmed past Gregory and Allouette as Zonploka's cry of outrage echoed behind them—outrage that turned to burning rage, shouting, "Down upon them, or die in agony!"

"That is my summons." Quicksilver twisted between Allouette and Gregory, drawing her sword as the clatter of hobnailed boots sounded in the passage ahead. She swung her blade up just in time to meet the warriors who rounded the curve of the rocky spiral and stabbed serrated blades at them. She recovered as Geoffrey parried a thrust from Zonploka's human guards.

Human, but they scarcely looked it. Their bodies were half again as wide as Geoffrey's, one soldier filling the whole width of the tunnel but others visible behind him. Their skin was pallid, their faces swollen, their eyes staring with gleeful anticipation of the pain they could cause as they attacked with gloating smiles. They wore black tunics with blood-red trim and stabbed with swords that gave off the gleam of bronze.

Cordelia held her glowing ball high and those smiles vanished; the soldiers had planned to do their work in the dark. But the narrow tunnel scarcely allowed room for one of them at a time—one sword against the two that Geoffrey and Quicksilver wielded, side by side, and the roof was low, so there was no room to slash; they could only thrust, and they faced expert swords that could parry and riposte far more quickly than they. Nonetheless, the first managed to recover and thrust a second time.

Quicksilver caught his sword in a bind and Geoffrey struck down at it with all his might; the bronze blade broke under the impact of the steel, and Allouette thrust deep into the man's vitals. "Back!" she cried, and they all retreated a pace, enough for the soldier to fall—but the next charged them.

Charged, tripped on the body of its mate, and fell. Geoffrey's blade rose and plunged; the soldier screamed, then was silent.

"Withdraw!" Geoffrey cried, sending his thoughts so that whatever language they spoke, the soldiers would understand him. "Withdraw, for you cannot win! We can stand here all day and slay you one by one—and when one of us tires, another can come to the fore in his stead!"

The soldiers backed away, muttering; then one called back a stream of words that were unintelligible, but they could read his thoughts; he was saying, "True enough, but you cannot go forward either, for we block the tunnel. What do you mean to do—walk on our dead bodies?"

"Why not?" Geoffrey retorted. "You would! And be assured, we shall keep our footing quite well."

The soldiers were quiet in consternation. Then sudden belly cramps doubled the companions in agony; the soldiers howled and charged.

Allouette managed to counter Zonploka's telekinesis with her own, and the cramps went away just in time for Geoffrey and Quicksilver to chop down the next two soldiers, leap back to let them fall, then stride over their bodies even as they had said; the footing was unfirm but the tunnel walls stabilized them when they stumbled. Still, Allouette stole a leaf from her enemy's book and sent her thoughts ahead, to make belly muscles spasm; grunts of pain answered her as the soldiers doubled up. Then Gregory reached into their hindbrains, activating a primitive panic that made the soldiers cry out with horror and turn to run, shoving against one another in their agony to be gone.

"Quickly!" Geoffrey shouted, and ran after them.

Up the tunnel and out into the cavemouth they ran, with Gregory, Allouette, and Cordelia countering Zonploka's thought-traps at every turn—first another round of cramps, then numbness in the legs, then sudden pain around their hearts. Finally Gregory struck back with a wave of dizziness that made the sorcerer reel in his underground cavern, long enough for the companions to sprint down across the rocky beach, between lines of huge soldiers bent over retching from the last round of belly cramps, and into the portal before the rising sun had quite managed to evaporate it.

They landed one by one, diving and rolling, then sat up, panting and staring at one another wild-eyed. Finally Allouette said wonderingly, "We are alive and whole!"

"Only a temporary state if Zonploka has his way," Alain warned. He looked around at his friends. "What shall we do now?"

"Stand ready to defend," said a familiar voice, "for surely they shall not let you escape so easily."

The companions looked up in surprise and saw a lean and thoughtful young man with lank blond hair neatly combed, looking down at them from a tall warhorse. His face seemed a thinner version of Alain's. Behind him six men-at-arms stood ready with their spears.

"Diarmid!" Gregory jumped up. "You are well come indeed! My dear, this is my chess mate Diarmid; Diarmid, my bride Allouette—oh, but surely you have met at Quicksilver's trial?"

"I would surely remember so fair a flower," Diarmid said gallantly but with no heat.

Allouette remembered him quite well, for as Duke of Loguire he had been Quicksilver's judge—and her own. "I was . . . disguised, Highness."

Diarmid gave her a small bow. "I hope we shall have the opportunity to renew acquaintance, but at the moment there are more immediate matters pressing."

"Aye, an invasion of monsters!" Alain stepped forward. "You are well met indeed, brother."

Diarmid smiled down at his older sib. "You did not, I hope, think I would sit at home and twiddle my thumbs while you went riding off to adventure and glory."

"I had something of the sort in mind, yes," Alain agreed. "Nevertheless, brother, if it is adventure you wish, you are likely to have more of it, and soon—for the morning mist is almost gone, and if Zonploka seeks to stop us, he will have to send his army through in minutes."

"Surround that knot of mist, men of mine!" Diarmid called, and the footmen spread out in a semicircle, archers and spearmen alternating, their weapons aimed at the whirlpool.

"Quicksilver, let us and Alain meet them with steel." Geoffrey drew his sword. "Let Gregory, Cordelia, and Allouette fight with telekinesis and whatever other spells they can fashion."

"I am surely as well trained in fighting as yourself," Allouette protested.

"True," said Geoffrey, "but you are also a most powerful projective telepath, and should be able to wreak far more havoc with that gift than with a sword."

Allouette blinked, uncertain whether to take the comment as a slight or a compliment, then decided to take up the issue after the battle was done, if the two of them still lived.

Monsters exploded out of the vortex with howls, roars, and baying.

"Loose!" cried Diarmid, and bowstrings thrummed. Arrows sprouted in monsters' throats, but they only roared with anger and pain and kept coming.

Alain, Quicksilver, and Geoffrey immediately formed a triangle, facing outward, swords at the ready.

The gigantic bull with pointed teeth lowered his head and charged the trio; the dire wolf and the giant scorpion closed in from the other two sides. The rest of the dozen, though, went right past the trio and charged the soldiers.

The gigantic scorpion's stinger flashed down at Quicksilver, but her sword swung even more quickly, chopping it off. It fell short but gouged her shin; she screamed but swung again, chopping off a pincer.

Geoffrey jammed his sword down the throat of the dire wolf, then yanked it out a split second before the great jaws clashed shut; he spun to chop off one of the scorpion's claws. The dire wolf fell back, coughing blood; Geoffrey kicked the stinger at it just as the wolf bounded forward again. The stinger's point caught it in the chest and it fell, jaws snapping at the pain.

Allouette glared at the oncoming menagerie of giant snakes, gargantuan spiders, ogres, goblins, and trolls; a huge dragon exploded into existence before them, sweeping them with a blast of fire.

Alain sheathed his sword as the bull charged again. He dove, catching a horn in either hand. The bull tossed its head, bellowing in anger, and Alain let go, somersaulting into a seat on the bull's neck. He whipped out his sword as he seized one horn again, lay flat, and slashed his blade under him, across the monster's throat. The bull's bellow turned into burbling as it pivoted in rage, snapping its jaws, trying to reach the man just behind its own skull. It failed, of course, but one pointed tooth did score Alain's leg. He shouted with pain but hung on grimly and stabbed behind his own knee, sword piercing between the bull's ribs and into its heart. Blood gushed from its throat as the monster fell to its knees.

Alain vaulted off—and his right leg crumpled beneath him. He stabbed at the ground, using the sword as a cane to push himself up, and hopped back to take his place in the triangle.

The squadron of monsters fell back from the dragon's fire, screeching and chittering; then a troll bellowed, "Not real! Can't hurt!!"

Cordelia stared at the dragon's mouth, thinking of molecules speeding up their dance to a frenzy.

The troll charged forward, then screeched and fell back, its hair burning. The other monsters skidded to a halt.

"Loose!" Diarmid cried again, and the bowstrings thrummed, sending razor-sharp broadheads to pierce hide and fur. The monsters screamed again but charged in anger. The dragon roared and half of them fell, writhing in agony; the other half charged onward.

The archers managed one more volley, but the giant spiders and giant snakes came on. The spearmen gulped but braced their spears, then stabbed as the nightmares came upon them. One went down, ichor streaming over his chest from a spider's fangs, but the monster made a grating noise and retreated away, turning to scurry back toward the vortex but falling in a tangle of legs on the beach.

Another spearman stabbed straight into a snake's maw, then dropped his spear and leaped aside; the snake thrashed about in blind pain. The soldiers dodged its loops, but its eyes were already filming over in death.

The third spearman's point went into another snake's nose. It hissed in anger, sounding like a boiler blowing, and struck at the man again—but the spearman held it off with his weapon, though it forced him back and back. Then it threw a coil over him. His companion archer loosed arrows at close quarters, feathering the monster, but its coil tightened inexorably around the spearman, whose cry of horror grated into choking.

Diarmid galloped up and chopped down. The snake's head fell and the coil loosened as the huge body began to whip about in its blind death-dance.

Quicksilver shoved her shoulder under Alain's arm. "Lean on me and walk, Highness!"

"And you upon me," Geoffrey said, throwing an arm about her waist.

"Where are you wounded?" she cried in alarm.

"On my left arm," he answered, "the one you are now guarding. Advance!"

So, supporting one another, they hobbled up behind the monsters who still crouched before the dragon, waiting for an opening. The companions began to slash and stab.

Then, suddenly, the dragon was gone and the wounded fighters stood staring around at dead monsters.

Cordelia dashed up, crying, "Allouette! A rescue!" She touched her hand to Alain's leg and began to knit muscle fibers back together.

Allouette set her hand on Quicksilver's shin and frowned intently. "Poisons . . . I must change the molecules to benign ones . . ."

Quicksilver bit her lip, choking back cries of pain.

Gregory knelt by one fallen spearman, resting a hand on

the wound in his abdomen, then shook his head and turned to the other fallen man. He placed a hand to either side of the fellow's chest, beginning to knit fractured ribs back together and close the walls of the bronchial tubes in a pierced lung.

The remaining spearman stared at the huge carcasses, awestruck. "How came we to slay such horrors, my lord?"

"Because," Diarmid told him, "your spears and arrows are tipped with Cold Iron, which is poisonous to any creature of faerie."

Alain was taking experimental steps, staring at his healed leg in amazement. "You are a wonder, my love!"

"And you were so brave you nearly stopped my heart." But Cordelia held her brother's wounded arm in her hands, glaring at the slash.

"Thank you, Allouette." Quicksilver took stiff steps, her healed muscles seeming to thaw by the second. "Surely this cannot be all the force Zonploka could muster!"

"Now they are wounded! There are only a dozen of them!" a voice screamed behind them. "Kill them! Rend them! Hack them apart!"

Whirling, they saw Zonploka, mounted on a beaked lizard with horns stabbing from its forehead, clawed feet, and a snake's lashing tail. He rode out full tilt against them, and behind him rode rank upon rank of over-wide human forms with distorted faces, grinning in anticipation of their victims' agonies.

CHAPTER
-17-

"It is an army!" Cordelia cried. "How can we stand against them?"

"You cannot!" Quicksilver snapped. "Fly, witch, while you may!"

"And leave you to face them alone? Never!"

"Even so, sister-to-be!" Alain set his shoulder against hers as he raised his sword. "We live or die together!"

"Aye, together!" Geoffrey cried, setting his shoulder against Quicksilver's and pulling Allouette up on his far side. She stared at him in surprise, then grinned in determination and turned to face the enemy with nothing but the dagger from her sleeve.

Then, behind them, a bugle blew and dozens of horses came thundering down upon them. The companions spared a quick look back and saw a fully armored figure with the royal coat of arms on its shield, riding at the head of scores of knights and hundreds of footmen, charging down upon Zonploka and his men with lances leveled—and pointed with Cold Iron.

The two forces met with a deafening crash. Instantly it turned into a melee, monster-man against steel-clad knight, bronze swords clashing against Cold Iron. Then the footmen came charging in their hundreds, pikes stabbing upward to unhorse Zonploka's half-armored riders, halberds chopping into the huge oxen and giant lizards they rode. The alien soldiers howled with anger and tried to defend their mounts, but steel weapons chopped through bronze and left the invaders unarmed.

Through it all rode the knight with the royal arms on his shield, shouting for the leader to stand against him in single combat, but nowhere could he be found—until Alain caught at the knight's bridle, pointing toward the river and crying, "There!"

The knight turned his visor to follow Alain's pointing and saw Zonploka, standing alone in the vortex as it closed about him, shaking his fist and shouting threats that nobody could hear above the din of battle.

On the slope above the riverbank, Cordelia stood holding her brothers' hands in her right and Allouette's in her left. Her mother Gwendylon held Allouette's other hand while her father the Lord Warlock stood before them with Quicksilver, guarding them as the witch-folk chanted a verse in a language that Zonploka could never even guess at—and as they chanted, the vortex closed, shimmered, then disappeared completely.

The army of horrors screamed with one united voice, then fell to the ground and, before the astounded eyes of the royal soldiers, melted away into a noxious steaming brew that evaporated and was gone.

Cordelia turned and fell into her mother's arms. Gwen reached out and gathered Allouette in, too. Rod Gallowglass turned toward them grinning, his left hand holding Quicksilver's high in triumph. Then Geoffrey was there to claim her, wrapping her in his arms.

Gregory gazed at Allouette with longing but said only, "Praise Heaven you have come, my father! How did you know?"

"You don't think Tuan was about to let the six of you go gallivanting off without a small army to back you up, do you?" Rod asked. "And when he found out you were going up against the supernatural, of course he told your parents!"

"I am mightily glad he did," Gregory said, then saw Lady Gwendylon relax her hug and the two young women step back. "By your leave," he muttered, and strode forward to embrace his fiancée.

Rod smiled and went forward a bit more slowly to take Gwen's hand just as Alain swept Cordelia up in a bearhug. Behind them, the royal knight rode up, sheathing his sword and lifting his visor to reveal the face of King Tuan, beaming down at them.

When Alain and Cordelia finished a very long kiss, the prince looked up at his father and asked, "How did you know?"

"Diarmid was good enough to leave word," Tuan answered, "though he was clever enough to make sure he had a full day's start on me. I have been tracking him ever since, and the six of you along with him."

"Of course." Tuan grinned up at him. "It would never do for the land to be left without a crown prince, would it? Or even his younger brother!"

"And it would never do for your mother and I to be left without a son," Tuan answered, reaching down to throw a steel-clad arm about Alain's shoulders, "either of you."

A few hours later, when the wounded had been tended and the dead prepared for their final journey, Gwen and Rod sat with Tuan, watching the younger contingent, who seemed to be in engaged in a very animated discussion.

"Here is a new enemy come upon us, then," Gwen said, "one whom our children have found and driven off almost without our help."

"They have found and confounded this sorcerer by themselves, and held him at bay until he unleashed a whole army," Tuan agreed. "They are a brood of whom you may be justly proud, my friends."

"Thank you, my liege," Gwen said, smiling, "and proud of them we are. But your sons have shown to advantage in this, too—and from what Geoffrey tells me, Alain has finally begun to show the qualities that will make a strong king, those which he has inherited both from you and from Catherine."

"Still so humble in the showing of them, though." Tuan shook his head with a fond smile. "So anxious to be sure no one else will rise to the occasion before he intrudes! Where could he have learned such overweening modesty?"

Gwen and Rod exchanged a knowing look, then beamed on their old friend, who would never acknowledge his finer qualities.

"Thank you for kind words, though," Tuan said, "and I am deeply proud of the lad, almost as proud as I was when he showed such excellent taste in his choosing of a bride."

"Thank you, my liege," Gwen murmured.

"I am quite proud of my younger son, too," Tuan went on, "both for his courage and for his determination not to let his brother face danger alone."

"Not to mention his carefully delaying the message to you," Rod said, "which showed responsibility and a certain yearning for adventure."

"Which I had thought he would never evince. Yes." Tuan nodded. "You must be proud of your future daughters-in-law, too."

"Yes, indeed," Gwen agreed, "but I am most proud of their accepting Allouette so completely into their fold."

"Yes, she had proved quite treacherous in the past." Tuan frowned. "To the Crown also—but how can we condemn a woman who has reformed so completely as to help save both crown and country?"

Gwen fairly glowed—Allouette's reformation, and the cure of a twisted heart that underlay it, were the greatest feats of healing she had ever undertaken, and she was rightly proud of them—but even prouder of her children being so ready to forgive.

"We can't condemn such a woman, of course," Rod said,

then sighed. "I do wonder, though, how Magnus will react to her when he comes home." *If he comes home* . . . but he put that thought away.

"If your eldest is as good-hearted as ever he was, he will give her as fair a chance as the others have," Tuan predicted, "and she shall prove herself just as true a friend . . . What do they wish now?"

The younger generation were coming toward them, all seven together. Tuan smiled with benign interest—excellent acting in several ways.

"My liege," Alain said with no preamble, "we have been discussing the likelihood of the sorcerer Zonploka making another attempt to conquer the land."

"He surely will." Tuan tried not to sound too proud. "He has lost little in this attempt; in fact, one might think he was merely testing us to learn our strengths and weaknesses."

"So I thought," Diarmid said, "wherefore it behooves us to develop new strengths and close old weaknesses."

"Well thought." King Tuan nodded. "What have you determined?"

"First," said Cordelia, "to press the Royal Witchfolk into service, maintaining guard over this place, and any others where Zonploka might try to establish a portal."

"Assuming that he can," Gregory added. "It may very well have come into existence by accident."

"I mistrust accidents," Diarmid countered.

"Accident or intention, it could very well happen again," Tuan agreed, "and from what you have learned of the land of Trahison, if Zonploka is not near to the portal there, then another lord who is as bad as he, or worse, shall be—so set your sentries indeed. What else do you propose?"

"To discover the reason why Cold Iron injures faerie folk," said Allouette, "and to try to invent an antidote—for surely Zonploka must already be doing exactly that."

"Do so, by all means," Tuan encouraged her. "Is there anything more?"

"Only to let the peasant folk know the tale of this encounter," said Quicksilver, "so they shall know to call for help when nightmares like these start, and not to perform the Taghairm or invite the monsters in any other way."

"Well thought indeed. How shall you do this?"

"We shall compose ballads telling of these events," said Geoffrey, "and give them to minstrels to sing throughout the land."

"Well planned." Tuan nodded. "It will require some among you to wander singing for a space, to interest the minstrels and let the songs take on a life of their own. Damsel Quicksilver, to atone for your rebellion, you were sentenced to wander the land helping the poor and weak. I hereby declare that your service to the Crown and the people has fulfilled that sentence; you are now free to settle where you will."

"I—I thank you, my liege," Quicksilver gasped, eyes huge.

"Yet I will ask you to wander some months more in the company of your knight errant," Tuan said, "to spread word of these events."

"My lord, I shall!" Quicksilver turned to Geoffrey. "Shall I not?"

"Indeed you shall," he said, smiling and gazing deeply into her eyes.

Tuan laughed softly. "Yes, for having her to yourself and the people is far more to have her to yourself, than to share her with our court." He turned to his son. "What more, Your Highness?"

"That is all we have thought of thus far, Majesty," Alain said.

"And well thought it was." Tuan turned to his most trusted advisors. "Lord Warlock? Lady Gwendylon?"

"There is some chance this Zonploka may find or make another portal and bribe a poor man, or a discontented lord, to turn traitor and invite him in," Gwendylon said.

"Well thought." Tuan turned back to Alain. "Set spies throughout the kingdom, seeking signs of such treachery." He turned to Allouette. "Do you ponder what manner of signs they should seek, damsel."

"My liege," she said, overwhelmed, "I will."

"I thank you." Tuan inclined his head to her, then turned back to Alain. "Do you confer with your friends, now, about ways to set all these matters in train."

"Majesty, I shall." Alain bowed.

Tuan rose, grinning, and threw his arms about his sons. "I am mightily proud of you both! Go now to plot and plan."

Somewhat dazed, the seven young folk moved off. After a few minutes, Allouette offered, "I cannot thank you all enough, and am amazed at your kindness!"

"Kindness forsooth!" Quicksilver laughed. "You have saved each of our lives this past week, lady, whether you counted it or not!"

"And it is even more to your credit that you did not," Cordelia agreed.

"How could we think of you as anything but a friend now?" Geoffrey asked, grinning.

Allouette looked down, blushing, but Gregory's hand squeezing hers gave her the courage to say, "I do not deserve such kindness."

" 'Tis more than kindness," Quicksilver said with a touch of exasperation. "You have saved us and we have saved you, and we have all depended upon one another in battle—for our very lives! There is only one bond closer than that."

"There is?" Allouette looked up wide-eyed. "What bond . . ." She felt Gregory's hand tighten again and blushed. "Oh . . ."

"We have become six parts of one whole now," Alain said, "and I think we shall have to include Diarmid in our schemes in the future, for I begin to see we may not be able to do without his wisdom . . . Lady! What have I said? Why do you weep?"

"Why, because I cannot believe my good fortune," Allouette said through her tears, "to be so intimately accepted by those who . . . have reason to hate me."

"Come now, sister-to-be." Cordelia put an arm around her shoulders. " 'Tis not good fortune, but a place you have earned—by your courage, your skills in battle and in healing, and by your good heart."

"Aye," Quicksilver agreed. "Accept the fruits of your goodness, for you were quick enough to claim the wages of wickedness!"

"You cannot claim the one without the other, love," Gregory said gently.

She turned to throw her arms about him and sob into his shoulder. Gregory stared in surprise, then smiled slowly as he brought his arms up around her.

The other five did not turn away, as perhaps they should have, but only beamed fondly at their little brother and their newfound shieldmate.

When her tears had stopped and Gregory was tenderly wiping away the last of them, Quicksilver turned to Geoffrey. "You three men had best marry us quickly, sirs, for we have already become sisters under the skin!"

"The ceremony does seem to have been delayed overlong," Geoffrey agreed. He turned to Alain and Cordelia. "What would you say to a triple-ring ceremony?"

"Why not?" Cordelia smiled around at her sibs and their fiancées. "Life for the six of us will certainly involve three rings of some sort!"